MORE TIME TO KILL

MORE TIME TO KILL

BIRTH OF HEAVY METAL™ BOOK 9

MICHAEL TODD

MICHAEL ANDERLE

DISRUPTIVE IMAGINATION

LMBPN Publishing
PMB 196, 2540 South Maryland Pkwy
Las Vegas, NV 89109

First US edition, November 2021
Version 1.01, December 2025
eBook ISBN: 978-1-68500-537-5
Print ISBN: 978-1-68500-538-2

DEDICATION

To Family, Friends and
Those Who Love
to Read.
May We All Enjoy Grace
to Live the Life We Are
Called.

Thanks to my Beta Readers
John Ashmore and Kelly O'Donnell

Thanks to my JIT Readers
Deb Mader
Dorothy Lloyd
Dave Hicks
Diane L. Smith

Editor
Skyhunter Editing Team

CHAPTER ONE

"I thought these training sessions were supposed to be some kind of challenge or something." The young mercenary looked around the open area, her hands on her hips and her expression a little dubious.

Matt Davis looked up from the security system and wondered if he should share the fact that she'd almost had her ass shot off by the resident AI. Connie had thrown a fit over what she obdurately referred to as "invaders" and wouldn't listen to reason. Anja usually knew how to handle the fucking AI but in this case, she was being annoyingly quiet on the matter.

Connie didn't like having new people in the Heavy Metal compound. She evidently also disliked being told to, "Build a bridge, bitch," when his patience ran out.

He chose to not fill the newcomer in on how close to a challenge she'd come. There was time enough to introduce her to AI if she joined the team. "Right. Kelly Oliver, I presume?"

She nodded and stepped away from the Hammerhead they had been driven in on.

"My friends call me Kay. Or KO when appropriate."

"When...is it appropriate?"

"You'll figure it out." She turned as the rest of the group began to approach.

Six newcomers all told had arrived and Gregor had taken the time out of his day to pick them up from the US base. It seemed a good time to look at growing Heavy Metal's ranks. Many people were looking for work these days with the whole economy of the region in flux.

The recent hellish Zoo outbreak in Niger had left the international community reeling. In the wake of this, governments had bowed to public pressure and forced the research companies to relocate to the Zoo area. Of course, the higher-ups everywhere were still trying to find a way to make money from the jungle without everything going pear-shaped. It was the type of situation where rushed decisions would end with people dead and things had slowed noticeably.

This meant a fairly substantial pool of candidates, but Sal had told him to select those he knew best or who at least had recommendations from people he trusted. It was the kind of responsibility he tended to avoid. He had been a sergeant for years, though, and one of the few who had been in the Zoo longer than Madigan.

It meant he'd seen enough and learned enough to have a good instinct for those who would pull their weight and be able to work as a team. He'd also lost part of his leg to the incursion into the old Russian base, but he hadn't let that stop him yet. As such, he was the kind of leader the on-the-ground fighters would identify with, which even he had to concede made him a good candidate for his current role.

He grinned at a sudden useless thought that a movie would be made about him one day. His choice to play the role of Matt Davis would be Tom Holland. He'd matured as an actor over the years. They would have to get someone young to play the part of Salinger Jacobs, though.

"So you don't think this is a challenge?" he asked and pushed up from the desk he was leaning on.

Kay shrugged. "Well, you brought people in who have already been in and out of the Zoo before, so I assumed you were putting a team together for something special."

A young man with curly brown hair approached, and Kay greeted him with a bump of the fist.

"Come on. You have to admit that Heavy Metal has gained a reputation for being at the forefront of the bigger messes and the clean-up required," the new arrival said with a grin. "That whole situation in Niger especially. From the way some people talk about it, one might think that Heavy Metal considered themselves way above us ordinary mercs."

Matt's eyebrows knitted together and he tried to decide whether the kid was being openly disrespectful or if they all felt a little out of their depth and tried to show how tough they were by a pretense that they were unimpressed.

He would give them the benefit of the doubt for now and see if they settled. Either way, they would find working with the Heavy Metal team required heads on shoulders and eyes on a constant swivel. His instinct told him each of them was prepared for that challenge and responsibility.

That said, he didn't mind those willing to speak their mind. Strong personalities were a bonus in their line of work when each team member needed to be able to sustain themselves and not be a drain on the others. Honesty built trust because you knew where everyone stood.

Still, it was time to nip this in the bud and move on to the real reason why they were all there.

"The Niger operation was a massive military undertaking, as I'm sure you are aware," Matt said and his dry tone caught the attention of the other four members who were inspecting the defenses around the compound. "We did go deeper inside than most because it needed to be done and we were equipped and experienced enough to do it, but we weren't the only teams in there."

He paused to give them time to consider his message. "Anyone who says Heavy Metal has put themselves on a pedestal is talking from sour grapes and if you dig deeper, you'll likely find they wanted to join us and were turned away. Yes, we set a high standard for ourselves and anyone who joins us. That isn't because we think we're better than everyone else. It's because it keeps us alive." He grinned. "And yes, also makes us better than most who aren't so particular."

The newcomers laughed.

"What my friend here is saying," Kay responded when they settled, "is that we expected this to be a one-off situation, which usually doesn't call for any...uh, desk-type training, especially since we're already Zoo vets. We were prepared for something a little more strenuous."

"Yeah, I imagined obstacle courses, base schematics, and animatronic versions of the beasts we'll probably face." The young man pulled his hair back and bound it in a tight ponytail to keep it out of his face. He smirked and darted Matt a teasing glance. "Maybe even floor plans for a bank or something."

"Bank?"

"We know you guys like to hang with the McFadden crew. You must have heard the rumors that he knocked over a couple of casino armored cars in the past and made a fortune from it."

Davis snorted. "Don't you love social media? It never ceases to amaze me how they will tout as fact information that has never been verified." He narrowed his eyes before he checked the paperwork again. The young man's name was Kolton Tate and people called him Kolt. He could have been Kay's brother, except her head boasted a buzz cut of bright red hair—almost orange—and her face was covered in freckles. Of course, they could have a different father and the same mother or vice versa. It would explain why they liked to work together.

Or maybe there was another reason.

His notes said he was friends with Kay, although the nature of their relationship wasn't quite stated and he would need to dig into that. As uncomfortable as it was, it was good to know if people on the team were sleeping together.

It might be a little hypocritical given the relationship Sal and Madigan were in, but at least he trusted them to be professional about things.

Despite his instincts, he didn't know shit about them except for what had been sent in the recommendations. While he had the authority to make decisions, it carried significant responsibility too. If they had the type of hangups or weaknesses that would put the Heavy Metal team in danger, he needed to catch it and send them on their way before they joined their ranks.

"So, you're looking for a permanent addition to the team?"

Matt turned as a tall, dark-skinned, and powerfully built man approached. He had met him a couple of times, although his recognition came from watching the man play linebacker at the Navy Academy.

"Jedediah Morrison. I'm glad to see you accepted the invite." He proffered his hand and managed to not wince when it was almost crushed in the handshake that followed. "I've heard good things about your work in the Zoo. Word is you have one of the best records of getting people out of that fucking place alive in situations where they were engaged by the cryptids."

"Please, call me Jim." He finally released the handshake, although the ex-sergeant knew the time to put ice on his liberated hand would come later. "Honestly, parents who call their kids Jedediah ought to be prosecuted for child abuse."

Davis chuckled. "There is that. But to answer your question, yes. We need more people to join the Heavy Metal team and this seemed like the best time to do some recruiting—while things have slowed and people are looking for work. Given the attack on the Japanese base and the incursion into Niger, we decided we'll need a few more members."

"I thought you guys worked with McFadden's group." The only one of the recruits who could match Jim for size stepped away from the Hammerhead and joined the others who moved closer. Matt recalled Malosi Leota—who answered to Leo—easily since he'd had to make sure he had the details right while checking for possible candidates. Few New Zealand Special Air Service members worked in the Zoo and he looked the part—built like a rugby player, with his long, curly hair dragged into a bun and a beard thick enough to almost be armor.

"The McFadden and Banks team have retired from active operations. Their focus is now to train the people who will head into the thick of it," Matt explained. "It's news to almost everyone, but I don't think anyone's surprised that the bastard's had enough for the rest of his life. Three lifetimes, maybe."

"I think it's safe to say we all believed the leprechaun would keep going in until he fucking died," Kay interjected.

He nodded. "Yeah, they said you had worked with him a couple of times. That was part of the recommendation."

She narrowed her eyes at him. "Are you working off recommendations?"

"Any shithead with half a ball sack can survive runs into the Zoo," Gregor commented as he turned away from the Hammerhead and approached the group. "There's a difference between surviving and thriving in there and between scraping by or making the Zoo know you were in there by the body count alone. We are looking for the people we know we can trust. Most of the best are already running their own crews, so we asked for recommendations."

"Yeah," Matt agreed. "If it gets thick in there the first time out, we need to know if you'll be a liability or will carry the liabilities."

"Shouldn't we have a way to know if the Heavy Metal team will be a liability instead?" one of the other men asked.

The South American member of their new crew was the one Matt had the most questions about. FARC was not an organization that had a good reputation these days. They'd gone quiet during the twenties but became active again. While they claimed to fight some kind of revolution, everyone knew they were financed by drugs and kidnappings, thanks to the very subtle training offered to them by the CIA.

It was a huge controversy that had threatened to bury the careers of hundreds of politicians involved all around the world, but they were saved when the Zoo appeared and caught international attention.

"Octavio. I'm glad to see you made it. I thought you were running with the French crew near Casablanca."

"They were killed in the Niger fighting. I'm the only survivor of the people who went in, and they can't afford to pay me now that most of them are somewhere in that fucking mess. I'm looking for a new crew and you are it. I thought you could use a real Colombian jungle specialist to improve the Heavy Metal team. And you can call me Juice."

"We'll let you know if we need any of that famous Colombian snow from the Colombian specialist, eh?" The comment from the last member of the group was delivered with the kind of dry humor that was bound to draw attention.

Although Sonja would have captured interest even without her humor. She came from Navy Intelligence and had been one of the best, a communication specialist who landed in trouble with the CIA. It wasn't something you thought about when you first saw her. Matt wondered if that was a sexist way to think but in the end, women like her tended to be the best fighters more often than not.

Tall, blonde, athletic, and with a military background, she had headed into the Zoo often and had been a private contractor at the US base for months.

"I'll assume you all did the meet and greet on the drive over," he stated brusquely to move the meeting forward. "This is the part where you will learn what we do at Heavy Metal."

"The last I heard, you were all about playing the hero game." Sonja folded her arms and regarded him steadily. "And being paid top dollar for it too."

"Is that why you dropped the gig you had at the US base to come and fight with us?" he countered and raised an eyebrow. "Because if it is, I would advise you to head back and keep the cushy job. Being a hero is what comes from being on the front lines, and that means you'll be on the hook for hard, dangerous work before anyone decides you're who they think of when they talk about Heavy Metal."

He paused to let that sink in. "Salinger Jacobs might not strike you immediately as the kind of person who pulls that off, but the records of beasts coming out of the Zoo these days that help to keep you assholes alive? He wrote half of those and edited the other half. That kid's forgotten more about the Zoo than most of the mercs who go in and out of that fucking jungle will ever know."

The group looked around. He knew he was dealing with people who had been out there a while, some of them for years. Treating them like newcomers wouldn't work. This would be a whole new challenge since they would have to unlearn a whole pile of shit. The Zoo was a whole other animal now.

"So seriously, what is the situation here?" Kay asked and approached him again. "Do you want us to do trials? Fight or spar or whatever so you can choose the best of the best? Is that what this is about?"

Matt shook his head. "There will be no trials, no training, and no prep. You wouldn't be here if we hadn't already vetted you. Not only that, you wouldn't have stayed for longer than a minute if I'd had even the slightest reservation when meeting you."

He folded his arms and looked at each one long enough to meet their gaze and for them to see how serious he was. "As far as we care, you guys are in it for the long haul as soon as you take our money. Heavy Metal consists of the one-legged wonder"—he pointed at his prosthetic —"Francesca Martin, former FFL, Gregor over here, Jacobs, Kennedy, and Monroe, who also has major business interests to take care of overseas. You all come with the highest recommendations and enough experience to justify your positions here. We merely want to make sure you know what you're getting into. We don't want to have to do the recruitment run twice."

"Come on." Juice growled impatiently. "We're not new to this."

The ex-sergeant leaned back against the desk and let the silence hang for a moment before he spoke. "Everyone's new to what's coming out of the Zoo these days." He gestured to Gregor, who nodded and jogged into the garage. "It will continue to change and evolve and people who don't accept and expect that will die. And worse, people who don't understand it get other people killed. It's what happened in Niger and it will keep happening. That clusterfuck happened because people messed with the Zoo without grasping what it was capable of. I can't fix everyone, but I'll be fucked before someone pulls that bullshit on my crew."

Gregor emerged from the garage and used a trolley to bring a crate out. He grunted under the weight, even with the help, and hauled it forward to position it in front of the recruits.

Matt drew a quiet breath and settled his focus. He didn't like to pull this kind of shit without someone ready and on standby in a suit, but Connie had already activated the perimeter guns and had them trained inside. In all honesty, he had been against bringing any of the Zoo shit into the compound, but he bowed to Sal's superior knowledge and the fact that they needed a real-life example to shake the newcomers into the right frame of mind.

He gestured to the crate that now had the undivided attention of the team. "Before we dig into our little treasure trove, you need to grasp that the Zoo problem is way bigger than what the heavies would like us to believe."

Kolt stirred and opened his mouth to say something but snapped it shut when the ex-sergeant looked sternly at him. "I know what you planned to say," he told the kid bluntly. "Things have all but ground to a halt around here, so the governments and the corporations and everyone in between must have finally seen the light, right?"

This drew chuckles from the group who now seemed a

little more interested in what he had to say. He took that as a good sign and hurried on. "Wrong. There's a delayed demand for Zoo specimens because the research companies have to move to the Zoo area. You can safely bet your balls that once their fat asses are safely ensconced in their new facilities, it'll be back to normal. There's too much fucking money to be made for them to shut the industry down. Not only that, but we need the research to keep us ahead of that goddammed jungle so we can stay alive. Why? Because that bitch keeps changing and we have to keep up."

"But that's no different to how it's always been," Juice pointed out. Out of all of them, he seemed the least inclined to listen to the full explanation.

"Yes. But what most people don't know is the extent of it." Matt wished he'd had a presentation ready with slides, but that could follow if they chose to stay. "For now, know that this remains between us. Anyone who discusses this out of turn will see how Heavy Metal deals with people who can't keep their mouths shut."

He looked at each of them in turn, enough to draw a small nod of agreement, before he continued. "A couple of you mentioned that we worked with McFadden. He was largely involved in dealing with Zoo incursions outside the Zoo area—the States and Europe, mostly—and I can promise you, Niger was not unique. The M and B team dealt with a similar outbreak in the Czech Republic that we believe was started in the same way Niger was, although they are still investigating the cause. They faced cryptids in the States, Norway, Italy, and Germany, among others. How many of you have heard of those?"

"Only Norway," Kay responded thoughtfully. "That photo of McFadden was a classic."

"Once you've made your decision, we can fill you in on some of the details we think you need. Until then, we've brought in some proof from a little closer to home to show you how quickly the Zoo is moving and changing. We haven't gotten around to naming this little baby yet." Matt approached the crate as Gregor stepped closer. "Well, Sal has, but his name is half a mile long and all in Greek, Latin, and maybe a little Klingon mixed in there. So she doesn't have a real name yet, but I've taken to calling her Christabel—one of the new additions to the Zoo that's appeared lately."

His weapon was tucked comfortably into a holster under his arm. The snap was off and so was the safety. If anything happened, he could join the defenses in a moment, although maybe Connie would make sure he didn't need to. Hopefully. The AI was sufficiently pissed at him that he wasn't willing to bet his life on it.

"You have a fucking Zoo creature out in the open like this?" Sonja asked and stepped back from the box.

"Not...not exactly."

He pushed the seal open and dragged the top off the crate. Something pushed against it as he moved it and as soon as the lid was clear, the vines slithered out.

"I'm sure there's a Japanese cartoon girl out there whose true love this is but for the moment, we've been studying it. She's still a baby, but we'll have to put her through the incinerator before too long, given how fast she's growing. I'm almost attached to the little bitch, you know?"

"Seriously?" Kay asked and stepped forward. "This is

your grand show and tell? It's a goddamn plant, Davis. Why the hell do you think we should worry about this?"

His focus slipped for a moment, so it was probably his fault. Then again, maybe he shouldn't have treated them like adults who knew what the fuck they were doing.

As he turned to look at her with a witty retort at the tip of his tongue, he realized she had come a little too close. The vines had begun to spread as they did naturally to push out of the shade and toward the sun. Unfortunately, it was also toward the mercs and she was in striking range.

"Don't—"

His warning came barely in time. She had good instincts, and the moment one of them lunged directly toward her, she jerked back. Still, it was a matter of inches as it snapped viciously and looked more like a snake when it rose almost three feet. The bud at the tip extended and opened a flower tipped with dozens of needle-like razor-sharp teeth that protruded outward. What looked like five or six cat tongues flailed out for anything and everything they could find.

Kay jumped out of the way, inches away from having her throat ripped out. The vine snapped back when it ran out of slack. She didn't quite show fear but instead, reacted instinctively to the adrenaline-inducing situation and was instantly ready to fight. He could see it in her eyes and the way she moved—the healthy side of the flight or fight response.

She might not have any real military experience, but the ginger was a fighter, no doubt about that.

"I guess I should have told you that we've had little Christa here on a diet these past few days." Matt chuckled.

"Fuck yourself," she snapped.

The others laughed but it didn't take them long to turn their attention to the vines that issued from the crate. The laughter stopped quickly and Matt saw that as the time to bring things to a close.

"Something is going on in the Zoo. Between you and me, I don't understand half of it, but the people who do are running scared. This new, aggressive trend from the jungle is the indicator for something big—something we're not sure we can stop."

"But we'll go ahead and give it the old college try anyway," Kolt commented.

The ex-sergeant nodded. "We're flying by the seat of our pants on this. There ain't nothing in the world like what we're seeing in the Zoo, and it's getting more dangerous by the minute. This new, aggressive trend is the kind of thing we need to be very cautious of. It's moved past simply being here to make money and keep the bitch under control. The day is coming when what we do might well save the whole dammed world, and Heavy Metal wants to be ready."

"I don't like this." The British merc scowled as he tried to peer through the mass of vegetation that denoted the perimeter of the Zoo.

"No one likes this." His teammate sounded resigned rather than impatient.

Damon looked at where the rest of his team still pushed forward. "I liked it better when the Zoo was merely a fucking cash cow. We came in, killed monsters, and walked away with thousands every time. Now, we've got to be careful."

"I bet you we all hate that shit as much as you do," Stone muttered and kept his rifle trained on the tree line. "I managed to get my pension fund up and running. A nice little nest egg is waiting for me at home with no wife or kids or family to share it with either."

"You did? I assumed all the guys around here lived like they expected to die tomorrow."

"Well, that's fun for a while, but once you survive a couple of rounds in the Zoo, you realize that even if you don't get out of here, it's always good to have plans in place just in case."

"So you already have the nest egg ready, right?"

"Sure."

"You've got the savings. Why the hell are you sticking around now that everything's gone to shit and there's less money available?"

His teammate paused and focused on the teams of flame throwers who burned the Zoo encroachment to push it back.

"Honestly? I'm not sure. I can't pin one reason down as more important than the other. I have nothing waiting for me at home except a pile of cash and I'm not sure I'd fit in there now. The way I see it, I'd head back there, end up depressed, go to Atlantic City, and drop it all on a couple of weeks of partying and end up here again. Plus, I'd feel bad leaving this mess to the newcomers, you know?"

"That…is many reasons, Stone. Did you write them all down?"

"I had too much to think about after I saw what the Zoo did to the fucking Japanese base." Stone shook his head. "Between you and me, I even saw the base shrink a couple of times to be safe and got all my feelings worked out. I laughed, I cried, and then I decided to stick it out with you newbie assholes until the situation clears or I'm dead. And for the moment, the Brits are handing out the most cash to their mercs so I'm good with that."

"I'm very sure you'll die before the situation clears, my friend. You must have heard all the talk about how the Zoo is kicking into overdrive, not to mention the crazy conspiracy theorists who insist the jungle is the aliens attacking and shit."

"I'm not sure I agree with any of that, but—"

"Movement! Movement in the jungle!"

Damon sighed. "Four words I hate the most for a hundred, Alex."

"What?" His teammate sounded thoroughly confused.

"Oh, come on. Don't tell me you never watched a little daytime television."

Predictably, the state of daytime TV in the US these days lost appeal given the considerable movement now visible from the jungle. It was always considerable. Someone had pumped steroids into the bitch and the dumb fucks on the ground paid the price.

"Get the fire team back and be ready to give us cover fire!" Stone shouted over the comms to direct the response as the first of the locusts broke out of the trees.

It always started with the locusts. Occasionally, a couple of panthers lurked in the branches, hoping to surprise someone who came too close. The hyenas would inevitably back them up. When it came to starting the fights, the Zoo was still predictable.

Some of the mercs believed this was the jungle's way to test the defenses. It certainly produced enough of these mutants to provide large numbers of cannon fodder. Once the probing was done, the real fucking could begin.

"We got something bigger coming from the left side," one of the fire guys warned.

They pulled back and Damon activated the shoulder-mounted rocket launcher he had on his heavy suit. He focused to make sure it was ready as his seismic sensors confirmed the presence of something large approaching.

"I bet you it's a gorilla-rhino." Stone hated those.

His teammate shook his head. "The steps are too soft. They always beat the ground before they attack. This is one of those goddammed lizards with the tails that can cut you clean in half."

They were both wrong. The creature looked almost like a sloth but one about the size of a horse, and it didn't appear to move as slowly as a regular sloth either. It straightened on its hind legs and a long, sinuous tongue flicked out to taste the ground as it brandished claws the size of daggers.

"What in the holy fuck is that?" Stone asked.

"Damned if I know. We'd better get some footage of the critter so the specialists can take a look."

Damon realized that its eyes were too small for the head and it didn't appear to use them to see the humans in its path. The smell and the sounds were enough to guide it and it suddenly bounded forward by almost twenty feet before it began to charge.

The rockets launched almost before he realized what he was doing. It was the right call even if he had done it on instinct, and they hammered into the creature and drilled holes through it. Surprisingly, it wasn't fitted with any of the armor like most of the other creatures that big.

Although he had no doubt that it would do some serious damage if it was allowed to sneak up on someone and strike from above.

He cringed inwardly. It wasn't the nicest thought in the world.

"Look out!" Stone yelled.

Damon immediately shifted away, although the suit was due more credit for it than he was. He hadn't even seen the danger or noticed the creature that emerged from the sand. The new trick from the Zoo was for many of them to move underground. Based on the records, it had started in the Japanese base but this time, it hadn't lain in wait to catch anyone in a trap.

It looked like a cobra of some kind, but the head was about as big around as a widescreen TV. The fangs extended outward and something thick, green, and viscous streamed out of them as he pulled the trigger.

This mutant had no armor either, and the bullets punched through and out the other side. A spray of purple blood splashed across the sand.

No alarms warned him that his suit was compromised and he shrugged and turned to the ongoing fight.

The locusts were very much in evidence, but the sensors confirmed that nothing else had made an appearance. Nothing bigger meant this wasn't a real attack, merely a reminder from the Zoo that it was watching and it wasn't pleased that they attempted to stop its progress.

He'd first considered it a little weird that he thought of the Zoo as sentient and living these days, but he had decided to not ask the many questions. Too much evidence existed to support that line of thinking.

"It looks like we're in the clear." Stone growled with satisfaction as the last of the creatures was eliminated. "I can see nothing more on the sensors...huh. It looks like that snake tagged you, though. Is it acid?"

"If it is, it had no effect on the armor," Damon answered and inspected the area. "Honestly, I have nothing to report. It's like it spat some silly putty at me before it died."

"Why the hell would a Zoo monster spit silly putty at you?"

There was no real answer to that, but he didn't feel comfortable laughing anything off. The Zoo always did something with a purpose, even if they had no clue what it was yet.

"Do you think you can get this shit off me?" he asked. "I know the mechanics will charge me an arm and a leg for the work."

Stone stepped closer and tried to rub the substance off but from the way he moved, it wasn't an easy task. He grunted, shook his head, and pulled away.

"Fuck. All I managed to do was get some of it on me instead." He turned to the fire team as they approached the trees again. "Hey, boys. Why don't you give us a little of the devil's touch over here?"

They were only too happy to help. Mercs willing to work as gunners for the fire teams were at a premium, which meant the privates running the suits had orders to not antagonize the hired help.

The fact that they protected the privates might have had something to do with it too, but Damon didn't particularly care. They made ten times what the kids did, even if it was a fraction of what they used to earn from the jungle.

"All right, hit me," Damon instructed and checked his sensors as the flames licked his suit. Nothing triggered immediately but after three or four seconds, the alarm bells started.

"Me next."

They started to work on Stone while Damon looked at the damage.

He could find no trace of any, which was the good news. The bad, as it turned out, was that the gunge wasn't gone either. All the fire had managed to do was turn it dry and solid, but it still clung obstinately to his armor.

"Shit." He shook his head and grimaced when the whole suit reacted to the simple gesture. "Don't let them get too enthusiastic with those things. You don't want your sensors fried."

"Already done, amigo, and we have more trouble on the way."

"Fuck."

Nothing was ever easy with the Zoo.

CHAPTER TWO

Franklin sighed inwardly, certain that this new downside of his position would finally push him over the edge. He was paid the big bucks, but it meant he was the one the people being paid even bigger bucks talked to when shit went sideways.

Sideways was about the only way things went these days. Who would have ever thought that half the people who loved to bludgeon him with demands and complaints would now be on his goddammed doorstep?

The US base commander drew a deep breath and curbed his irritation as yet another specialist joined the video conference. He had no idea why they insisted he do this given that he already knew everything they would tell him. It was like they thought he was a judge, which meant their lawyers had brought in all the expert witnesses to sway him.

"Commander Franklin, don't think we don't appreciate the situation you're in," Samson, one of the CEOs, commented and leaned forward. "Being in charge in a place like the Zoo will always be far more difficult than people give you credit for."

"Don't give me that bullshit, Eric," he snapped. "If you want to play the good-cop-bad-cop routine on me, feel free to play the bad cop. You're much better at it."

Samson chuckled and shook his head. "We know we're making your job more complicated than it might be, but you must understand the difficulties we have to work with and the kind of pressure we're under to move all our research facilities to the Zoo area. The level of protection we'll need is critical. We're trying to coordinate with you and make things a little less complicated for you down the line."

Franklin snorted. "You don't give a shit about how complicated my life gets. You don't give a shit about the bodies I've had to commit to preventing the Zoo from being a worldwide disaster, and you don't care about how many of those bodies are cold when they come out of the jungle—if they come out at all. You can make noises about feeling bad and try to sound as contrite as possible but in the end, all you care about is the numbers you present to your respective boards of directors. So, now that we're all past the political bullshit, let's get down to the business of this."

"We can't say we're happy about the situation," Fontes commented and ran his fingers over his bald head before he adjusted his glasses and dabbed his forehead with a napkin held in the other hand. "If we could rethink moving our personnel to the secure areas inside the wall, it would be much easier to get everything done."

"No non-military personnel inside the walls. No exceptions. End of discussion." He had said those very words three times already in this meeting.

"Come on, Franklin. You have to meet us halfway here."

"I have to do no such thing. On the contrary, I have to keep my people safe. I have to find a way to contain the alien Zoo that is on the warpath." He could see a couple of the CEOs already preparing their objections. "Yeah, yeah, I know that's a culturally insensitive term to use. My point is what you want is for me to help improve your bottom line and quarterly reports. You get your bonuses, throw year-end parties, and everything's right with the world. Now that you're being held accountable for the bullshit you've pulled, you want me to meet you halfway? Please tell me you're joking."

The CEOs all looked around and he could tell they were angry and wanted to retaliate, but they still needed to convince him to take their side. Maybe the last guy who wore his shoes would have gotten into bed with them in a heartbeat, and maybe that was the reason why they were in the situation they were in now.

"Fences are being erected to enclose the area on both sides of the base," he continued, having regained his composure somewhat. "You will all be responsible for erecting temp housing and labs until changes can be made to the wall to house your staff and facilities there."

"Are you fucking kidding me, Franklin?" Samson growled and finally showed his true colors. His career in hockey had made him a fortune and his business degree added to it made him one of the most coveted CEOs available, but anger issues had already landed him in court a couple of times. "You intend to hold us responsible for the goddammed building now?"

"Our budget was cut the moment they decided that the Zoo wasn't making enough profit for you bastards," he retorted coldly. "I assume your lobbyists had a part to play in that. Either way, we can't afford to have thousands of your people leeching off our resources. The space will be strictly apportioned according to the reports provided to us of your needs and will be allocated on an alphabetical basis in the interest of fairness."

That did not go over well, and the entire group immediately began to protest at the same time and tried to talk over each other. He leaned back in his chair and decided to not bother to even attempt to answer any of them. The decision was made and it was final. He didn't have the money to house all the researchers from across the planet. If they couldn't spare the cash, maybe it was better that they didn't handle any Zoo shit.

The impulse to tell them all that they now finally had to live with the danger the people who went into the Zoo experienced daily was strong, but this was not the time to open that particular can of worms.

"Regarding security," Franklin continued bluntly once they'd all quieted, "we will have patrols in the area. We already do, in fact, and I'll allocate additional troops to the rotation. It's been enough for the bases and if it's not enough for you, I won't be held accountable for whatever costs you might incur if you choose to hire mercenaries. This is the way things will be. I've been given control of the move and the relocation, and I have orders from the highest echelons. If you have a problem with that, you might want to reconsider having your lobbyists cut our funding again. This is on you and I'm done taking shit for it. Are we clear?"

Maybe it wasn't the best idea to antagonize them, but he was tired—more tired than he'd been in his entire life— and it would get far worse before it got better. Part of his daily report was to check the lists of the people who had died in Niger—military and non-military personnel—and there was an entire section in the US that was dedicated to trying to find the dead and connect them with their families, or at least confirm their deaths for a little closure.

It was the kind of nightmare scenario that no one considered when there was an outbreak like that. He still had difficulty sleeping as a result.

Franklin cut the connection when the silence began to annoy him, drew a deep breath, and regretted his pledge to stop smoking. A cancer scare had prompted the decision but these days, it wasn't guaranteed that he would live long enough for lung cancer to have its say on how he died.

Still, the headaches with the CEOs would only get worse soon. Dramatically too once the relocation was underway.

"What do you think of the new guys?" Matt asked as they pulled up at the edge of the Zoo.

Sal looked up from the data feeding across his HUD and made sure their operations leader was on a private feed. He wasn't the kind of person who liked talking about people like they weren't in the same Hammerhead with them, but if they did, they could at least show the common courtesy to make sure the conversation wasn't public.

"Did you have a look at how they handled their suits?" he asked and started with the obvious question.

Davis looked at him, which would make it obvious that they were having a conversation to anyone who watched them closely. "Sure. As we expected, they are far above the basics, but I picked up a couple of bad habits—nothing major and we'll continue to work on those when we get into the Zoo. Still, there isn't much we can learn about them until we put them in front of a horde of Zoo fuckers. I look forward to that."

He nodded slowly and noted that a few of the others looked curiously at him. They knew they were having a conversation but probably assumed it was about Heavy Metal and needed to be private.

Which it was and did.

"Okay, so do you have a feel for them?" Sal asked. "We all know I'm the expert when it comes to Zoo shit, but my social skills…"

"You don't have any."

"Right. Which is why I count on you and Madigan to make the personnel calls."

The young scientist wasn't a micromanager when it came to this kind of thing. Madigan didn't involve herself in his business of writing white papers and he trusted her to keep the combative side of Heavy Metal operational. They made a good team.

It took Matt a few seconds to reply. He always thought about what he would say, a reassuring trait that brought trust and respect.

"They're tough and good for a fight but I do have some questions, mainly about the Colombian and the smuggler. But they come with the recommendation of people I trust who say they're good additions to the crew, so I'm willing to give them the benefit of the doubt if you are. It's a shit-load of pressure to make me run this. Madigan usually has a better eye for talent."

"She trusts your judgment far more than you know, man. It's not like you to feel like this. Is everything okay?"

"It's all good. You don't need to worry about me."

That drew a laugh out of Sal, although he was able to stop his suit from jumping halfway across the Hammer-head as a reaction to his jerked movements.

"Do you remember my first day in the Zoo? This dumb kid shows up off the plane and is dropped into a fight for his life. You were running the team I headed in with. You and Madigan."

"It seems much longer ago than it is, but yeah, I remember."

"I trusted you with my life that day and you haven't broken that trust once. The moment you do, we'll talk and then we'll, like...duel to the death or something but until then, I know you've got my back. No matter what."

"Damn straight, kid."

Matt was the only one who still called him that. Madigan had a whole litany of names and nicknames she used when he was involved, and everyone else called him Sal or Dr. Jacobs. None of those changed the fact that he was one of the youngest people in the area who didn't wear a private's arrowhead.

Kid seemed appropriate, no matter what letters he put in front and after his name.

The Hammerhead came to a halt and Madigan yanked the doors open. They poured out, their weapons at the ready and trained on the trees in front of them.

Sal paused and settled his gaze on the swathe of green. There was a time when he would have felt a thrill of exhilaration every time he saw those trees but lately, things had reached the point where all he could feel was an achy, bitter feeling in the pit of his stomach.

He couldn't change the fact that he'd been exposed to the Zoo shit. His DNA had been altered at a core level and he still had no idea what all the changes were or how they would affect him. Maybe he would attack everyone around him in a couple of weeks.

Nothing had happened so far, but that didn't take away the possibility that something would, not to his mind.

"Did you and Davis have a good talk?" Madigan asked on a private channel as they secured their position and waited for the Zoo to react to their presence.

"I think he was dealing with the pressure of making personnel decisions on his own. You're usually with him for things like that."

"I trust his judgment. It's better than my own when it comes down to it."

"Sure, and I do too."

"And what's that supposed to mean?"

Sal froze in place and his eyes widened when he realized what he had said. "I…you… It's not…you need to—"

"Shut the hell up, dumbass, I'm kidding. But yeah, he'll

second-guess his decisions. It comes with being a critical thinker but that merely makes his decisions better."

He knew that she was right but something different was going on with Matt. Ever since Niger, a shadow lingered in his eyes that Sal didn't quite know how to address. Maybe Madigan thought she saw it too. If so, that was likely why she handed dealing with the newcomers to him. If they gave him a solid win, it might settle him.

It would resolve itself in time, hopefully. The scientist grasped his assault rifle a little tighter and left the extra limbs in his suit tucked into the back for the moment. They would come out when they had to, along with his sword. It was generally best to not break the big guns out until they were needed.

"Shit," Francesca warned over the open comms. "We already have movement on the border of the jungle. Do you think they were waiting for us?"

"Yeah," Gregor joked. "Someone tipped them off. We have a rat in our organization."

The team chuckled but the humor was as short-lived as her warning was timely. A small horde of the creatures already waited for them as they approached the trees. They appeared to be mostly cannon fodder, which the Zoo tended to send out to harass the fire teams, but even they had begun to pose the kind of challenge they hadn't before. The sheer level of aggression and numbers thrown into the seemingly meaningless attacks revealed that they wanted to maintain the pressure on the humans who tried to contain them.

Gregor had talked about it and mentioned how it was a tactical decision that many different organizations had used. Sal had discovered that the Russian was something of a history scholar and he had gone on about it for a couple of hours. He'd drawn an obvious parallel to how one side could apply consistent pressure on an enemy to wear them down if they had no issues with throwing bodies into the bullets until there weren't any more bullets.

It was what the Russians had done to the Germans in the battle of Stalingrad—ancient history at this point, but it still felt relevant.

"We have a big critter moving in on the right," Madigan warned as they stepped into the trees. She was already keeping track of the movement and her HUD spread the word to the rest of them regarding the location of the beast.

"What are you thinking?" Francesca asked as the first of the locusts appeared from between the trees. "Killerpillar?"

"It's not big enough," Sal answered and indicated for the rest of the team to take their positions. "It's something heavy but with short legs and low on the ground. My guess would be a lizard of some kind. Open fire on my mark and not a second sooner."

It was plain that the newcomers ached to get into the fight and were more than ready to get it started, but they didn't want to waste unnecessary bullets for one kill. The Zoo liked to attack in groups, and if they could kill three or four with every bullet, they would start ahead and hopefully stay ahead.

The beasts surged at them, while the larger one held back and waited for them to be distracted.

"Madigan!" Sal shouted.

"I'm on it. Clear out the little ones. The big fucker's mine."

It didn't mean she couldn't help them with some covering fire. The automated guns on her heavy suit could thin the herd enough while she kept her focus on the larger one, watched its movements, and made sure it wouldn't flank them while they were engaged with the horde.

Skirmishes like these happened every day in the Zoo, and Sal knew that even a shallow run was a massive risk at the moment. Most of the merc teams weren't willing to commit to going into the jungle and limited their efforts to helping the fire teams outside it.

The people were there to contain the Zoo, but it wouldn't be enough. They needed information and from intel filtering in from the people in the buffer zone, more monsters had appeared for them to document. The one he wanted to see was the damn snake or whatever had spat the green substance.

It wasn't the first Zoo creature to emerge from under the ground to attack them and this was a disturbing trend. He had a feeling they would have to find a way to develop sensors to pick up any of the creatures who tried to attack them from below.

Sal pushed that line of thought aside to focus on the fight ahead. The locusts had gathered and in seconds, they swept forward. He set up a marker that would show on all their HUDs and give the signal when it was time to open fire.

The creatures seemed as anxious as his team to engage so it didn't take long.

He clicked the button with his chin, pulled the trigger

with his right hand, and moved the left to draw the sword on his back. The rest of the team added their firepower, the newbies a little slower on the draw but only by milliseconds, and the clatter of gunfire filled the jungle.

Madigan's shoulder-mounted mini-guns sprayed into the trees to make sure those mutants at the back were able to only provide minimal support to the front ranks. The larger creature was already on the move and now circled to try to flank them. Its new trajectory would take it directly to where the recruits stood.

"I got movement!" Leo shouted and drew back to where Madigan waited. "You got this covered?"

"I've been killing goddammed dinosaurs for years now. I'm very sure I can deal with an oversized Komodo dragon. Keep your eyes on the trees. We have leopards in the branches."

He nodded, aimed his assault rifle at the cannon fodder, but drew his pistol and looked around for any sign of the creatures above.

The lizard barreled through the underbrush, whipped its tail into one of the smaller trees, and cut through it with the ease of a buzz saw. The trunk dropped to where the group was positioned but they had scrambled clear and Madigan had her rocket launchers up and ready.

Tongues of fire spat behind her and in half a second, the thump of an explosion rocked the ground, followed quickly by two more as the rockets hammered into the beast. The shrapnel rapidly turned the rest of the area into a hellscape of flying metal and shredded wood, together with a mess of vaporized animal body parts.

Very little of the lizard was left after the explosives, and she began to reload the launcher chambers. Her mini-guns selected their targets automatically to clear the area systematically.

"Something above us!" Sonja yelled

Sal's initial thought that it was the panthers looking for easy kills from above was quickly set aside when he realized it was considerably larger than the mutants they were used to dealing with.

From the shape, he assumed it was one of the sloths people had reported seeing in most Zoo sectors. Those encounters had all happened at the perimeter where the jungle met the buffer zone, so no one had any real idea of what fighting them inside the jungle would be like. It looked like they were about to find out.

"Look out!" Sal was already on the move when he shouted the warning, and it took him a second to realize that his suit had reacted faster than he could have. The limbs on his back had activated and carried him out of the way as something heavy dropped onto the jungle floor. It rivaled a damn bear in size and claws the size of his arm swept through the air he had occupied not a quarter of a second earlier.

He already had his sword out and as he switched it on, it shuddered a few micrometers at a time. It wasn't much but certainly enough to cut through almost anything like it was butter. He pushed forward and in his suit, New Connie increased the pace. The AI had worked with him long enough that they no longer needed to communicate all the time and she could simply anticipate what he needed in many situations.

The beast was still recovering from its landing when he

opened fire. It could almost have been a wampa straight out of Hoth except for the greener and browner hues of its fur, rather than white.

Still, it was a threat and he had no intention to risk trying to take it alive. The claws lashed out at him, and he slashed his blade down to slice them off at the root. The extra limbs lifted him up and over to give him a clean strike and it would not be wasted.

Sal stepped forward, let his arm follow through with the swing, and his sword cut through the beast's neck. A light red mist followed where it came out and the massive sloth toppled with a heavy thud and showed no sign that it would get up again. Still, there was no point in being cavalier about it. Too many times, they had felled a beast or monster only to have it spring up the moment their backs were turned.

Madigan yanked a grenade from her belt, shoved it into the creature's body, and set the timer to ten seconds, which allowed them to move clear of the area while they eliminated the last of the monsters. It was the type of species grouping that generally waited to harass the fire teams, but they had been more aggressive over the past weeks.

Despite this, the attack wasn't quite as large or intense as they had expected, especially since the Zoo liked to attack anyone who stepped inside the jungle as hard as it could. But he knew better than to relax naively into the sense of optimism and assume the Zoo was settling.

"Okay, that wasn't too bad," Kay noted and checked her rifle as they moved on from their current position. "It seems like the Zoo doesn't mind having us in here. We might want to take advantage of it and see if we can come away from this with some pita flowers. The prices for even the bruised petals have skyrocketed lately."

Sal shook his head. "And I bet you this is a ploy—something to keep us off-guard. This is only a quick study run so there is no need to commit to a position where we might not be able to beat a hasty retreat."

The rest of the team nodded. It felt like they might have been a little afraid that he would make the call that made the most financial sense and were relieved to hear that he was committed to keeping them out of the thick of it.

This was a shallow test run and nothing more. It had been a while since he and the team had been able to move through the Zoo like this without having a major crisis to deal with. Something stirred in the back of his mind—a sense of something happening beyond where he could see it—and it annoyed him how it had become so familiar that it no longer surprised him. He'd long since put it down to the goop he had ingested and left it at that.

An urgency underpinned it this time, however, and seemed to press against him like he was being driven by something beyond what he could understand. The adrenaline in his body climbed and made him more eager for combat and bloodshed.

He recognized it as nervous excitement that demanded action but thankfully, also knew he was able to control it.

"Are you good?" Madigan asked, again on a private channel.

"Yeah. The adrenaline is pumping, is all."

There was no way to be sure she believed him, but she chose to not question him.

"I don't know," Leo commented. "If we can make even

shallow runs like this, we might be able to have some effect on the goddammed creatures and maybe draw at least some of them away from where the fire teams are working. And if we can make a little more money from it, we might as well take advantage."

Jim laughed. "I like this guy. Are you sure you never played cornerback?"

"Nah, man. I play rugby. It's kind of like football but it's played by men."

"That's some sexist shit," Juice protested, although from the laughter among the group, it didn't sound like any of their female comrades would make any complaint.

Sal wondered if he should check in with them. Or maybe Madigan, although she was the type who could whip out a metaphorical dick whenever it was needed. Maybe he should leave it to her. She was better at it than he would ever be.

"I've watched a little rugby. It's fun but looks like checkers while football looks more like chess." Jim checked his weapons again before he took another step toward the edge of the jungle. They were close enough to be out in under twenty minutes if nothing happened to delay them.

"I've never played either of those games." Leo swung his rifle over his shoulder.

"That does not surprise me."

"Enough!" Sal snapped when his irritation heated and surged through his body. There was no reason for it, but their good mood grated on his nerves. Madigan turned to look at him but the others continued and followed the path he'd plotted for them. "We have to keep moving. Believe me when I say we do not want to be caught out here when the sun starts to set."

He wasn't sure what happened inside the Zoo at nightfall, at least not lately. None of those who had tried longer or overnight trips came out. Besides, there was no time to think about that. Madigan knew his outburst was out of character and she would no doubt talk to him about it later.

For now, they had to focus on the mission. She would recommend that he stay out of the Zoo again, and he knew that he would have to talk her out of it.

"How can you have never played chess or checkers?" Sonja asked.

Leo shrugged. "It's nerd shit."

"You say that like it's a bad thing."

"Yeah," Jim agreed. "What's the problem with nerd shit?"

He paused and looked at each of them in turn. "I intended to say that nerds would never make it in the Zoo, but I assume we have two among our number."

"Three," Sal interjected.

"Right. I guess it's time to reevaluate my stance on... nerd shit."

The scientist nodded and worked hard to keep himself under control. It was difficult to stay focused on the mission with them chattering like that. The challenge was even worse when he attempted to determine what the Zoo was saying without letting it into his head.

CHAPTER THREE

The general consensus seemed to be that the French sector was the most peaceful since the Zoo did not focus its attacks there and so allowed them to gain the most ground in pushing it back.

If this was peaceful, Ariel seriously didn't want to know what the other sectors had to deal with. Their teams had gone through their bullets and thrown them around like candy on Halloween, and the jungle continued to throw its creatures at them.

"Corporal Lipschitz! You'll want to come and see this!"

Her parents hadn't given her much of a chance growing up. Even with moving to Israel a few months after she was born, naming her after their favorite Disney character had been a low blow and the surname wasn't much better. Still, it wasn't like she would change it. She'd learned from an early age to simply grit her teeth and take it, although it had earned her merciless teasing while coming up the ranks.

She wasn't even a fucking redhead, for crying out loud.

Still, her men knew better than to refer to her by name, especially when they were on patrol. She had to stop gritting her teeth every time she heard it. There were only so many times she could tell people to simply call her Corporal.

"What do you have, David?" she asked and pushed her suit into a jog to catch up with the rest of the troop.

"A tunnel. It looks like it's been here for a while."

She paused and scanned the area. It looked like the small section had once had a gate in the past. If that were the case, it probably didn't have the underground sensors like the rest of the wall did—something easy to overlook once the gate was removed and the construction sealed. An access point like that could have been used by a construction or mercenary crews and most likely came from a time when they didn't have the issue of the Zoo trying to push past Wall Two.

"Fuck," she whispered and shined her flashlight into the tunnel. "Get a report back to base and see if there's anything about this in the schematics."

David nodded and immediately activated the long-distance comm lines. They were lucky the Zoo hadn't pushed hard into this sector already. If the jungle had reached the wall, communications might be affected—although not to any degree for concern on the outside of the wall. The interference, if any, would merely be irritating.

It was late afternoon and the sight of the sun casting surreal shadows over the dunes was always a sight to see. The Sahara had always been somewhat mythical to her. She knew it was in the world and not too far from where she'd grown up and spent her whole life. At the same time, it would always be a place that she was more than happy to see in textbooks and inspirational posters.

Not live and in real time as she did now.

"The signal's a little choppy," David called. "But it's not Zoo interference."

They all paused and every gaze focused on the tunnel, where the movement of something enormous could be detected.

"To hell with that," Ariel snapped and drew her assault rifle from the holster on her back. "Get connected. Now."

They had to find a way to stop whatever was emerging but in case they didn't, she wanted to make sure that knowledge of this tunnel didn't die with them.

"Connected. Message delivered," David confirmed.

"Send them a live feed from your HUD," she ordered. "Everyone, defensive positions!"

She knew what was coming. They'd all seen the footage recorded by the McFadden team while retaking the Japanese base. Ariel made a note on their HUDs to look for any sign of the monsters hidden in the sand where they would simply wait, ready to spring some kind of trap. Once they had eliminated those in the tunnels, they could drop grenades to force the bastards out from underground.

"Target acquired!" one of her men yelled.

Every member of the team tensed and their weapons locked on the target immediately as it drew closer to the exit. The aperture was narrow and the lack of light contrasted by the light coming from behind them made it difficult to see exactly where the creature was. It looked like the tunnel had been created with pillars and outcroppings that gave anything within cover as it moved toward the entrance. Unfortunately, it meant they had no way to tell how many mutants were present. At least they would have to emerge singly, which would give her team the chance to choose their targets.

"Get away from the entrance!" she shouted and motioned them back a few steps in case the bastards rushed through and used their bodies as shields to block the attacks.

It didn't look like they would be able to kill any of the monsters inside, and she sure as hell wouldn't go in to hunt them without a bigger and better team behind her. Still, if they could draw them out into the open, it was one way to target them clearly and effectively.

"Oh, shit!" a private yelled in near panic.

It was about the only warning they would get and she spun as the sand around them was kicked up. She somehow hadn't expected that the beasts had already established themselves in the sand. While she knew to check for them, she hadn't once considered the possibility that the obvious threat might be a distraction. With all their attention drawn to the entrance of the tunnel, they hadn't looked for signs of their presence.

David was already being enveloped by one of the mole rats and so were two of the others. The massive teeth dug immediately into their armor, ripped it off, and exposed the soft and vulnerable humans inside.

They were already dead, she accepted dumbly. It was only a matter of how long it would take, and she wouldn't let it last. Aside from the fact that all she could do for her men was end it mercifully quickly, she also knew the monster inside the tunnels was about to rush out.

She snatched the grenades from her belt, let the automated feeder slot them into the launcher attached to her arm, and directed the first at the mole rat closest to her.

The grenade detonated on impact, ripped a hole in the creature, and tore half of David apart as well. She adjusted quickly to eliminate the second, then the third.

Their deaths would be mourned later—hopefully, they would live long enough to do so. For now, it was her responsibility to make sure none of the others met the same fate.

It was easy to guess that the vibrations from the explosions would rouse those that were still underground and sure enough, five more of the creatures thrust from the sand. Their six limbs flailed and lashed at any movement to catch those who had positioned themselves so conveniently in their traps.

"Kill them!" Ariel shouted and focused her attention on the mutants that tried to take advantage of the humans' distraction to attack them from behind.

Her last grenade hammered onto the nose of the lead mole rat and removed the head and about half the torso in a splatter of blood and viscera that spewed on those behind. Only two or three of them remained, and she chose her targets carefully. They were difficult to kill but particularly weak to explosives, as most organic shit tended to be.

It was easy enough to launch one of the new, automated claymores so it landed behind the creatures and blocked their path into the tunnel as she unleashed a salvo of armor-piercing rounds.

Once the mutants were where she needed them to be, she dropped to a knee and activated the mine. A little cover was all she needed as the air was suddenly filled with around seven hundred ball bearings launched at around four thousand feet per second. There wasn't much left of the group when she looked up again and tried to determine if any more threats would emerge from the tunnels.

If there were any, they soon decided that the danger waiting for them outside was not worth the effort. Ariel turned to see what her team was doing but they had taken a page from her book and now fired their claymores to turn the whole area into a kill zone.

She barely had time to duck again before the explosives detonated and spewed smoke, and the sickly smell of it mixed with burned organic matter.

The soldiers wouldn't meet her eyes. They were all new to the Zoo and it made no sense that the three who were killed in her little troop were those who had been around the longest.

Against all odds, the newcomers had survived and looked at her like they knew why she had done what she did but they still didn't like it.

In all honesty, she didn't like it much either.

"Do you know if David's message went through?" she asked once they were sure that the area was secured.

"It did," one of the survivors commented after he took a second to check. "The message you wanted, plus the footage from his HUD right up until...well...uh, until..."

"Yeah," she whispered and shook her head. There would

be an investigation into that later and she would probably be called in for a hearing or two to make sure she hadn't acted improperly and killed her people instead of trying to save them. Her explanation would be that they were dealing with an attack from both sides. Even if she had tried to save them, it would have resulted in all of them dead instead of only the three.

It would be on her superiors to decide if she had acted improperly, but Ariel was not too worried about how it would end. They knew that those in the Zoo had to make choices that the "normal" military never faced. Even if they thought that she hadn't done the right thing, they wouldn't risk losing one of their most experienced Zoo officers.

She smiled despite the heavy feeling. It hadn't taken long for the distinctive thwump to indicate the approach of the helicopters from the direction of the base. No one wanted to deal with a tunnel like this and before five minutes passed, three choppers carrying a handful of men each hovered over the site. The soldiers dropped in immediately and the aircraft remained in position with their guns aimed at the entrance of the tunnel.

"What's the situation?" one of the officers shouted.

"We have…eight of those giant mole rats dead," Ariel answered and highlighted the bodies for them. "There might be more of them in the tunnels but I can't be sure. We had three fatalities while dealing with the fuckers."

He nodded and gestured for the reinforcement to form up around the tunnel entrance once they had finished sweeping the area for more mole rats hidden in the sand.

The major finally finished checking the area and turned to his communications aide. "With the possibility of escaped cryptids, we need to alert the other bases to tell them to be on the lookout for any more tunnels near the walls. Perhaps we should get the Heavy Metal team involved too. They cleared these shits out the last time."

It was the McFadden team—Ariel was an avid student of how the situation had been handled—but there was no point in correcting him. Besides, both teams often worked together, so it was understandable that many people simply used their names interchangeably.

He nodded when the man acknowledged the order and turned away to set his equipment up. "I'll contact Franklin to see if the HM squad is available."

It wasn't something one could expect to forget. Sam had a feeling that an abundance of nightmares proliferated and as many people needed therapy, although there was no telling if they would get any.

Soldiers were expected to tough it out and walk it off, no matter what damage witnessing a whole city being ripped apart by the Zoo did to a person's psyche. Of course, he wasn't a soldier. Neither was Elke or Chen, for that matter.

Despite this, people still expected them to show the same kind of toughness. He didn't want to look weak but he wouldn't deny that the image had left an imprint in his subconscious.

One, he acknowledged ruefully, that would never truly go away. The ENSOL teams had volunteered to support the rescue and had largely worked with the survivors and refugees. As such, they had been spared the worst visuals that those who worked hands-on in the rampant jungle had experienced. It had still exhausted and chilled them to the core, but from what they had heard, it had only been the tip of the iceberg. They'd saved a few hundred out of possibly millions killed.

Millions of people with families and friends. Social media was awash with requests for people to confirm that they had survived the attack, but reports were that less than ten percent of the expected survivors had checked in.

Of course, that might have had a little something to do with the fact that people had lost their phones, computers, and all other means to interact with social media. Nevertheless, the resounding silence that came after the storm was almost more deafening.

He could see it in Elke's eyes and Chen's too. They felt the same way and like him, they tried to play tough and look like they weren't affected by it. Once things had returned to a semblance of normality after the event, they'd returned to their previous mission of building and reinforcing the walls since there were enough troops to protect them again.

Elke looked like she had thrown herself into her work to avoid thinking about the very real possibility that they wouldn't ever leave this hell.

"If there's one good thing about what happened..." she said and kept her voice low so no one else could hear what Sam knew would be an unpopular opinion. She glanced around before she continued. "It's that no one's dragging their feet over getting the wall finished, especially in the Sahara coalition."

Chen snorted. "They should be the most determined to finish it. If the Zoo breaks free, their countries will bear the brunt of the first attack."

Unlike Elke, the young man hadn't kept his voice low and Sam realized that a couple of the nearby mercs were listening to their conversation.

"They've committed almost twice the number of mercs to protect us and engineering teams are working around the clock," Elke muttered and glared at Chen before she focused on her tablet. "ENSOL had better get a fat bonus for coordinating all of this. Hell, in another day, we'll be able to move everything to the second campsite."

"They're practically throwing money at us, begging that we fix the problem," Fix muttered and scratched his chin. He hadn't had time to shave and a thick beard had begun to make an appearance. As much as he liked having one, it wasn't his most professional look.

Chen nudged him in the ribs and pointed at a handful of Hammerheads that pulled up outside their camp. The newly installed security team was supposed to make sure they were alerted well in advance of any possible attack on the camp but also keep them apprised as to where any newcomers came from.

The insignia indicated that they were from the Algerian base, although it looked like they had a few mercs with them.

A lieutenant exited one of the vehicles before they even stopped moving and flashed his credentials to the guards who approached before he strode to where the ENSOL group waited for him.

"We're always glad to be reminded of the patrol presence around here," Sam said, took the man's hand, and shook it firmly. "Is there anything we can do for you?"

"This is merely a courtesy call," the lieutenant answered in almost flawless English. "We picked up a couple of mercs leaving the Zoo without any permits."

"Permits?"

"They have been required ever since security locked down. We have to make sure that no one leaves the area with anything that might cause another outbreak."

That seemed reasonable enough, although it was the first Fix had heard about permits. They'd been buried in their work so much that they were bound to miss a few developments here or there.

The mercs themselves looked sullen at having been caught. They were poorly armored and both scratched their hands and arms almost compulsively, although he couldn't see any signs of a rash or insect bites to justify it.

"What will happen to them?" Elke asked.

"We'll send them home, most likely," the officer answered with a chuckle. "We don't have the budget to keep prisoners."

"Are you sure that's wise?"

"Well, if they intended any foul play, we would have simply shot them and dragged their bodies into the Zoo to be rid of any evidence."

Sam drew a deep breath. He didn't like the idea that he might one day get used to the concept of dropping bodies in the Zoo. It had been a while now, but he still didn't have to remind himself that he was very much complicit in the deaths of the raiders. They weren't necessarily good people, but there was nothing that said they were terrible people simply because they were raiders. He still recoiled from the stark reality that he might as well have killed them himself since he was, in effect, justifying those who had.

His regret was real, though, and he wondered if he would ever stop feeling guilty about what happened. Part of him hoped he would start believing the rhetoric that he tried to feed himself. A much larger part hoped it would never happen.

CHAPTER FOUR

"We will need more than six people for this," Sal muttered.

Madigan shook her head as she poured fresh coffee into her mug.

It had improved, interestingly enough. Sal wasn't sure how it had happened. Maybe the people in charge had begun to demand that they send better coffee. The worst part was that he was afraid he was merely getting used to the god-awful one.

It was one of his biggest fears, foolishly. Maybe that made him a terrible person, but he was coming to terms with the fact that he had numerous irrational fears about spending this much time around the Zoo. If he knew anything about psychology, he would say he was sublimating and transferring his very rational fears onto the irrelevant shit.

Something like that—it sounded suitably shrink-speak.

"I looked at the names and I did my research." Matt took the coffee Madigan offered him and sat in the living room. "Most of the names at the top of the list are either already otherwise engaged or they are no longer available. We lost far too many people between the Japanese base and the Niger incident. There are others who know what they're doing in the Zoo and we might bring them in from time to time to boost the numbers, but as permanent members of the Heavy Metal team? I don't think so."

"What was the problem?" Sal asked.

"A variety of things. Issues with greed or aggression, a history of trying to squeeze people for better prices, that type of shit. While it's not the big stuff that would put black marks on their records, it is the kind of thing that would be problematic in the future. You asked me to make judgment calls on them and I did."

"I still don't know why we need more people," Madigan argued and sipped her coffee. "At this point, we might as well look around for freelancers to take the work and be less selective about the people we bring in full-time. We can afford it but holding onto a standing army like this feels like overkill. Plus, we'll poach the people other mercenary groups want to hire. They won't be happy about that."

"We will have to deal with an upswing in Zoo activity before too long," Sal answered patiently and rubbed his shoulder. "If we have to hire our work out to people, we'll find ourselves caught in a waiting period. We won't be able to respond as immediately to emergencies that need more people—like having to wait for Taylor to fly here. Of course, we can no longer even hope for that."

"You can't be sure of any of that," Madigan protested. "I say we start hiring people when we need them. This isn't a company that needs to study market value."

"We know the shit will hit the fan soon, and this is the

point where the price for hiring new people will be at its lowest."

It wasn't the first time they'd had this discussion and it likely wouldn't be the last. Courtney was involved in managing her business in the States and left most of the issues on the ground for them to deal with. Even had she been there, it was only a matter of time before they ran into an issue they would not be able to agree on.

From the way Matt watched them warily, Sal could tell that maybe it was time for them to make their discussion a little more private. Involving him like this probably would not end well.

Before they could say anything, they were interrupted when the phone rang. Sal raised a finger to pause the discussion, answered it, and put the call on speaker.

"Heavy Metal. This is Dr. Jacobs."

"Dr. Jacobs, this is Major Aaron Peretz with the IDF, and we were directed to contact you about an ongoing matter in the French sector. Am I correct in assuming that you are not otherwise engaged?"

"We can't be, not if it's an emergency," Madigan pointed out and leaned forward. "This is Madigan Kennedy. What's the situation, Major?"

"Some of our forces found a tunnel leading under the wall. The troop there engaged a small group of those mole rat creatures that have appeared ever since the Japanese base was overrun. An effort will be made to contain the situation as much as possible but we are concerned that mutants might have already escaped. Franklin confirmed that we should contact you to join us. It should be a simple seek and destroy mission, but you of all people know how much the Zoo likes screwing around with us."

Sal looked at Madigan and she nodded firmly.

"We're in, Major," she assured him. "Although it should be noted that you will have to extend your current search area. The Zoo creatures won't be restricted by darkness or a need to rest. They could already be miles away by now."

"Understood. No real pushes will be made today, but we hope to be ready to move as soon as the sun rises tomorrow. I can scramble helicopters to bring you over at first light."

"It sounds like a plan, major. We'll see you then." She leaned back in her seat.

The line disconnected as a roar of engines was heard in the background and Sal scratched his jawline.

"Don't you fucking say it," Madigan warned him and pushed from her seat.

He realized he was smirking and erased the expression quickly from his face.

"This is merely one incident, and we've dealt with this kind of shit on our own already. It doesn't qualify for your little...doomsday prediction," she pointed out.

"I didn't say anything." He fought his grin

"You thought about it."

She was right on that account. He was willing to admit it if only to himself.

"Do you think we'll be able to get McFadden in on a job like this?" Sal asked and looked at Davis. The man had worked with the crazy leprechaun the most and would have a better idea of his state of mind.

All Matt could summon was a shrug. "We could ask him

about it but Niki made the situation very clear the last time you spoke to her. "

"Yeah, she said they won't go into the Zoo unless the whole fucking world hangs in the balance and like I said, this doesn't quite qualify as doomsday." Madigan shrugged.

"I guess we can't blame her." Sal sipped his drink and seemed both disappointed and a little excited. "Niki's pregnant and her first priority is the little McFadden on the way."

"This might be the end of the world," Madigan commented wryly. "I'll believe that Taylor's a dad when I see that little kid's bright red hair with my own two eyes."

"Why do I have a feeling that comes with numerous stories involving you kicking him in the nuts?" Sal's brows furrowed.

"Come on, Sal. A lady should never kick and tell."

"There are many words I'd use to describe you, but ladylike is not among them."

She tilted her head and nodded. "Okay, fair enough. Still, though. I wonder if they will get married?"

"With them, who knows?" Matt laughed. "My gut says no but they might surprise us. I can imagine there will be a baby shower, though, and I don't doubt Niki will expect us to drop some serious gifts for it."

"Yeah, I can see that." Madigan nodded slowly. "Although Courtney might be in a better position to spoil the little one with gifts. Assuming Taylor and Niki don't want us to suit their kid in a pint-sized suit of combat armor."

"Knowing Taylor, he'll probably at least make the suggestion," Davis commented. "Niki is the smart one so she'll probably shoot it down immediately, but even she will have to consider it, if only for a second."

"Well, we'll keep that idea in the back pocket." Sal grinned, tickled by the idea. "If they are interested, I'm sure Amanda would be more than willing to help us with her expertise."

It had been a while since he had talked to Amanda, but Anja stayed in touch regularly. The hacker said the armorer had been swamped with work orders and considered bringing more talent into the French base. Maybe she would be interested in working with Bobby Zhang in Vegas.

He made a mental note to mention it, but he would have to make time for that later.

"Right." Madigan sighed and closed her eyes for a second before she settled her gaze on Matt. "McFadden might be playing daddy and won't join us, but he might know someone who will, right? Doesn't he have that team of freelancers on the payroll?"

"I'm not sure." Matt shrugged. "They have a thriving business with their little…Camp Cryptid. The Niger situation raised awareness and governments from all over have sent their troops to be trained there. They have their hands full and already have built a reputation with him as the instructor and some new sim software."

"Are the freelancers part of their training program?" Sal asked.

"I'll check if you like. If not, I'll ask for their contact info. Things will have gone quiet now that the companies are forced to move all their research to the Zoo area. They might be willing to join Heavy Metal, at least temporarily."

"Do that." Madigan studied her cup of coffee like she contemplated having another one. "Get Gregor on the horn. He and Francesca can help us get prepped and hopefully, we can get a couple of hours of sleep and be ready to go. We'll make do with what we have here."

"You're spending way too much time on that shit." Stone sounded irritable.

"And you're spending way too little time on your shit." Damon pointed at his armor. "That gunk is still on your suit too, so you might want to take a look and stop complaining. Trev got himself in some serious shit over tracking Zoo shit in. They confiscated his suit and made him pay for the replacement. Do you think I have fifteen grand to drop on whatever bullshit they have on hand here?"

"That was at the US base. They're a little laxer about that here and you know it. This is about you being obsessive about cleaning your suit. Ten quid says I see you scrubbing the nooks and crannies with a fucking toothbrush before you're done."

He wasn't wrong about that, but it didn't change the fact that they needed to be more careful about cleaning their suits.

"I don't understand why you're putting that much work into it." Stone turned his seat so he could face his teammate. "It's not like it damaged the suits at all."

"And you don't think that's even a little weird?" Damon motioned one of the other soldiers over to check.

"The Zoo attacks us with something that does no damage?"

The soldier approached and picked a rag up. They were used to helping each other with their suit maintenance and it was almost an unspoken rule. When the work needed to be done, they would all do what they had to do to help each other.

"Did you have trouble with this?" he asked with a confused expression.

The other two looked to where he sat and brushed his rag over the section of armor that had the gunk on it. Startled, they leaned closer as he repeated the motion and the gunk slid off like it was dust.

"What...the fuck?" Damon pushed his seat forward and realized that Stone studied the spot a little closer as well, his eyes narrowed.

"You should have put these things in quarantine," the soldier commented and dropped his rag. "It might have done something that we can't see—like maybe the Zoo version of some disgusting STD and you walked it into the base."

"Hey, it's only some fucking gunk." Stone nodded, almost as if he needed to convince himself. "The Zoo wasn't finished working out the kinks. It's probably the kind of acid that's supposed to melt through our armor but didn't react the way it should."

"That or we brought the Zoo equivalent of the clap to the base," Damon interjected with a grin. "We might as well go to the medic and check on the state of our dicks before they start to drip a little too much." The other soldier laughed with him but Stone scowled.

"You're both fucking disgusting is my point."

"Yeah, we got that." His friend slapped him on the shoulder

"Are you guys going to report this shit, or should I?" the soldier asked as he stood.

Damon sighed and shook his head. "I'll report it, don't worry about that. We'll probably need to run our suits through decontamination or some bullshit, but better safe than sorry these days, right?"

None of them thought about collecting the dust that had been brushed off the suit while they gathered the pieces and sealed them for the purposes of inspection. It didn't even occur to them and even if it had, someone with a broom would likely clean it all up before too long.

They left the tent without looking back. The residue was caught by the slightest air currents and drifted into the desert sand in moments. Once there, the organisms detached themselves from the dust-like carrier, crawled beneath the surface, and burrowed deeper.

Expansion was the goal coded into their DNA, and they were there to push for that. Beneath the sand, they immediately began to mitose, divide, and grow under the sheltering desert. Only a few organisms had survived the trip, but as they dug deeper and began to multiply, they produced the potent goop that seeped into the barren landscape. Slowly and inexorably, it transformed the sterile waste into a secret but fertile hotbed ready for the Zoo.

CHAPTER FIVE

The Israeli major certainly knew how to time his choppers. Sal had no idea how he managed it but true to his word, they heard the rotors only a few seconds before the sun appeared on the horizon.

He was happy that they managed to have all their equipment prepped and ready for departure the night before. There was no way that they could have done it all in the morning. From the looks of their little group, no one was a morning person and all were already in the mood to kill the Zoo, merely for making them wake up this early.

They were used to it, of course, having been in the military and all, but it didn't mean they particularly liked it. He sure as fuck didn't and Madigan was as far from a morning person as anyone could be. The only one of their team who generally seemed energetic early in the day was Anja, and that was only because she had a habit of working a full twenty-four hours for a few days and nights in a row before she crashed. Once she woke, she would get right back to it.

She was honestly a fucking machine. That was the only way to describe the Russian hacker.

Three helicopters appeared and settled onto the open ground outside their gates. Madigan motioned for the team to get their supplies moving and loaded before they boarded themselves. The helicopter rotors didn't even have an opportunity to slow before they elevated again and in under five minutes, they were in the air.

In the rush, Sal didn't pay much attention to who was in the chopper until they were up in the air. He had missed a tall, broad-shouldered man with his face clean-shaven and his short hair showing a few signs of gray here and there.

The most important detail to note was the major's leaves on his uniform, easily identifiable.

"Major Peretz, I presume?" Madigan asked. "I'd shake your hand, but…"

"Thanks, but I have no desire to have my hand crushed by the heavy suit." Peretz didn't look like he was joking but Sal wasn't sure if it was merely dry humor.

Maybe he was a little too tired to think about this shit.

"What's the situation?" Madigan asked as the helicopters gained their full speed and the strip of green grew bigger on the horizon.

"There are no reports of Zoo activity on the desert side yet," Peretz answered and took hold of one of the grips as the helicopter banked a little. "The other sectors have been notified so we can hope that the mole rats were the only escapees."

"Well, it's nice to be able to hope like that," Sal muttered. "Have you guys swept the desert?"

"With as many eyes and sensors as we could muster.

Nothing's been found but we know better than to assume that means nothing got through. We'll maintain the sweeps for as long as we can and hopefully, the other bases will get the same message out to their people."

He nodded. "I'm very sure all the base commanders are desperate at this point to avoid being the ones who are remembered for all eternity as 'the one who let the Zoo in' so they'll contribute. Hopefully."

"Still, you never know when someone will end up being stupid," Kay commented. "You can't ever account for human error in these kinds of scenarios. I've made a great deal of money from people who simply didn't pay attention. Or were a little too greedy for their own good."

"You...made a great deal of money?" Peretz asked with a bemused frown.

"I used to work as a smuggler and occasional thief and made a living off of the criminal side of the Zoo."

"That's...uh, interesting. And now you're reformed?"

"Well, I still do that shit but for the good guys now." She shrugged. "It's a matter of perspective, I guess. I never worked for the very bad guys like North Korea and the other real nasties, but I did operate in situations where morality came in many shades of gray."

Madigan turned to look at the redhead. "You sound like you've practiced that speech for a while."

"Yeah, a little. How was it?"

Sal held his hand out flat and tilted it from side to side. "A little rushed but I think you got the message across."

"Thanks."

Peretz tilted his head and studied them all for a

moment. "Are you always this light-hearted before you head into the Zoo?"

"Sure," the scientist confirmed. "It's a good way to keep your spirits up before you go into an area where monsters wait to spit acid in your face and break every bone in your body. You have to have a sense of humor about these things or you'll end up going nuts. And...well, I suppose at that point, you end up having a sense of humor about every-thing or nothing."

"It's kind of hard to not make a joke of everything from the inside of a padded cell," Leo interjected over the comms from one of the other helicopters.

A few questions might need to be addressed about the complications of mental health issues, but it was some-thing for another time.

Besides, any number of issues would arise for them to work through over the next few months. If they weren't all dead before the year was out, they could have a nice long talk over beers about how complex mental health was.

Sal shook his head. He was overthinking things as usual. It did stop him from thinking about the Zoo, which grew bigger with every second that passed.

The pilot knew better than to come within range of the trees. He no doubt wanted to avoid being the subject of the next footage that uploaded to ZooTube of a helicopter dragged down by hundreds of locusts.

People were learning, amazingly enough. Sal didn't bother to draw his assault rifle but his gaze was fixed on the tree line. The moment they saw any movement from the jungle, he would be at the door and play the part of the gunner straight out of a Vietnam war movie.

Nothing moved, but he could see that the Zoo had begun to burgeon out and showed signs of it starting to press from its confines again. It was happening in all sectors, signs of the jungle growing at a higher rate than it had been before.

"Chopper team, chopper team, do you copy?"

He looked around and focused where he thought the signal came from, a point near the wall and a few degrees east of their original heading.

"We read you," Peretz replied over the drone of the helicopter rotors. "Tunnel team, what's your situation?"

"We need assistance as soon as you can land. We see and…attacking…need reinforceme…now!"

Sal knew where the interference came from. If it was that strong, it meant the team was caught in the middle of jungle growth that had begun to press on their position.

"We can redirect to your position," the major told them briskly and motioned to the pilots, who had already advised the choppers to bank into a new flight path to where the signal came from. "Hold your ground and we'll touch down momentarily."

Any attempt to land was complicated and so out of the question. This was a burgeoning section of the Zoo, where the trees had begun to advance. It wasn't quite a jungle yet but the trees grew like literal weeds and seemed to transform the sand miraculously into soil to support the other vegetation.

There was no room for the helicopters to land. Volleys of gunfire came from all around, which told them the ground team was already engaged.

The choppers hovered for a moment and allowed the

newcomers to drop from the aircraft and land heavily. The ground was still soft from so much growth in that little time but the suits kicked up from it almost immediately.

Madigan had already begun to organize the team and tried to get them into some kind of formation. Even the scattered trees were enough to give the Zoo creatures some cover as they advanced on the group that had landed.

"Movement, three o'clock—give us some cover fire!" she shouted. Her suit knocked a handful of trees over as she moved and the mini-guns activated almost immediately. The IFF systems in their suits told them where the ground teams were pushed against the wall and fought hard to prevent the monsters from overwhelming them.

The jungle was not quite mature yet and the trees were barely as tall as Sal's head, but they made up for it by growing thicker than they generally did. It expanded far more rapidly than it had in the past, but the process was about the same.

Oddly enough, it looked almost like a fairly narrow spur rather than a wide-fronted outbreak. On the other side of the wall, an entirely new section of growth had emerged and had pressed forward to the wall, where about a dozen soldiers from the original team still tried to hold their ground as they were attacked from all sides.

It had likely all grown in the night but only gained speed once the sun was up. They had to find a way to get fire teams into the area but with how aggressive the monsters were, Sal doubted it was a realistic approach until they'd cleared some of the local fauna.

By then, however, it would likely be too late. The only

way to burn the Zoo back was when it was still growing and in the early stages. Even with the plasma throwers, when the trees were fully grown, there was almost no way to burn them down. Even cutting them was a complicated process that was almost never worth the time and effort that went into it.

"Get to the ground team!" Madigan shouted and motioned their group forward. The helicopters remained where they were for a while and gunned down any of the monsters that came too close, but the beasts had almost reached the point of frenzy and it wouldn't be long before they began to throw themselves at the aircraft.

When that happened, the pilots would withdraw. It was always best to not be an easy target.

Sal left his sword on his back for the moment and moved with the team as they pushed to where what remained of the ground team was waiting for them.

They looked like they had sustained heavy losses and a little coordination let the Heavy Metal team step in to join their fight almost seamlessly.

"Where is the rest of your team?" Matt shouted and drove his boot through the skull of a panther before he kicked the body into the path of the other creatures that rushed at them.

"Spread out," the corporal shouted as she stepped into formation with her troop. "I'm not sure how many of them are still alive. We tried to fight through to them, but we were isolated quickly. The jungle appeared almost as soon as the sun came up. I'm not sure how that's possible, but fuck it, right?"

That seemed to be the anthem for everything that came out of the Zoo these days.

"What happened to the tunnel?" Sal shouted over the gunfire all around them but the answer would have to wait. He ducked and let Madigan take the center of their formation as he drew his sword. It activated and he charged at a handful of horned gorillas that rushed from the underbrush.

The two limbs extended from his back and enabled him to jump clear of the first one. He opened fire into its side as it passed and whipped his sword to cut the legs out from under the second one that approached them.

It dropped and scrabbled on the soil in an attempt to stand before he pressed the barrel of his assault rifle against its skull and pulled the trigger. A three-round burst drilled directly through the bone.

The creature shuddered, sagged, and its eyes closed as the life left its body.

"We blew the tunnel last night," the corporal shouted once the second gargantuan cryptid was dealt with. "But it looks like they excavated it again, which explains why the bastards aren't too concerned about using the dense jungle to cover their movements."

It seemed they wouldn't be given any time to catch their breath. On the bright side, this kind of fighting was just the thing to get everyone up and ready for the day ahead. It was better than a cup of coffee.

The fact that the mutants were able to get to the other side of the wall so quickly was a concern and Sal had a feeling they would have to act quickly or this would be merely the start of something much bigger.

"Major, are you still with us?"

"I'm heading in with extra troops," the man answered and the interference seemed a little worse than before. It wasn't the best sign, given the side of the wall the incoming troops were on.

"We could use fire teams on both sides of the wall," Madigan shouted. "We need to cut the new growth—both outside the wall and the Zoo spur—off from the jungle proper or we won't be able to block the tunnel."

"Understood. I already have eight fire teams on the way with more being scrambled as we speak."

Depending on how things went on the ground, Sal wasn't sure if they had time for more teams to be scrambled.

He paused suddenly and tilted his head before he flicked his sword to bisect one of the locusts that managed to get through Madigan's cover fire.

His eyes narrowed as he returned his focus to what had caught his attention before the locust distracted him. The new pita plants were already present. He'd never seen the blue ones growing in the newer sections of the Zoo. The teams always had to travel in for a few hours before they found the goddammed things.

These had the red-and-blue petals, though. In his mind, they were clear indicators that the Zoo intended to push its expansion out as quickly as possible. He could only see a few but it was possible that the rest were either hidden by the underbrush or had been trampled during the fighting.

Sal caught his breath when a sharp tension seemed to freeze everything around him for a moment. He had no idea how he sensed that this was the Zoo's reaction to the presence of the fire teams. Like an elastic band stretched to its utter limit, it suddenly snapped and released a surge of primal bloodlust that was almost exhilarating.

It was a common enough reaction but always terrifying to see as though everything touched by the Zoo, plants and animals, were suddenly driven into a frenzy. This time, however, he was oddly even more aware of it and somehow felt it more acutely. A powerful rush of adrenaline erupted in his chest, his mouth went dry, and a vibrant tingle touched his extremities.

The feeling wasn't at all pleasant. It was like the taste of bile made into a sensation that pressed forcefully through his body.

He'd only started to notice the sensation lately—and never to this extent—but looking back, the sudden release of pheromones from the Zoo had been present from the very beginning, whenever it felt like it needed to defend itself.

The only difference between then and now was how much stronger the release was.

Tongues of flame already began to burn the growth back and the monsters were suddenly distracted from their attacks on the ground teams, their attention drawn to those on the perimeter instead.

It wouldn't last, but it at least gave them a moment to draw a breath and decide what their next move was. They couldn't stay where they were or they would be caught in the fire along with the Zoo all around them.

"Did you have anyone guarding the entrance to the tunnels, even after you blew them?" Madigan asked and checked her weapons before she launched a couple of parting grenades at the creatures that were moving away.

"Two men." The corporal nodded and gestured in the direction of the tunnel. "I'm fairly sure they're dead now, though."

"The mole rats that did the digging," Sal interjected before his partner could ask any other questions, "did you burn the bodies? The protocol is to make sure all the larger creatures are plasma'd when possible. Did that get done?"

The soldiers exchanged a look that answered the question without the need for words.

"Fuck me," Matt hissed. "How many goop sacs do you figure were in the creatures?"

"Two each is what we found in those we've dissected before," Sal answered quickly and reloaded his assault rifle. "Do you know if they were intact?"

"Well...we did use grenades and claymores to clear them out so...I'm not sure," the corporal answered with a shrug. "Wouldn't we have been swarmed yesterday if we broke them"?

"Not necessarily," Sal replied, his expression grim. "I don't think it's ever been put to the test. The only time these bastards have been killed in a way that might damage the sacs is during a major outbreak, which is when the Zoo is in a frenzy anyway."

"I don't see how they could have been intact when we killed them," another soldier added. "I was here, but I doubt we would have noticed it in the carnage."

Sal nodded. "All right, I guess that makes sense. We need to get out of here while we still can. The rest of the teams will do some serious burning, and I always prefer to be audience to that shit from the outside."

"Agreed." Madigan motioned for the combined teams to ready themselves again, this time in a formation that would allow them to move quickly.

Given the time that had already passed, it would allow the militaries to conduct their searches and for them to be called if anything was found. If the major did his job, all the bases and the surrounding areas would be on high alert, with regular sweeps conducted to make sure there were no other attempts by the Zoo to get clear of the wall.

Their sector was, after all, in Niger and no one wanted a repeat of that particular clusterfuck.

It was easier to deal with the other base commanders than the corporate executives who filled his schedule almost every day. Most of them didn't even respect the sanctity of office hours and called him at all times of the day or night to try to gain any advantage they could.

It was pathetic, honestly. Franklin knew it was their job and every call could mean millions gained or lost, but it was still annoying to hold their hands after the amount of damage they'd already done to the planet by spreading the Zoo around like it was manure.

The rest of the base commanders all had their problems and flaws too, but he found he could respect each and every one of them. They were mostly military and vets of the Zoo as well, and each one had intimate knowledge of what would happen if they failed in their tasks.

That type of thinking had a way of focusing the mind and brought them common ground. He could work with that and was even grateful for it because he had almost none of it with the pompous executives who demanded his time and attention.

"Between us and the Internet gods, allow this call," the British base commander said and sipped her water. "I don't know which is worse. The Zoo starting to encroach on the areas beyond the wall or the corporate overlords who think they can touch down and have everyone around them kowtowing to their every whim and need."

"The Zoo is certainly the worst of the two," the French commander retorted and ran his fingers through his hair. "The line is much closer than one might think, however."

"It's good to know that we all share a common hatred for the nuisance arising from having to move all those assholes into our backyard," Franklin muttered. He understated it somewhat. Before too long, they could probably open a support group for the trauma of dealing with the bastards.

"Unreasonable demands and unreasonable expectations are essentially part of our day-to-day routine," the Japanese commander added and shook his head. The man looked like he was recovering well from the attack but was still a little weak. It was almost like the poison pumped into his system had aged him ten years. "The most concerning part is the growing demand for specimens of the latest Zoo additions to be obtained for their study."

"Well, at least it confirms that the shits truly are crazy," their British counterpart said and shook her head. "Next, you'll tell me that they want us to deliver these specimens alive and unspoilt."

"I've dealt with that too," Franklin admitted. "Honestly, at this point, I have my speech on our new regulations regarding live Zoo specimens memorized. I can have my assistant write it up if you all want to have a look and get some ideas."

"As much as we might dislike the idea of handing the keys to our bases over," the Sahara Coalition commander stated and leaned a little closer to the camera, "we can all understand their primary motivation. Greed. They never know when the next pita plant gold mine will present itself and they want to be on top of the situation so they can profit from it before their competitors do. It's despicable, but I think we can take advantage."

The US commander sighed. He'd had a feeling this would come up and all he could say was that he was glad that he wasn't the one to say it.

"We need intelligence," the Brit commander agreed. "Information will be the key to our surviving the next few months. The Zoo sometimes appears to have taken a breathing space after its push into Niger, but there are still considerably more attacks on teams that venture in or even approach the fucking place."

Agreement rumbled among them but Franklin waited, unsure where she was going with her line of thought. They all knew the Zoo was far more aggressive these days, especially with people who went inside the jungle. They'd lost enough teams before they decided they would have to put a stop to even shallow runs.

"What are you getting at?" he asked finally.

"Only to the point that it's a matter of time before these attempts to get beyond the wall are far too common for us to deal with consistently. These two recent incidents in the French sector might well be the start to whatever is next on the Zoo's agenda. Honestly, it feels like it's testing our defenses and studying where we are at our weakest."

Gone were the times when she was the voice who complained about them anthropomorphizing the jungle. Those were interesting times when he had to fight tooth and nail to get these people to sit at the same table as him to negotiate some kind of action. These days, they were almost too willing to get shit done.

There were limits to that, of course, but like the Zoo, he would test the limits of what he could and couldn't do, if only to have a proper reference point for the future.

Franklin leaned forward and drew a deep breath before he spoke. "Good points all round. All that coupled with the increase in new species of flora and fauna that have appeared everywhere has been noticed by the experts in Zoo biology. It might seem like the place is throwing everything up to and including whatever passes for a kitchen sink to see what sticks, but Dr. Jacobs is very keen to point out that nothing the Zoo does is without purpose. I have a feeling we've only had a taste of the kinds of monsters we'll have to deal with in much larger numbers."

There was also the feeling that the Zoo was throwing their cannon fodder creatures—the locusts and hyenas—at them with greater vigor than before. Sal had been quick to note that not all the creatures were willing to rush at the bullets and some were even quite passive about it all. The smaller simians, in particular, seemed like they only got involved in the violence when they were dragged into it, usually on those rare occasions when someone pulled a pita plant from the ground.

"We've also had a couple of reports from our people in the field," the British commander continued, slid her glasses on, and studied something on the table in front of her, out of sight of the people that she was talking to. "A couple of men made note of something that looked like a cobra springing out of the ground and spitting some kind of gunk at them. The report says it stuck to their armor and even fire couldn't remove it. I'm honestly not sure what the point was because later reports pointed to this... gunk as being quite easy to remove once it dried."

"Did you collect any samples of this?" Franklin asked

"None have been noted. It doesn't appear to have any real purpose."

"Appear being the operative word here," he insisted. "Just because we don't know what the purpose is doesn't mean it has none. If I were you, I would start insisting that your people keep any organic material from the Zoo isolated. If they can get it to the labs, we can study it a little closer and see what it does in a sterile environment."

"I have a feeling this statement has been made dozens of times all around the world," Kimura pointed out. "Right before their houses came crashing down and required the efforts of experts to clear the outbreaks. I don't see how any attempt to bring organic material out of the Zoo can end in any other way but disaster."

"Therein lies the monkey's paw," Franklin muttered and scratched his jaw. "We need to know everything we can about the Zoo and the only real way we can study it is in a lab. But no lab, no matter how high-tech and no matter what kind of security we put around it, can guarantee that it will be able to hold off any incursions from turning into an outbreak. We're caught between a rock and a hard place here."

He could see that his idioms sailed over the heads of a couple of the members present for the call—those for whom English was a secondary or even tertiary language—but he appeared to have made the context clear enough for them to understand it.

Generalized mumbling followed and a couple of the commanders discussed the matter with assistants off-screen. The idea was for these meetings to be confidential, but there was no way for him to enforce that in an environment where line of command needed to be preserved with some people briefed and ready to take over should anything happen to the base leader.

"I think there is not much of a choice," Kimura stated finally with a deep, troubled sigh. "We will have to acquiesce to these demands for new samples from the Zoo or we risk falling behind in a war for intelligence—information that might have won us this fight if we had acquired it in a timely manner."

None of them liked it, but Franklin could see that the agreement was practically unanimous.

"We need to understand these suckers if we're going to kill them properly," he agreed and tried to ignore the tiredness at the back of his eyes. "But how the hell can we acquire these new specimens for them to test?"

"The answer is obvious enough," his Russian counterpart—who had been silent for most of the meeting—interjected. "We'll have to change our stance on runs into the Zoo. They will have to be shallow and with the express intention to gather new specimens to be studied in a lab."

"In other words, we'll commit our troops to missions that have a high possibility of leading them to their deaths." Franklin growled his frustration. "All in the hopes that those who survive will be able to drag something out that might be able to help future efforts survive?"

Solodkov rubbed his jawline for a moment before he nodded. "It is a risky venture and likely will not be a popular one. I would say we need volunteers, possibly from the mercenary ranks, and we will need to find a way to incentivize them despite the high risks. I think we might be able to convince these corporate *cyka blyats* to pay these fees themselves, given that they are the ones who insist on it."

That was a good idea, although Franklin knew there would be considerable whining and complaining about that too. These people were trained to fight against any additional expense that threatened their bottom line. It was practically pathological.

"It's a calculated risk," the British commander stated finally and shook her head. "The kind of thing that we will always face in positions like these, but I doubt any of us anticipated the scale when we first accepted the promotions. I'll see what I can do about passing the costs along to the people who can comfortably pay them."

Once again, unanimous—if disgruntled—agreement was uttered by the other commanders, and they began to sign off, likely with the intention of gathering their notes and data to see that they had beefy arguments to support their new decision.

Franklin didn't like it. Committing men, even if they were mercenaries, to this much risk would always weigh heavily on his mind, and it was the kind of thing that would surely backfire.

He didn't know how, when, or where, but it would blow up in their faces. And when people looked around for names to put to blame, theirs would be at the top of everyone's lists.

That would also be a calculated risk on their part. He had taken the job knowing the risks, and while it had begun to hit him a little harder than he thought it would, he intended to continue to fight the Zoo every step of the way until they put someone else in charge.

At this point, being recalled to answer questions in front of the Joint Chiefs almost sounded like a vacation.

"Fucking shits," he muttered, pushed from his seat, and stretched carefully.

He wasn't sure who he had directed the insult to. Maybe everyone and maybe only himself. There might be some questions about that too.

After a moment to collect his thoughts, Franklin gathered the paperwork. There were numerous mercs to choose from, the daredevils who wouldn't mind a little extra risk as long as there was a hefty payday waiting for them on the other end of the run.

If he could convince the best to join, others would fill the ranks quickly. The veterans were those who brought the real crazies in on their missions, and if they could all get their shit together and pull off a couple of successes, it wouldn't be long before the others joined the fun.

It was a place to start if nothing else. He ran his gaze over the names and noted those he thought were essential to these operations.

When he reached the Heavy Metal team, he smirked and circled the whole group in red. If anyone was crazy enough to get involved in this, it was them.

CHAPTER SIX

Things could have gone better. They had been dropped into the middle of an incursion and if they had arrived there a little earlier, the chances were they could have saved those who had died. It was the kind of hard fact that always needed to be considered, no matter what the final outcome.

Sal didn't like to think of it as dwelling too long on the guilt he had no reason to feel but rather as a way for him to analyze the situation so that they could be better prepared for when it happened in the future.

Then again, it could have been far worse. If they had been an hour later, they would have been faced with a massive outbreak on the other side of the wall. That would have been a disaster. Thankfully, they were in time to prevent that, which meant the other bases were already committed to more sweeps and patrols to watch for signs that the Zoo was attempting the same thing again.

It wasn't a guarantee that it wouldn't happen, but at

least more people were involved. In addition, the merc companies had more work , which would keep them around instead of forcing them to find work elsewhere.

"Sal?"

He looked up from his computer screen, tilted his head, and scanned the details of the report he was typing. Most of it seemed to come without thought these days, which made it much easier to multitask when he needed to. It had reached the point where he could keep up with the shows the streaming sites brought to the Zoo bases on the big screen while he worked on reports and white papers.

But it did mean that he needed to give everything he worked on an extra look with his full attention to catch any problems and editing issues that should be addressed before he submitted them. In this case, there wasn't much for him to study. They had dropped in, killed monsters, pulled the teams out in time for the fire teams to clear the area, and all before the Zoo established itself.

Mission done. All's well that ended well, right?

"Sal," Anja called over the intercom again. "You'd better not be taking a fucking nap."

"No, I'm here. I'm focused on getting the reports in," he answered. "What do you have?"

"I've got a call from a captain heading up the Israeli contingent. He wants to talk to you. He's calling from the French base?"

"Yeah, they're stationed there."

There was a pause over the line and Sal simply waited.

"Yeah," she answered. "I'm aware. Do you want me to put them through? Or are you too focused on your reports?"

She wasn't in a great mood and he could understand it, and him explaining something she already knew was the kind of thing that would make a bad mood worse.

"Yeah. Sorry."

"No worries. Call coming through."

He leaned back in his seat as the call was transferred to the app on his laptop that let him see where it was coming from and hear the different voices in the background in real time. Anja had some help setting it up, but she had been the mastermind behind it, mostly as a way to keep track of the people who contacted them.

Once again, he reminded himself that he needed to give her a raise.

"This is Sal Jacobs," he announced as the line opened for him.

"Dr. Jacobs?"

"The one and only. How can I help you?"

The man was Israeli but to Sal's ears, his accent almost sounded French. He wasn't sure why.

"I am Captain Jesse Gasko, and I was directed to contact you about reports of Zoo activity."

And Madigan thought they didn't need more people. Sure, they had a heavier cash flow with it, but there would come a point when they needed to have two or three teams on call for when shit started to go extremely bad and the A-Team was off on another mission that had come up a little earlier.

The only question that arose was the fact that Gasko contacted him from a location that was nowhere near the Zoo—or the wall for that matter.

"Explain."

"Reports have come in from people who believe mutants of some kind might have holed up in the Aïr Mountains inside the Niger border. They were seen last night, but the only description we have describes the beasts as extremely large hippos, although some of the locals also added that they have large tusks. Not quite as large as an elephant's, by their description, but larger than their canines should be and even larger than a warthog's."

Sal was under no impression that hippos were as cute and cuddly as their portly appearance might lead one to believe. It was one of the first lessons learned when you looked into what the creatures were capable of. He was surprised that the Zoo hadn't used some variation of the terrifying creatures already. Maybe it was something it had saved for later—or it was something that even the Zoo was terrified of getting mixed up in.

He shook his head. "Right. Are there any other reports?"

"A few mentioned that the creatures are scaled too, but no one truly believes that. I merely thought I'd mention it since it was a part of the original report."

"No, I mean have there been any other reported sightings." The creatures already sounded like something he probably should run away from, along with all other sane people in the area.

"Not many. By the sounds of it, these creatures appear to avoid the local settlements."

That made Sal breathe a little deeper. "Settlements? As in more than one?"

"That is correct, Dr. Jacobs. There is a significant number of population centers in the area, which is why we need specialists on the job as well."

It wasn't something he had expected to hear. All other incidents involving the Zoo saw the creatures putting every effort into adding more biomass to their growth. It didn't add up that they avoided human settlements in the area, which meant there were other elements involved. These mutants either had nothing to do with the Zoo—which raised a whole other series of worrying questions—or they were tasked with a purpose that differed from the norm.

He wasn't sure which one was more worrying and he didn't want to get caught up in any assumptions until he had a better idea of what they were dealing with.

There was no need to get all worked up if these people were merely facing a bloat of hippos wandering the landscape. It was certainly a possibility and easily the best-case scenario. People were still freaked about the Zoo so if they saw any new animal life in the area, they would let their fears take hold of them and the stories would get worse with every retelling.

It wasn't even that people lied about things. All they had to do was let their fears take over and it would warp their concept of what they'd seen. The weakness was rather common among humans, as it turned out.

"What about the US base in Niger?" he asked and leaned forward. "Shouldn't they be the first responders to anything appearing in the region?"

"They have sent troops in but you and your Zoo specialists have been approved and specifically requested. The funding to hire you is in place, and helicopters are standing by to take you from your compound to the area in question."

"Well, if the funding's been approved, we'll be more than happy to investigate the situation."

"Right. You might want to know that there is water in the area. I thought that might be an important detail."

Given that they were dealing with hippo-like mutants, Sal could understand why the man felt the warning was appropriate.

"Shit." He sighed deeply and rubbed his temples where the first twinges of a headache had materialized. "Right. Our team will be ready when the helicopters arrive."

"Excellent. I'll send the word."

This had begun to feel like the good old days.

Not that the good old days were good or even that old for that matter, but it felt like forever since they had been given the go-ahead to enter the Zoo with a team of researchers. There was no mention about whether they were supposed to collect pita flowers, but the mission parameters were to collect samples from any and all new species they could find, both flora and fauna.

That probably included the pita plants. Given the prices they were sold for these days, even one flower would be enough to see them well-compensated for this mission. It would likely pay for their food and drinks for a couple of months at the very least.

Marcel gripped his assault rifle a little tighter as something moved in the trees above them, and he checked the movement quickly on the sensors. There was nothing bigger than the simians that had taken to watching them wherever they went. His every impulse told him to shoot the fuckers, no question about it. But their priority was to continue with the shallow run for as long as possible, which meant keeping the gunfire to a minimum.

That was also reminiscent of the good old days. Back then, they had moved fast and only fired when they had to. While it almost seemed strange to think of it now, it was how things were done back then.

It was interesting that he was the only one of the mercs willing to be there. Marcel didn't generally think of himself as desperate for jobs, but none of the other mercs were willing to work for the Chinese. They had a bad reputation, but he'd worked with them for months and had seen no justification for it thus far.

He chose not to advertise it, however, as the Chinese were the only ones who paid good coin to their mercenarie, and he wanted to make sure that the market didn't saturate. That was a sure way to make the prices drop. For now, it was him, Sarai, and Bets on their payroll, and if anyone else wanted in on the money, they needed to get over their misconceptions—without his help.

Although he would be the first to admit that working with the Chinese was a little difficult, even if not through any fault of their own. Language barriers were always a bitch, and very few of their soldiers spoke any English. Hell, he would have been happy with French or Spanish. A couple of them did—mostly the officers—but the rest made him rely on the translate function installed in his HUD.

Still, it was worth it. He currently led a twelve-man

team into the Zoo—not one of the shallow trips—to escort three researchers in. He wouldn't complain about the work. If current rumors were to be believed, there would be more for the mercs in escorting the research teams. The decision taken at the highest level to ensure that they had all the intel on the monsters coming out of the Zoo would mean an improvement in the work on offer.

A hand was raised by one of his men and the group came to a halt. Marcel swept his weapon quickly across the perimeter to make sure they weren't under attack before he focused his attention on the man who had called for their group to halt.

"What's going on?"

The soldier said something in his native language but his gesture at the researchers in their hybrid suits provided the reason before the translation came through.

"Right," Marcel muttered. "You told them the last time they stopped that we had to ward off a horde of the fucking monsters, right?"

A second passed as their translators kicked in and the man laughed, nodded, and replied. *I said it, but they said they needed to collect samples, so we stop,* read the translation.

"I can't argue with that." He shook his head and scanned their surroundings again. The last time, it had only been a pack of hyenas. These beasts were a Zoo staple and it would honestly be a bigger surprise to not encounter them.

He wasn't one of those people who thought the whole Zoo was working on some Gaia shit with everything connected, but whatever was happening, it knew how to coordinate and stay connected with all the creatures in the jungle. There was no way to tell if the mutants knew where the team was, but he guessed that the monkeys that followed them in the trees somehow sent word to where the rest of the monsters were waiting.

It was an unsettling feeling and honestly drove him to want to gun the little beasts down where they stood, but the orders were to hold off on that kind of thing. It would be a waste of bullets, in all honesty, and he wasn't sure if he could hit the little critters if they skittered into the high branches.

Still. He scowled at the little bastards and resisted the urge to flip them off before he turned his attention to the ground.

"Something tripped the sensors," one of the men shouted and he could see it reading across his screen. "Animals on the move!"

The translations were always technically correct, but there would always be a little wonkiness since they made literal translations. Maybe someone needed to design an AI that could interpret idioms in different languages.

He didn't have the technical skill for that bullshit, but many bright people around the world could make considerable money with that.

Instead of telling his people where they needed to be, he highlighted the positions for them. It was important that no point was left open for the monsters to get in because someone didn't understand what he meant. In this situation, less was most certainly more, and Marcel gestured for them to be ready to open fire at his signal.

"Hey, geek squad, what's the situation?" Marcel shouted.

"We are almost finished."

"Well, I'll be sure to let the monsters know that you need a second."

It took them a couple of seconds, but they worked a little faster as they collected their samples carefully from a nearby tree. They were working on what looked like moss, and while it seemed like a huge waste of time, he wasn't part of the geek squad. He would have to trust that they knew what to look for better than he did.

His attention was immediately caught by two panthers that approached them from above. They waited for an opening to strike at the people below, and he wouldn't allow them to have support from the ground creatures.

Marcel was only too willing to open fire first. He squeezed the trigger and his rifle kicked back with a three-round burst that drilled through the first of the panthers and clipped the shoulder of the second. It toppled from its perch on the trees and plummeted.

He didn't bother to finish it off as the rest of the creatures rushed forward. They no doubt felt that any surprise they might have had on their side was gone and they might as well throw themselves into the thick of it.

There were locusts for the most part, although a couple of those with scorpion tails tried to push through a flank. He eliminated those immediately and acted as the sniper for the team, letting them handle the bulk of the kills while he dealt with those that posed a greater threat if they managed to get in close enough.

Sooner or later, the Zoo would decide it had enough of throwing monsters into a veritable barrage of projectile damage and it would all be over. For the moment, they still had the advantage of being able to keep the monsters at bay while they were at a distance.

From the moment it had started, he could tell that their heart—or whatever the equivalent happened to be—was not in the attack. They didn't have the numbers to over-whelm the twelve and they had likely hoped to pick off one or two and soften them up for when the real attack came. It had been an admirable attempt, but it wasn't long before they were all taken care of and their bodies piled around fifteen paces from where the team was situated.

"Clean up!" Marcel called, raised his index finger, and made a circular motion with it in the air. "If anything else is in the area, I want it dead. We move out of here with nothing on our backs!"

He could tell that the translation hadn't been effective as they paused and discussed what he meant until they decided on what made the most sense and got to work. With them busy, he moved to where their researchers were still huddled and now peered at something close to the base of a massive tree.

"It looks like none of you took any damage," Marcel commented but checked to make sure. It was his job to get them back alive and uninjured, after all. "Do you want to talk about what's taking so long?"

"We found the spitter."

He tilted his head and tried to decide what that could mean until he circled to where they were stared so intently.

"Oh...you mean it literally."

They'd all seen footage of the creature or plant that had sprung up out of the sand on a British team and spat some unknown type of gunk. It was the kind of thing that was circulated even if it wasn't displayed by the group for the purposes of education.

Everyone wanted a closer look at what these little creatures or plants were, and it seemed they had one on the ground in front of them. This one, however, looked much smaller than the one that had spat at the Brits.

"Why didn't it attack us?" Marcel asked and examined the thick bud intently. It did look almost like a cobra with what could be called its head tilted toward the ground and what appeared to be a breach ready to spit something out at anything and anyone that stood in front of it.

"It's not old enough. Maybe it's a baby."

"Or a sapling," he retorted. "Or…whatever the hell these things are when they're young. Do you think you can take it out? Like…transplant it?"

"That is what we are trying. If you do not have any more interruptions to add."

The statement meant they didn't want him to bother them while they were working. It looked like they were putting probes into the ground around it, possibly to determine how deep the roots went and if they could pull it out.

A few minutes passed before they retrieved a containment box and what looked like a long knife, although he had no idea what they would do with it. He lost interest at that point, satisfied that the plant itself posed no danger to them. Honestly, he didn't give a fuck how they got it into the box, only that they did—and soon because he had a feeling they had already been there way too long.

Thankfully, they worked efficiently and the sample was

secured—and about damn time too given that something had tripped the edges of their sensors. They moved forward again and Marcel scowled when he noticed one particularly large mutant instead of the tiny fuckers that had attacked them before. Maybe the timing was off and it was supposed to attack with the rest of them.

Still, it was possibly the kind of monster that could take them all on without any real help. He'd seen it before, especially when squads of weaker beasts rushed in for a few easy kills to soften the humans up for the larger creature to attack.

"We all stay together. When we have a target, I'll let you know."

Green checkmarks appeared over all their heads in his HUD to confirm that they understood as they continued as quickly as they could. Should the worst-case scenario happen, they were less than five minutes from the edge of the jungle if they pushed hard. They would be able to leave the whole damn place behind and race to the edge where they could call in the Hammerheads—or the knockoffs the Chinese had brought over—that had guns mounted on top that would help escape the area even faster.

But one monster didn't feel like it would warrant that kind of response. Marcel grasped his rifle a little tighter and inched closer so he would be at the front lines if and when the creature decided to attack.

It didn't wait long. He decided it was some kind of lizard from the way it walked. The shorter, stubby legs could move it quickly enough, especially through the dense underbrush.

Finally, the sensors revealed a clearer indication of what

tracked them and it was one of those that could kill them all if it managed to catch them by surprise. The damn Komodo dragons were hard to predict since they could kill two or three people at a time with a sweep of their tails and were able to kill even more if they got in close with the acid they could spit.

Thankfully, that was the kind of two-edged sword they could take advantage of.

"Focus on the acid sacs around its throat," Marcel warned them and highlighted the point on the creature's silhouette as it began to rush toward them. "And keep an eye out for that tail, because it will—"

His warning came a second too late as it skidded to a halt and the whole body twisted and snapped the tail around. He was already diving to the ground as it whipped toward them. One of the Chinese was a second too late in hitting the deck and the appendage glanced over the side of his helmet. He sprawled awkwardly and while he appeared to be alive, he also looked like he'd been poleaxed.

The other soldiers opened fire on the beast as it readied for another attack, even though most of them were still on the ground.

They managed to deliver three or four rounds into the acid sac before it was able to attack them again, although he was surprised that instead of the beast's acid devouring it, it merely rolled harmlessly over its skin. Only once it fell did the substance begin to react with the biological material it found on the ground.

New and improved Zoo monsters—just his luck. Marcel pushed a grenade into the under-barrel launcher on his assault rifle and slapped it shut smoothly, locked on his target with a little help from his HUD, and launched it before the creature could whip its tail again.

The explosive drove into the beast's side, and it was enough to blast through its skin, shatter the ribcage, and gouge a gap to where its innards were now blackened and charred by the grenade.

It uttered one soft, pitiful roar—impressive since it didn't have much in the way of lungs left—and collapsed. Blood seeped into the dense bushes and leaves on the ground.

Interestingly enough, the researchers were the first to jump into action once the large beast was downed. They approached the carcass and chattered in their language about something his translator had a difficult time conveying.

Finally, he realized they were trying to determine why the acid hadn't burned through its skin like it usually did. He had that question as well so he joined them but kept his assault rifle trained on the perimeter in case something else decided to attack.

Nothing did, which allowed him to settle on his haunches and focus on what had caught the researchers' intense interest.

Their excitement grew as they inspected the dead beast and he could see why. A murky substance covered the scales. It was flexible and allowed for movement almost like wax, but it created an armor-like skin rather than only the usual scales that overlapped.

Once they had their samples, one of them moved to the tail, inspected it closely, and chattered animatedly as he took another sample of skin, this time from the tail where the beast had struck their man in the helmet.

"It came off here!" said the translation.

He zoomed in on it and noticed with surprise that the waxy protection had been knocked off where it had made contact. Marcel looked at the soldier, who was being helped slowly to his feet. He'd certainly sustained a concussion but was lucky to come away with his head still attached to his neck.

Still, they were effectively a man short. He gestured for them to start moving again.

"If we stick around here for too long, we might as well build a damn fortress because we will be besieged. Come on, let's go."

They understood him well enough and once all the samples were collected, the men gathered in marching formation. The man who had been hit still twitched and growled about something that his translator had no success with.

"What the hell is the matter with him?" Marcel snapped to one of the men who stood nearby.

"He's saying that the hit must have dislodged something in his suit," the soldier answered through the translator. "It must have because he says there are mosquitoes inside."

"Mosquitoes?"

The man nodded to confirm there was no error in translation. Maybe the concussion was the source of the so-called mosquitoes. He wasn't sure if that was possible, but he recalled the few times he'd been knocked out in his boxing matches when he'd woken feeling tingles all over his body.

That must surely be it. Marcel nodded and grimaced when his suit wanted to jerk with the motion. He took control before it did.

With all that said, however, he wanted to get the men out. One man injured who thought he was okay would be a weak point for their enemies to make use of. He saw no need to put his people through that kind of risk, not in these already dangerous times.

CHAPTER SEVEN

"What in the actual fuck?"

Courtney realized she was yelling when her assistant jerked in his seat and turned to see if there was anything she needed. He even went so far as to stand from his desk and motion to ask wordlessly if she needed him.

She waved him off quickly and shook her head.

It wasn't like she was stalking them or even keeping that close an eye on them. Heavy Metal wasn't a subsidiary of Pegasus but as one of the partners, she still got monthly reports of their finances. Most of the time, Sal and Madigan managed to ensure that the company produced a heavy profit so she didn't have to be involved in micromanagement—or any management at this point unless they specifically needed her input or expertise. She was still technically a founding member, but her focus was on her US business interests and she had to delegate.

For once, however, she saw that Heavy Metal was in the red—spending more money than they were making—and that alone was why she needed a little more information. Not because she was micromanaging or anything like that.

The fact that she needed to justify it so hard to herself said a little about issues she probably needed to address sooner rather than later. Still, it was annoying to see that Heavy Metal had allocated most of their spending for the month under *Recruiting*.

She drew a deep breath, calmed herself, and set the glass walls in her office to their opaque mode—being the boss had its privileges. When reason had reasserted itself, she keyed her computer into the secure line Anja had set up so she could contact them without any chance of it being overheard.

The hacker didn't respond immediately. This wasn't surprising given the hours the woman kept. She had talked to her before about the possibility of changing her schedule to something a little healthier, but the Russian had replied that it would be far more stressful to change lifetime habits this far down the line.

It didn't make staying up until she crashed, sleeping for hours, and getting up to do it all over again with a pot of terrible coffee and the few energy drinks that were sent to the Zoo a healthy practice. Courtney's opinion hadn't changed but she could at least respect the amount of effort Anja had put into making Heavy Metal what it was today.

Finally, the hacker's alias pinged on the server and she connected to the call.

"Courtney. It's been a while." Anja sounded like she was multi-tasking. "How are things in your neck of the woods?"

"People say the city is a concrete jungle, and I think they mean Philly when they say that," she answered. "It's nothing like the jungles you and I are used to dealing with, though."

"No indeed. But is it weird that I prefer being here than there? Most of the time, anyway."

The Pegasus chairwoman turned in her comfortable chair and stared at the view of the city below. "If I said I don't miss being in the thick of it with you guys from time to time, I would be lying. But I have to say that sticking it out in civilization, getting home to a real bed every night, eating good food—"

"Yeah, yeah. There's no need to rub it all in our noses."

"I wish someone was rubbing it in my nose. Or I was rubbing it on someone's nose."

Anja cleared her throat. "All right, I'm ready for a change of subject. Is there any reason why you called me or was it simply to make me uncomfortable?"

"It's always fun to make you uncomfortable, but I need to chat to Sal or Madigan."

"Oh, they…well, neither of them is available. They have gone to a situation in the Air…Aïr Mountains, in Niger. Reports are that a few hippos have been seen in the area and they had to deal with."

"Hippos?" Courtney wasn't sure she'd heard correctly.

"Sal isn't sure that cryptids are involved," the hacker explained quickly. "He says it might be regular hippos that have the locals running scared. And they have reason to, all things considered."

"Yeah, I think everyone has heard about what happened in Niger—oh, and you could mention to them that Pegasus donated substantially to the effort of finding survivors in the area. But the real reason for my call is I looked at the financial report and saw that you guys are hiring and not merely paying mercenaries for individual jobs." She called the report in question onto her screen again.

"Oh...right. Sal said we need more people on our permanent roster—he talks constantly about how the Zoo will start something big and we should be prepared. Madigan doesn't see eye-to-eye with him on that particular opinion but she's going with his word on it for the moment."

Courtney drew a sharp breath and took a moment to push her irritation aside as best she could. "Why didn't you guys call me for this? You know you have at least one more member on the team to call on."

"Well, that was discussed, but we assumed you were busy on the Pegasus front. You might not have time to travel to the other side of the world." Anja sounded a little defensive.

As she'd listened to the hacker, her grasp had tightened on her pen to the point that it began to crack. Instead of releasing it, she squeezed a little more until it snapped and a glob of ink spilled out to stain her fingers and the desk a little too.

She didn't like people to make decisions like that for her. While she knew Madigan and Sal's decision had come from the best place, they should have included her in the discussion. With that said, she did appreciate that they didn't make her choose between what was happening at Pegasus and what was happening in the Zoo. This way, if she'd been unable to help by virtue of some dire crisis only she could attend to, she could feel like the choice was made for her and she could be mad at them without any attack of conscience on her part.

"I'm never too busy for my friends," Courtney finally stated when she'd regained some of her composure. "He knows that."

"I…uh, can't argue with that."

"Damn right you can't."

Anja sounded like she was uncomfortable again and she did the woman the favor of changing the subject.

"Right. What kind of people are they bringing in?"

"Matt was put in charge of that," the hacker told her. "He has connections all around the Zoo so would know the people who would fit with Heavy Metal. We talked to McFadden too, and he recommended the three freelancers he worked with in the US. They said they are willing to join Heavy Metal, at least on a temporary basis. For the moment, that makes nine new members fighting on our side."

"Let me guess—all gunners and Sal is the only scientist involved?"

"I…well, yeah." The Russian sounded like she wished she didn't have to answer.

Courtney sighed and shook her head. "Right. Send me their contact information. I'll arrange for them to fly with me."

"That sounds like something you should probably discuss with Sal and Madigan first, right?"

"They aren't the bosses of me. Pegasus is behaving for the moment. Andersen is more than capable of managing everything in my absence, and if he runs into any problems my board can't handle, he has Savage."

"Is he still working for you?" The hacker sounded surprised, which indicated that she only had contact with the operative when he was running missions that required her expertise.

"Sure. Never underestimate how useful having a security consultant on retainer can be."

Anja lapsed into a moment of silence and her chair creaked in the background. "Fine. I'll send you the contact details."

"And Anja?"

"Yeah?"

"Not a word of this to Sal. He'll try to talk me out of it and it'll be more difficult for him if I'm already there."

"I can't argue with that logic." The Russian's tone almost suggested that she wished she could.

There was no real assurance that the hacker wouldn't tell Sal anyway, but if the truth be told, she often felt a little bored with the civility of the day-to-day humdrum of running Pegasus. In the early days, it had been more challenging having to run things by the skin of her teeth and deal with the numerous people who wanted her dead.

Even that had ended. She needed action and it was a good time to kick some Zoo ass.

Sal's worst fear was realized as soon as they flew over the target area—many settlements were strung across the mountainous region to make the most of the fertile pockets. He shook his head in both surprise and concern as the helicopters brought them to the location. The mountains were rather beautiful and a blessed break from the duality of desert and jungle he was used to.

As the choppers climbed into the mountains, he had expected the settlements and farms to decrease, but the higher elevations had been no deterrent to those who chose to make this region their home.

"Are you thinking what I'm thinking?" Madigan asked.

"It's hard to say. If you're thinking there are way too many humans in this area, then yes."

"Yeah. What else would I be thinking?"

He chuckled. "Something that wouldn't be appropriate to talk about on an open comm channel."

She grinned and tilted her head without answering one way or the other.

"Why wouldn't there be humans here?" Juice asked and adjusted his suit so he had a better view out the window.

"Since they've recently suffered one of the worst Zoo attacks since this whole situation started, I expected to see far more people heading farther south," Sal answered.

"The locals have lived here since before there were cars, roads, or anything like that in the region. They've remained in their homes for that long. Do you think something as short-lived as a humanitarian crisis would make them move?"

This reply was both logical and understandable, but it was still something to think about. If these people weren't willing to move and no one could make them, their homes would probably be on the front line of the war against the Zoo when it overcame the human attempts to corral it. The fact that he no longer considered that a matter of if but rather when was a worrying sign.

"Well, if there's a Zoo outbreak, it's good of them to provide it with a nice nursery larder," he muttered as the aircraft finally began to descend to where he could see a small temporary base had been erected, with tents and defenses in place to make sure that nothing could attack them in the night.

He recalled the story about two man-eating lions someone had made a movie about, but that was a little farther east. They probably didn't have to worry about that there. He was about eighty percent sure about that.

Gasko was waiting for them, holding his cap down as the helicopters landed close to the camp where what looked like a collection of different militaries with a presence in the area was stationed. There were still enough of them left after the incursion not that long before, and they were more than willing to be included in any opportunity to deliver payback to the Zoo.

Colonel Amos stood beside him and both tried to hold a conversation over the drone of the rotors before they finally gave up and motioned for the Heavy Metal team to join them at a position away from the helicopters.

"We appreciate you being able to make it here so quickly," Gasko said and gestured for the full team to join them.

"Have there been any developments?" Sal asked and hunched his head a little even though they were well away from the rotors. It was a purely reflexive action based on the noise of the choppers and he barely noticed it.

"Nothing since we've spoken," Gasko answered as they approached the camp.

"Oh...I wish you hadn't said that," the scientist

muttered. "So, Colonel, what brings you this far from the center of the recovery operation?"

Amos shrugged. "The reports were worrying enough that it required my immediate attention."

He shook his head. "I didn't think reports about hippos being seen around these parts would have your attention."

"Because hippos haven't been seen this far north in Niger for hundreds of years," Amos answered and seemed unperturbed about his snarky reply when talking to a biologist. "That fact alone makes this a very unusual occurrence—one the Zoo might or might not have instigated, given the reports."

Sal suppressed a little embarrassment. Of course the man would have been given the details of the possible escaped mutants, and any military commander worth his salt would have been concerned. Still, as much as he wanted to make some clever excuse, there was no point in getting arrogant and defensive about the matter. He'd been wrong and it was time to take a deep breath and push forward.

And it did answer the one pressing question he had in his head. There was little doubt that these were not naturally occurring creatures.

"Right," he responded and turned to business. "We'll need troops to cordon off the area around where the animals were last seen."

"Do you think an evacuation is needed at this point?" Amos asked and motioned them to the command tent.

"I doubt you'd have much luck telling the locals to leave," Madigan replied. "At least not without very clear and accurate details of the monsters that will threaten them. I think our efforts are better spent making sure there is no threat for them to evacuate from first."

The colonel looked at the other men in the command tent and none of them disagreed. Or, at least, they didn't feel strongly enough about it to make their disagreement heard.

"If we can't find the monsters or at least ensure that they aren't infesting the area, that'll be the time to evacuate," Sal clarified. "It's a secure area for the mutants, and if they've moved from the vicinity where they were last seen, there's no telling what their purpose here is."

"Right then." The captain cleared his throat. "I'll arrange for Hammerheads to get you up there."

Madigan immediately shook her head firmly. "It's rough terrain, and if these creatures are avoiding the settlements, they'll steer clear of any sound of us approaching. We'll be quieter with only our suits and quicker too, depending on the terrain. Plus, there are numerous caves and ravines the Hammerheads won't be able to get us into."

Again, there was no disagreement from the group assembled, and she gestured for the Heavy Metal team to ready their gear. Something niggled in the back of Sal's head, a small voice that insisted the Zoo was probably working on something. He had no idea what and even if he did, how the hell he could explain it without Madigan sending him packing back to the compound?

"So, we'll hike up the mountains," Juice muttered. "I knew that signing up with Heavy Metal would take me places. I guess I should have asked if those were places I wanted to go to."

"If the worse comes to worst, you'll have a nice view of

the landscape before a mutant hippo guts and crushes you," Sonja commented with a grin.

"I've seen some nice views in my time," Jim noted as they gathered their weapons. "I climbed Denali during my last stint home and had a nice view of the Alaskan wilderness."

"I can't imagine there were many Zoo monsters to worry about up there," Kolt interjected.

"Nope. Well...fuck, I hope not."

CHAPTER EIGHT

There was no way to determine why he felt this way. Franklin had dealt with numerous people since he was put in command of the US base, and he had thoughts on every single one of them. Generally, the spectrum curled between like and dislike, although a few fell into the realm of disgust and fewer still attained the trustworthy spectrum.

Only one of them had ever dropped into the section of downright unsettling. Solodkov had a way of making people uncomfortable around him without even trying—and it was very likely that this applied to everyone who encountered him. He also never gave any indication if he knew of the effect he had on other people but since he was former FSB—the direct descendant of the KGB—he likely knew and took advantage of it. It was even very possible that he cultivated it very deliberately for this particular purpose.

The US base commander didn't like it. Having someone with no military background—and an intelligence operative, no less—among the commanders he needed to deal with on a daily basis made him wary and irritable, but he couldn't do anything about it. There was nothing concrete to complain about and even if there were, it was unlikely that the Russians would reassign the man based on an American's complaint. The worst part—one that made him constantly wary because he couldn't be sure of the motives behind it—was that he had been the most supportive when it came to changing the mindsets of the Zoo commanders.

Which meant he needed to grit his teeth and connect the line that would put him in contact with the Russian without any complaint.

"Commander Franklin." Solodkov answered with a polite smile. "To what do I owe the pleasure?"

The guy's English was so perfect, he could have passed for an American almost anywhere.

"I'm calling to discuss the memo I sent you yesterday. Your assistant said that you would need to confer on the topic?"

"Of course. There isn't much to confer on, to be honest. The bases around the Zoo already have the Heavy Metal mercenary team on call for any emergency in a practical sense. We might as well start paying them properly for it. Who knows what kind of foreign interests would be willing to give them a better offer when we're flooded with corporate presence around the Zoo?"

The Russian looked distracted, and a few men were speaking in the background although it wasn't clear what was being said.

"Did I call you at a bad time?" Franklin asked when it appeared as though his counterpart was paying more attention to the conversation happening away from the camera.

Solodkov didn't answer immediately and instead, snapped what sounded like an order in Russian before he returned his attention to the American.

"My apologies," he said finally. "There was an incident overnight that has required my attention."

"Do you need any assistance with it?" he asked and leaned forward. "You know our troops are yours the moment you need them."

"I appreciate that but for the moment, I think we can handle this ourselves." The Russian looked down as a tablet was placed in front of him. "Our surveillance planes picked up the fact that the Zoo had crossed the buffer zone and is now directly at the wall. It is only a section, which is the odd thing, not the full-length of the tree line in our sector. Like…the jungle reached an arm out, although it is wide enough to be a matter of some concern."

"It happened overnight?"

"I'm looking at the comparison shots, twelve hours apart." Solodkov held the tablet up for Franklin to see. As the man had said, one picture had a wide buffer of sand between the wall and the Zoo, and the second showed a narrow stretch of dark green stretching from one to the other. "I confess, I find it even more worrying than I usually would. Something seems…odd about it."

"What does the cryptid movement in the area look like?" Franklin frowned as he experienced the first stirring of concern as well.

"And that is another oddity. The mutants don't seem to

have massed in that section, at least according to our initial sensor reports."

"That can change from hour to hour." It somehow seemed important to ground this in what they could regard as "normal."

"Naturally." The Russian nodded. "The whole base has been put on high alert. We have teams preparing to head in, which might exacerbate the situation as well. They'll push at it with flame and plasma throwers to try to eradicate this seemingly pointless spur."

Franklin scratched his jaw and scowled at the screen in front of him. Logic said that if it had pushed to the wall, it fully intended to try to push beyond it and that always included hordes of the monsters. Aside from the frantic growth, however, there appeared to be none of the expected aggression at all.

"I'll advise you on any further developments, especially when our teams head out," Solodkov promised. "But we are going in on high alert. No matter how stupid something might seem, I think we are past assuming this is a pointless exercise by the jungle. My gut tells me there is some ulterior motive to this that will become clear moments before alarm bells start to ring."

"Keep me posted."

"Naturally."

The base was in a tizzy and had been since the team returned with the first live samples they had managed to get their hands on. From what he was told by their intelligence officers, they were the first live samples of the new creatures to be retrieved.

Sying would never understand the kind of mindset that drove the people who actively wanted to go into the Zoo. It had always been an unwilling decision on his part, and the moment they promoted him to the head of the biology division, he made sure he would never go into that damn jungle again.

Maybe it was a little selfish on his part, but he knew that every single one of the researchers would do the same. All things considered, with the way the jungle was going, it had been a good decision, even if it meant the crazy American Marcel Seymor was still going in.

Given that Sying had gained his masters in Berkeley, there hadn't been many chances for him to practice his English since he'd returned home.

They had arranged to meet for drinks later. He had suggested to the base commander that they bring all the people who went into the Zoo for rest and psychological evaluation to see if the jungle caused any psychological reaction in those who experienced it. They hadn't replied to him about it, which meant they had decided no and didn't want to engage him on it.

As usual, the soldier with the concussion would be the only one to receive any medical attention. He snorted and returned his attention to his current priority. They were examining what had been brought out. Dr. Han and Dr. Fa —the two men who had retrieved the samples—were part of the team and about a dozen others followed what they were doing on the cameras and took meticulous notes.

Another suggestion he had made was to make sure that

more than one team of researchers observed the tests to confirm the accuracy of the data and to make sure the Zoo had no effect on the people in contact with it, even if that contact wasn't direct. Isolation chambers and rubber gloves allowed them to examine everything inside a contained area without ever touching it.

Safety was paramount. Even more important was to ensure that the jungle had no opening to turn their lab into an incursion site.

"Approaching the chamber," Sying announced for the benefit of those watching. He had his gear on to add another protective layer between himself and the samples, and he approached the first of the chambers, leaned a little closer, and slipped his hands into the gloves.

He had the most exciting sample so far. The Brits' encounter with it had been considerably more exciting, but they hadn't brought a live sample of the massive creature-plant that spat the green goo at them.

His subject was considerably younger than the one they had seen in the feed, which had almost looked like a cobra pushing from the ground. His sample still resembled the snake but was much smaller. The bud at the tip was about as thick around as a table tennis ball and from what he'd seen in the video, he was sure there were rows of needle-like teeth inside. All he could hope was that the polymer in the rubber of the gloves would be enough to protect his hands from attack.

"There is no sign of it attempting to spit as I engage it," Sying muttered as he inspected the plant. "It appears healthy despite the transplanting."

He eased his fingers around the bud and tried to find

the breach he could use to open its mouth but nothing moved. It was the same species as the creature encountered by the Brits, he was sure of that, but more pokes and prods produced none of the results he'd hoped for.

"Shit." He sighed to clear the frustration from his body. If he couldn't get the creature to produce on its own, he would have to be a little more invasive and even break the scalpels out. He didn't want to have to do that since it would kill the only sample they had.

As a way to procrastinate, he looked up from his work to see what his colleagues were up to with the other samples taken from the Komodo dragon that had injured the soldier. Dr Fa had elected to work on the section where the protective, waxy substance had come off the tail.

It was practically a control group for their testing and there were all the usual reactions to the materials that it was subjected to. No one expected any surprises there.

What was interesting was the sample covered by the protective substance. They still had no idea what it was but were able to cut into it easily enough—as shown by the sample being taken from the dead dragon—and bullets penetrated it without any real issues. Based on that, the skin-like quality that seemed to change the creature's outer layer from scales to something a little more mammalian might be another kind of protection.

At least he wasn't the only one who faced frustration when it came to the new samples. Dr Han worked meticulously and applied an assortment of acids with measured care, but all of them rolled off harmlessly. More were used, all with the same result.

The scientist cursed softly as he expanded his list to

include things they might not ordinarily try. He now worked systematically to find anything that could dissolve or crack the layer without having to resort to brute force.

When he finally shrugged and used water, Sying thought they probably needed to stop, take a step back, and reassess what they were trying to do.

"This substance is something new," Han muttered as the three convened to discuss their options. "I would say it might be a protection for the beast that would allow it to survive having its acid sacs ruptured, but there is something else to it. I can't tell what it is, however, without breaking it down."

"We'll need to get closer," the lab head commented. "The isolation will have to be removed for us to obtain the results we need from the sample. If we can get closer, we'll have a better idea of what we're dealing with."

The two doctors in the room with him nodded their agreement and turned their attention to those who watched from outside. Those conferred for a moment before they contacted them over the PA.

"You are cleared to remove the additional protection protocols."

It was an easy decision for them to make since they were all well-removed from any of the potential problems that might arise, but given that Sying had suggested it himself, he was willing to put his safety aside in the name of science.

For the most part, at least. They were still in their hazmat suits, after all. He nodded and motioned his colleagues to their positions, drew a deep breath, and raised his hands to the bolt that secured the clear plastic box between the little vine inside and himself.

Automated features would activate the box again if needed, so everything was available to help him if it decided to grow up and attack. For that one moment, however, he couldn't help a hint of hesitation before he undid the bolt and let the box open.

Sying realized he was holding his breath as though he waited for something to happen as the sides of the box were lowered by the pneumatic arms. He leaned closer, narrowed his eyes as he approached the little bud, and simply watched and waited for any sign that it would attack.

From what he'd seen of the full-sized one, he had little doubt that its needle-like teeth could rip through his suit no matter that it was reinforced, and even something this small could take a finger off.

And if it did, it would be his fault since it had been his idea to begin with. He pushed his reservations aside, leaned even closer, and finally found the courage to touch the little thing. There was no visible reaction and he ran his fingers up the stalk until he stroked the bud.

"I know you have a mouth full of teeth and spit whatever that goo is, but you're still...kind of cute."

He'd always liked plants for some reason and even kept a peace lily in his living quarters as a way to remind himself that at least one living thing in the world wasn't determined to kill him.

Maybe it was a little weird on his part, but he felt it was important to have a little perspective. Too many people in and around the Zoo had difficulty seeing the forest—or jungle, in this case—for the trees.

It was one of his favorite English sayings but he always had trouble translating that particular idiom to his native language.

But, for all his fears, removing one extra layer of protection hadn't changed anything and there was no sign that the plant would do something worthy of being recorded. He shook his head and glanced to where the others had resumed work.

"So you have nothing for me, huh?" Sying sighed and turned his attention to the row of tools that had been set up for him inside the box. He had hoped that the little thing would put itself on display for him without the need for him to cut it open but if it was inert, they would need to do something drastic to get something out of the damn thing.

He collected the scalpel and looked closely for any sign of where he should make an incision. There were no visible seams and they didn't have the time to look for a microscopic section they could use. He would be called up for wasting time and resources when simply cutting would get what they needed. No one would understand that he didn't want to kill their only live sample.

Reluctantly, he pressed the scalpel to the bud and his whole body reacted when the plant moved suddenly out of his grasp almost like a snake would slither free.

"What the hell?" A surge of annoyance flooded him that it now decided it wanted to show a little life.

With a scowl, he approached it with the scalpel again but the bud opened like a flower might have from a similar position and the familiar sight of endless rows of teeth was exposed. Petal-like appendages flicked around like tongues looking for something to latch onto, but he snatched his hand away and dropped the scalpel.

The noise appeared to provide a good indication of where he stood and as he backed away from it, the whole bud turned, appeared to focus on him even though it had no eyes, and the teeth extended outward a split second before it spat something out.

It had only taken the span of a second or two, and he had almost no idea what had happened until the pneumatic arms engaged and the box sealed itself again. Alarms blared and the lights changed from clinical white to bright red as the other two containment boxes began to seal as well.

Sying's entire body tingled with a sudden surge of adrenaline. His heart hammered hard against the confines of his ribcage and he examined his hands to make sure he still had all his fingers. There was no sign of anything missing or that any of the teeth had managed to make contact with his suit, although he would put it under a microscope to make sure.

He still felt utterly shellshocked and by the looks of confusion from his two colleagues, they had no clue of what had happened either. Neither had seen the encounter and their only indication that something was wrong was when the containment boxes started to close.

"Are you all right?" Han asked and approached him slowly. "Did it get a piece of you?"

"I don't...I don't think so." Sying shrugged and looked at his suit. There was no sign of any kind of breach, although he had initiated tests based on the software in his HUD to tell him if there were any problems. If there were, he would need to quarantine until they determined that he was clear of any infection.

Or until he was dead. There was rarely anything that came between the two options.

"It looks like it got some spit on you," Fa commented as he stepped closer and pointed at his chest.

He wasn't sure how he'd missed it in his first check. Maybe he'd simply looked for bright red splotches, a sure indication that he was wounded, not something bright green that almost vanished in the bright red lights that seemed to glower at them.

"It looks like it," he whispered and brushed his fingers reflexively over it.

To their surprise, the gunk immediately desiccated, slid off easily, and became a powdery dust that drifted to the pristine white floor of their lab.

"What in the hell?" Sying whispered. "Quick, get something to collect it with. I want every fucking particle."

"Why? It's not like we'll get anything from it."

"Do your goddammed job."

While he waited, he resisted the temptation to look more closely and was careful to not even approach the little pile. He did not want to disturb it with even the air currents that came from them walking around.

His colleagues collected the dust quickly, isolated it, and made sure there wasn't even a speck left on the floor. The lights around them were still red, which said they were under quarantine until someone decided that they were good to leave.

It was for the best given the circumstances. The last

thing he needed was for a dozen people to rush in and make their work more difficult.

Still, by the time they had contained the gunk-dust, the lights turned white again when the AI detected no possible threat. Sying turned his attention to the bud that had reverted to inertness like its previous aberrant behavior had been nothing more than a nightmare.

"And to think that I thought you were cute," he whispered, disappointed with himself more than with the little beastie.

"What...what happened?"

Han's bewildered tone drew the attention of the other two scientists and they both looked at him. He inspected one of the samples of Komodo dragon skin. For a second, the lab head couldn't tell if it was the one that had the protective wax skin on it or not. The reason became clear a second later when he realized that the other sample didn't have any evidence of what they had tried to study either. Neither showed even a sign of it.

"We'll have to look at the video to see what happened," Sying commented and scratched his arm. The odd sensation of pins and needles prickled his skin but it itched more than it hurt. Given the high level of adrenaline still in his body, though, he assumed it was merely his nervous system overreacting and would pass.

He hoped so, anyway.

"What happened?" Fa repeated.

"We won't be able to tell until we see the videos," Sying snapped and scratched his arm again as he motioned to the men watching on camera.

That was their job, after all.

CHAPTER NINE

Sal had begun to wonder about the wisdom of hiking to the target location after about three hours into the climb. The mountains looked much flatter from the air but on the ground, it was impossible to avoid the ridges that required them to both ascend and descend repeatedly, and he was sure they'd barely advanced about a mile as the crow flew.

He had begun to take strain and even with his suit helping as much as it could, some effort was still required on his part. The other members of the team had a tougher time of it. They didn't have any extra limbs to help them through the harder places and he often had to go back to help the heavier suits.

The whole area was a little too quiet. He wasn't sure what he had expected from the mountains, but there wasn't much to hear beyond the wind whipping around them. Maybe he was too used to being in the jungle where nothing was ever quiet. Something always groaned, creaked, or growled and filled the senses with constant stimulation.

It was weird how he preferred the noise. Silence felt like he was missing something that could arrive and kill them all and he wouldn't have heard it. Or maybe he would since there was nothing to mask the sound.

He reminded himself constantly that something as big as a hippo would be easy to hear, but he knew better than to think the Zoo would make anything that easy.

The team was quiet as well. Whatever he felt seemed to affect them as well and made it tough to gauge what they were thinking and what was bothering them. If there was any wisdom to talking about it to them, Madigan would have already opened the conversation. The chances were she was as unsettled as he was and couldn't think of a good reason for it either.

"I fucking hate this," Sal muttered once he was sure he was the only one who could hear what he said. "I'm jumping at shadows."

Even mountains like this must have animals in them, right?

In that moment, he knew with certainty what the uncomfortable feeling across the whole team was. And why there were no other animals, not even the odd bird that liked to make their nests in the rocks.

"Shit." He switched to the common channel. "Madigan, you know what this means, right?"

"Yeah. I have a feeling I do." Her voice sounded a little strained

The rest of the team paused, unsure of what was happening or what was being discussed between the two of them.

"A trap?" He looked around warily and his gaze searched the shadows and rocky crevices.

"Oh yeah."

Matt approached and looked like he was a twitch away from hefting his assault rifle.

"We've passed three caves with nothing to show on the scans," Sal muttered, drew a deep breath, and tried to gather his thoughts. "The fourth is coming up ahead of us. There is no sign of any animal life in the region and there should be."

"And no sign of water either," Kay commented. "Are you sure you're not letting your nerves get the better of you?"

Sal was prepared to offer a rebuttal but the truth was that he was working on gut instinct.

Before he could say anything, Madigan stepped forward and stared at the woman until she raised her hands in apology.

"Your instincts have kept us alive thus far," she stated firmly as she turned away. "Don't think we'll start doubting you now."

"Yeah," Matt agreed. "You're fucking nuts but you have a good head on your shoulders."

He couldn't help a small grin at the show of confidence. "I appreciate it, guys."

"Sure." Madigan grunted to end that part of the conversation. "Now, what are you thinking here?"

"You and I can probably move in and hopefully spring the trap. Matt, you keep an eye on our position and if it turns out that we get ourselves in shit too deep, you can bring the cavalry in. Thoughts?"

"It sounds like as good a plan as we'll get." Madigan checked her weapon systems again more. "And it's about time. I'm starting to regret my decision to hike up here."

"We couldn't have gotten the Hammerheads over terrain like this," Matt pointed out. "Our only real option would have been to get helicopters up here, and if something that can fly is waiting for us, we would be sitting ducks."

He made a good point, and Sal was relieved that he hadn't suggested they fly to the different caves. Maybe there was a better way to map the area before they came, but not in the limited time they had. As far as they knew, they were on the clock.

"All right, we're good to go." Madigan gestured for the rest of the team to wait with Matt. "Davis, if it looks like we're about to be swarmed, you lead the team to rescue us, you got that?"

He laughed. "What, and risk my team?"

"I'm serious. I'm not in this for the suicide missions."

She knocked him on the helmet in passing before she directed her partner to cover her left flank as they began to close on the fourth cave they had seen. The rest of the team took their positions on the perimeter and made sure they had a clear line of fire should anything emerge to attack.

Sal tried to push away the annoying nagging that lingered and resisted its push to draw his sword. For the moment, his assault rifle was all he would work with.

Something was already moving inside the cave as they approached. The beast was large, with steps heavy enough to make the ground shake noticeably. It made no effort to stay out of view and probably couldn't hope to be stealthy even if it tried.

In all honesty, it showed no inclination to do so either. They might have woken it in their approach but it didn't seem disoriented or slowed. It moved immediately toward the entrance of the cave, which suggested that it had merely waited for them to move close enough and they hadn't surprised it at all. Madigan stopped their advance where they would have space to maneuver if they needed it.

The creature stepped out of the cave and it was immediately apparent that this was not the kind of creature they would find walking naturally on their planet, at least not without considerable CGI straight out of a museum, maybe. The description for it had been surprisingly accurate.

It did resemble a hippo with a heavy, burly body that looked a little fat although Sal knew it was anything but. The tusks were way too large, and the muscular structure of the mutant showed that it was not something that would be more comfortable in and underwater than on land.

Despite its size and structure, when it prowled toward them, the motion was almost like a lion. Small, beady eyes needed a second to identify them through the change in lighting, but once it caught sight of Madigan in her massive suit, it needed no encouragement and barreled forward.

However many tons of Zoo fury was not what anyone wanted to see rushing at them, especially not at that kind of speed. They already knew how to deal with these kinds of creatures, however, and immediately split up in an attempt to distract it and force it to divide its attention between two targets. Something that big, no matter how fast it was, would have to choose its trajectory since it wouldn't be able to change direction with anything resembling ease.

Still, they needed to be prepared for Zoo surprises. He'd hoped it would pause and perhaps be confused by what they were doing, which would give them a chance to attack it from its flanks.

Not this time, unfortunately. It had already curled its charge toward Madigan's larger figure. She opened fire on it and Sal did as well, looking for any sign of a soft target on the mutant.

The bullets struck and sank in, but all they did was anger the creature without inflicting any real damage. She shifted position to where she could shore it off with a rockface and give him a broad target to fire at.

Still, it didn't look like his bullets did much good. She launched a handful of grenades into the creature and they made impact with its skull but did nothing to slow it. At the last minute, she changed direction and her suit responded with surprising speed to jump out of the way as the tusks pounded hard into the stone.

None of them were surprised that the long teeth came away intact but gouged a chunk from the wall. The Zoo liked to make its bigger creatures more durable than their earthly counterparts. All Sal could feel was relief that Madigan hadn't tried to stand her ground against the hippo. She might have been able to hold her own, but he had a feeling that her armor would be missing a chunk the same way the wall was now.

It was his turn to shake the red flag at what easily

reduced even the most fearsome metaphorical bull to almost Disney-cute proportions. He exhaled slowly and drew its attention with a handful of rounds that glanced off the skull. That would make things difficult. The eyes were a weak point but they were small targets, especially when the creature was in motion.

Sal narrowed his eyes and realized that the creature had four more eyes parallel to each other, which gave it almost a full three-sixty view around it. Flanking didn't appear to be such a good idea after all.

Still, it was his turn. The extra limbs on his back extended and changed his direction barely in time as the tusk swept forward, inches from his armor as he swung his sword and aimed it at the squat and stubby neck.

The head snapped around and his whole arm jarred from the impact with one of the tusks. Suddenly—and with no idea how he'd managed it—he stood in front of the mutant.

"Oh, shit."

He had no time for any further thought before the whole five or six tons of monster bowled him over. The collision knocked the breath out of him, and he sprawled under it as it tried to trample him to death. The extra limbs, directed expertly by New Connie, worked faster than he could have to drag him out from where he was about to be crushed, armor and all.

Despite having narrowly escaped a gory end, he still reeled from what he assumed was what it would feel like to be hit and run over by a city bus—or maybe a trash truck. The fact that he was still alive was the most important takeaway.

His chest twinged painfully and his shoulder had difficulty with the full range of movement, but that would have to be looked at later.

For the moment, something massive still needed killing. He forced himself to his feet, grasped his weapons, and tried to decide how they could kill the bastard.

At a flicker of motion from the corner of his eye, he flung himself to the right with a curse. Two more hippos rushed from the bushes outside of the cave. Neither were quite as large as the first, but two-thirds as big was still too big in his opinion.

The ground shuddered as they rushed past him. His whole body felt like it was being wrung and stretched through his suit's movements—they kept him alive but were still as painful as all hell. It was time to take this fight a little more seriously.

Madigan stepped into the attack again and hammered her fist into the skull of one of the smaller creatures with enough power to lift it from its feet and upend it—a benefit to using one of the biggest suits provided to people in the Zoo. It didn't do much damage to the monster itself but getting it out of the fight even temporarily was worthwhile. She already had the rocket launcher primed and ready and two white plumes dusted the air as the first of the rockets crashed into the side of the smaller creature's head.

Sal didn't care how strong the bone was. If it wasn't steel-reinforced concrete, the strike would do what they needed it to. The blast crushed the skull and splattered brains and blood in a wide radius. The neck was broken too given the way what remained of the head flopped as it landed on the rocks.

It was a start, at least. The second rocket streaked across the small canyon they fought in and caught the larger creature in the chest. It wasn't enough to kill it, but the skin had peeled off to expose a few ribs.

Unfortunately, it didn't seem to slow the mutant but pushed it to greater rage, and it whirled with astonishing agility and raced toward Madigan. This time, she made no effort to evade the charge. It was a dumb move on her part but it looked like she was angry too. Maybe she was reacting to the creature almost killing him.

While it was endearing, Sal knew he would feel responsible if she was killed over him. All he could do was make sure it didn't happen.

The massive suit didn't quite stop the monster but she managed to stay with it and was able to slow it until it finally skidded to a halt when it pressed her against the wall and uttered a low, deep roar. It couldn't attack her with its tusks and tried instead to crush her into the unyielding rock.

The team opened fire and tried to lure the beast away from its prey as Madigan activated the other weapons on her suit. There was no guarantee that it would be in time or if it would even do enough damage to kill it.

Sal flicked his sword from side to side and attempted to coax more movement out of his shoulder. The suit could force the movement if he couldn't, but that would probably do more damage to the bone, muscle, and tendons injured by the mutant.

He could still fight, though, and he turned his attention

to the smaller creature that finally managed to regain its feet. When it roared at him, he raised his rifle and fired a three-round burst into its mouth. It wasn't enough to kill it and Sal began to wonder if they should have a look at the bone structure to see if it could improve their armor.

Determined to gain the victory, he yanked a grenade from his belt and as he approached it, the beast opened its monstrous jaws. He pulled the pin, lobbed it into the gaping maw, and bounced his boot on the top jaw as he raced past to thunk its mouth closed barely a few seconds before the device detonated.

The hippo jerked hard and closed its eyes with a bellow that was silenced abruptly when the blast savaged it from within. The explosion created a large hole in the center where it was enough to kill it.

It brought a grin of satisfaction but he knew the battle wasn't over. He began to move across the canyon and New Connie increased his speed as if she could read his mind. A yell surged from his chest as the sword shuddered in his hand. He launched forward as he swung the sword in a downward arc and drove it through the opening in its armor-like skin that had been inflicted by Madigan's rocket.

Maybe she didn't need his help. The rest of the team was ready to blanket the whole area in enough cover fire to rip through any living thing that wasn't human. The truth was, though, that Sal felt a little pissed off too and needed to direct it at a deserving target.

The blade cut through the ligaments, bones, and muscles. It juddered as it hacked through internal organs and finally resisted when he reached the bones on the other side of the ribcage and the skin to skewer it like a kebab.

It wasn't enough to kill it but it did distract it from its attack on Madigan. She was able to push it off and she lunged forward, jammed her assault rifle barrel through the mutant's eye, and flicked it to full auto. With what might have been a warcry or simply a pissed-off vent, she pulled the trigger.

She continued to fire until the rifle clicked empty and her suit started the process of its automated reloading.

Her method was effective, Sal conceded, pulled his blade out, and turned it on for a few seconds so it could clean itself before he approached her.

"Are you okay?" he asked but felt like it was a stupid question. No damage was visible on the outside of her suit while his had sustained noticeably more. Alarms blared in his HUD to warn him of breeches and damage. It was still functional but he would probably have to do a fair number of repairs and check the structure as well as the armor once they returned.

"I'm all good," she answered. "You?"

"I took a good hit. I'll survive, though."

"Yeah? Do you think you can take another hit?"

"What?"

She punched him hard on the arm. That answered the question at least although he gasped as the pain rushed up his arm and into his spine.

"That's for putting yourself in front of that fucking— Sal?"

He'd dropped on one knee and struggled to compensate for the blow and his unexpected reaction to it.

"Maybe...not a hit that hard." Sal wheezed and gritted his teeth for a moment. "I think the first one pulled something in my shoulder. I'll need some medical attention when we get back."

"You're goddamn right you will."

He nodded and recovered his balance and some semblance of composure before he was able to inspect the beasts they'd killed. The bones and the skulls, in particular, needed closer examination, and he wanted to get a good look at their structure, which was what allowed them to take the kind of punishment Sal and Madigan had inflicted.

It wouldn't take long to collect samples but he could sense the questions coming from the rest of the team as they approached.

"What in the fuck were these shits doing up here?" Kolt asked, his weapon trained on the carcasses like he didn't trust them to not miraculously resurrect from where they'd fallen.

"There could be any number of possible reasons," Kay answered, stopped beside the larger one, and nudged it with her boot. "It's not like we can interrogate them."

"Well, yeah, because they're dead," Leo retorted.

She turned to look at him with one hand on her hip. "Exactly. That's why we can't ask them any questions."

"And there's no need to be shitty. I was joining your joke."

"It wasn't a joke."

"Argue all you want," Sal interrupted, "but could you please stop moving the big fucker while I'm trying to take samples?"

"Oh." Kay removed her boot carefully. "Sorry."

His first impulse had been to snap at her and he'd barely controlled it. He reminded himself that it wasn't their fault that he was in pain and on edge. The ache was new but the edgy feeling had followed him for a while already. He wasn't sure how long, exactly, but he'd noticed it more often when entering the Zoo and that it seemed to have become stronger.

"The most likely explanation behind these is that they're carriers," he said, vacuum-sealed his samples, and stored them in his pack.

"Carriers?" Madigan approached him. "What are you talking about?"

"It's far-fetched, I know, but—"

"That's an understatement," Davis muttered.

He held back the impulse to snap again. "I don't know what they carried but they were here for a purpose. They brought the Zoo here and avoided all contact with the locals for a reason."

Madigan nodded. He wasn't sure if she understood because he sure as fuck didn't, but it was nice to know she was there to support him, no matter how nutty his ideas sounded.

"We need to get in touch with the Israelis." Sal groaned as he pushed to his feet. "They have to put this whole area to the torch, plasma and otherwise—everywhere around the caves that shows a trace of them. Of course, we can't know what they carried, if it's here, or if something is bringing it to the mountains. All we can do is neutralize whatever is here right now."

"I'll get on the horn with them," Matt answered. "Well,

as soon as I can. The mountains are playing hell with our reception out here."

"Assuming it's only the mountains," Madigan replied grimly.

Hopefully, the Niger contingent could make regular sweeps and warn the locals. At this point, they had no idea what they were looking for, which meant trying to look at all was a pointless endeavor.

CHAPTER TEN

No one liked being on the night shift. A few people assumed it was a punishment for the soldiers who were unpopular with the superior officers but in the end, it was a job and someone had to do it.

How people were selected for the job was a matter for debate, but Sheeran didn't mind it as much as the other soldiers did. He'd always been a night owl and it was cooler in the evenings. When day came around with the impossible desert heat, he could withdraw into the barracks where the AC was hopefully working and avoid the worst of it.

Still, he could understand why people hated it. The other men grumbled from the moment they woke and continued through the mess for breakfast and coffee, taking advantage of the fifteen or so minutes they had before they were expected to start their shift.

He merely let them complain. There was no point in rocking the boat by telling them to quit their bitching—

especially as a private—but he didn't have to join them in it either.

"There has to be some way for me to get back on the day shift," Setter mumbled and drained the last sip of his coffee before he threw the disposable cup into the recycling bin. "I don't care how—suck cock, run a thousand miles, it doesn't matter. I'll do it."

"Whose cock would you have to suck for that to happen? The last I heard, our commander isn't packing anything below the belt."

"Don't believe everything you hear."

"I honestly don't care. I'll suck whatever the fuck she wants me to suck. Put me on a civilized shift and I'll be a happy man."

Sheeran doubted that anything in the world would make them happy, especially not in the king's service. All he could do was shake his head as they began to pull their uniforms on.

"What's the matter there, Sheeran? Going to sing about how you're in love with the shape of me?"

"I could," he answered as he buttoned his shirt. "But then you will all complain to your COs about how you're being subjected to cruel and unusual punishment."

That got a laugh out of the group, and they didn't have any rejoinder for it. Maybe they were all too sleepy to start their usual nonsense with him, but it wasn't the first time his last name had reminded people of the singer who shared his name. He'd grown up with it and especially as a ginger. People constantly asked him to sing.

It was easy to tell that his parents hated him. Still, he was making a name for himself in the military, out in the

Sahara and as far away from the two of them as he could get.

It was for the best, frankly.

"All right, ladies," the sergeant snapped when they formed up and waited for him. "I know you're all too afraid of the dark to enjoy working at night, but I'll be fucked if that means we don't put our best foot forward. Short patrol sweeps and prompt reports to base. Anyone who takes a break to smoke, jerk off, or whatever before sending the report will run alongside the fucking Hammerhead, you got me?"

"Sir, yes, sir!"

The roared affirmation from all the privates was reminiscent of all their time in boot camp. It was more recent for some than others, but the general rule was that the new arrivals either headed out to the Zoo with the fire teams or they were on the night shift.

Sheeran knew they had come away with the better of the two options. The death toll was a little lower than it had once been, but teams still returned with fewer members than they had left with if they came back at all.

Maybe it was a little cowardly to wish to avoid that, but he had joined the military with the intention to survive. That couldn't always be guaranteed, of course, and he had always been a hard worker and even received a few commendations for bravery in combat, but he would never be one of those assholes who actively sought it out.

Their doors opened and the troop moved out. Miller was first and he suddenly tripped when he was three steps out of the door. The men laughed until Serra tripped too and was quickly followed by the three others who followed them.

"What the fuck is wrong with yo—shit!"

The sergeant joined the pile on the ground as the rest of the troop came to a halt. It wasn't like the whole group had taken clumsy pills, but it was still dark and they all needed a second to adjust before they saw what had made everyone trip.

He knew what it was—almost like instinct, something in his body immediately told him that maybe today was a good day to call in sick. Not that being sick helped much. He'd worked through all manner of colds and fevers since he'd joined the military, but this was the point when he would generally make a show of it so he was assigned some other work.

Evasion wasn't an option, however. They had stumbled onto grass—as common as the clap anywhere else in the world but in the desert, it was not what they expected to see and especially not in the middle of their base. Growing plants was particularly difficult, even for the people who knew how and had their little spaces once the commander allocated their homes on the base.

Of course, they weren't that far from where plants grew like weeds, and that was what made his mouth dry out. The Zoo had come to the base and no one had noticed it. The grass wasn't grass, he realized. It was what the jungle was before it became the Zoo. The plants grew thickly and close together, which allowed them to take over any area as quickly as possible.

How had it reached them? How had no one seen it?

"Holy shit!"

"Get the guns! We're under attack!"

"What the fuck is going on?"

Interestingly, that wasn't his voice but he wished he'd said it. The sergeant was the first one on his feet and his instincts kicked in.

"Shit! Get your asses together. Form up, or I swear to every fucking god on this planet, I will take your twisted knickers and use them to hang you on the flag poles!"

That was enough of a threat to ensure that every man and woman on the squad settled while he retrieved his radio and called the situation in to command. Moments later, lights came on across the damn base and alarms began to blare.

Oddly, the incursion was a small one with no signs of the bigger plants that usually followed the small ones. Even more importantly, it didn't look like any cryptids were involved as yet. The plants were still growing and the tallest one was only about as tall as Sheerans' waist. While the growth appeared to have spread to a solid third of the area, there was no apparent connection to a larger growth outside and certainly nothing leading to the wall and the Zoo beyond.

The base reacted quickly. Their patrol team was recalled and assigned menial work while the fire teams began to clear the incursion.

No one knew where it had come from or had any idea why it suddenly thrust from underground.

He didn't mind the menial work and willingly carried boxes to the area from which they were ferried to the fire teams. They hadn't had the time to prep for a long-term burn, which meant they needed to be fed constantly. And they were working fast. Ten or so teams were already involved and more would soon join them. It meant more menial labor.

"What's going on?" Sheeran shouted when a troop of men marched past them, not wearing combat suits.

"It looks like we got another incursion around the decontamination site at the wall," one of the soldiers shouted in response. "It wasn't there when we started but started coming up half an hour ago. We're meeting the Germans to take a look at it."

It was unfortunate, but it appeared the night was becoming something of a clusterfuck. He didn't have to wait too long before soldiers were directed to the supply trucks heading to the wall to supply the troops assembled there as well. He had a feeling there would be a horde of people too. The decontamination section of the wall was used by both the Brits and the Germans as well as the merc teams, which meant they all had something to lose if it was overrun by the damn Zoo.

With no recognizable reason or explanation, it was the kind of nutty situation that none of them could account for. But it was typical of the Zoo that seemed to constantly push out surprises and mutations to try to counter the humans' efforts. If mankind didn't catch up with it, they would be wiped off the face of the planet.

Many people said the Zoo was an alien attack and an attempt to terraform the planet and they had complete control of what it was doing, but he didn't quite believe it. He could agree that something guided the Zoo, but it felt more chaotic than a carefully planned and implemented campaign.

If aliens were behind it, he would expect the whole thing to simply work on autopilot with everything about it trying to adapt to life on earth while humans tried to profit from it. If he were an alien, he wouldn't have anticipated how greedy humans could be either.

"What are we looking at?" Sheeran shouted when he noticed a fair number of researchers in the area along with the fire teams involved with clearing the growth. All wore their light hybrid suits and it looked like they had been brought in to do their jobs instead of fighting monsters. They carried boxes of samples, although they were all sealed tightly and he couldn't see what was inside.

"Have a look for yourself," one of the German researchers answered and gestured for the privates to approach. "The floor inside the section was corroded and the fucking prefab tiles were eaten through. Nothing we know could have done this."

"That's what you got in those sample boxes? Prefab tiles?"

"We'll have to find something. And orders are that if we find anything, we take it in for study."

Sheeran nodded as the scientists moved on, not wanting to keep them. The whole section would be torched and rebuilt while people acted like nothing had happened, the way they did every time the Zoo burst out of control. It felt like the damn jungle was testing their defenses, but it wasn't like he could prove anything and it didn't fit with his perception. He'd failed biology in school so the best people were on the job already. If they came out with something believable, he would listen.

Pictures were being taken as the plasma torches started

to get a little closer. No one seemed to know what the hell was happening, but the lack of fauna on the rampage made it considerably easier to burn everything.

It was unthinkable that the Zoo had somehow penetrated their defenses and left no trace as to how. All they could do was kill the monsters should any appear, burn the trees, and pray to every god on the planet that it didn't happen again while knowing that it absolutely would.

The infernal buzzing dragged him from sleep. He knew his phone was ringing but his body couldn't seem to respond.

Sal's shoulder throbbed dully. The painkillers were effective but, as always, a faint background ache lingered. Madigan had wanted him to spend a few days in the hospital even though the doctor had assured them that nothing was torn or broken and he didn't need to remain for observation.

She wanted to teach him a lesson—like he'd intentionally put himself in the path of the charging hippo mutant. It was complete bullshit. She had slept in her bed that night, saying she didn't want to be tempted to jump his bones when he was so tender. He knew this was merely another version of the lesson she wanted him to learn. While she was good at so many things, communicating honestly about her feelings was not among them. These weird protests were her way of showing that she cared.

The phone had gone mercifully silent but it rang again, a sure sign that someone was determined to speak to him.

He groaned softly, rolled onto his side, and tried to

make out the name that appeared on his phone. His eyes were too blurry and wanted to stay closed for a little while longer so he simply gave up and pressed the button to answer it.

"Yeah?" His voice sounded like a frog croaking.

"Sal? it's Franklin."

"Franklin?" Sal opened his eyes and managed to register the time on the phone screen. The US base commander sounded like he'd just woken up too, and given the hours Anja said he was keeping, interrupting his sleep was a bad idea. "It's four in the morning and I'm officially on recovery."

"The Zoo's timing will always suck. It's about time we get used to that shit. How official is your recovery?"

It was a good question. When the doctor prescribed the painkillers and anti-inflammatories, he had said he needed time to rest, but no hospitalization meant he was good enough to go if he was needed.

"That depends on why you're calling me."

"There's a situation at the British base. A few mercs tracked some gunk in that was spat on them, and it looks like the Zoo's been springing up everywhere they've been."

That was the kind of news to wake anyone up.

"It what?"

"The situation is already being controlled. They caught it early so it was only flora and no fauna and they've collected samples. I assume everything will return to normal very soon."

"So...if everything's getting back to normal, what the hell do you need me for?"

"That's the main reason for my call. The ZCP committee

finally voted to approve my recommendation to appoint the Heavy Metal team to investigate these incidents and try to find answers—our resident experts, if you will. The Brits were the only ones who dragged their heels on this, but the shock and confusion were enough to get them to capitulate and agree. The remuneration won't be quite as good as your usual fees, but it'll be more regular and on top of everything else."

"I appreciate that, and honestly, at this point, making a profit comes second to saving the world. As long as you guys can cover our costs, we can discuss the fees."

Sal chose not to share the fact that this was a perfect answer to something that promised to be a dilemma in their attempt to learn more about what the Zoo was up to. No matter what the issues were, he had expected there to be far too much dick-measuring and people complaining about how Americans needed to stay in the US sector.

This way, there wouldn't be as many ruffled feathers.

"So does this mean we have to drag our asses out of bed and go to whatever sector happens to have a Zoo scare whenever it happens?"

Franklin laughed, although there wasn't much mirth in the sound. "That's what you'll be paid to do. I'll talk to you later."

"Later."

The call ended and he stared at his phone for a few more seconds and wondered if he could simply go back to sleep and then go to the British base. Six and a half hours was not bad but his meds made him want to sleep more.

"Anja, I assume you listened in on that?" He pushed to a seated position.

"Of course," the hacker answered over the PA.

"Wake Madigan and tell her to get the rest of the team ready."

"You mean the two of you didn't sleep in the same room? Is there trouble in paradise?"

"Shut the fuck up and wake the others."

Sal groaned softly as he pushed off the side of the bed and registered a slight twinge of pain from his shoulder as he pulled his clothes on.

His shirt was on and he was working on his pants when the door opened behind him. No knock meant it was Madigan.

"Everyone is getting ready to move out," she stated, closed the door, and leaned against it while she watched him struggle to dress.

"Anja filled you in on the details."

"Sure, but is there any particular reason why the whole team has to suit up for what will be fact-finding with very little shooting?"

Sal shrugged and regretted it immediately. "As impressive a specimen as I am, I won't be able to be everywhere at once. We might as well give them a crash course on what to look for in my absence."

He almost fell when his foot missed his pant leg and he had to try again more carefully.

"Oh yeah, a real specimen of manliness, that's you," she muttered. "You know they don't have your scientific knowledge on the biological makeup of the Zoo, right? I'd be surprised if over fifty percent of them even graduated high school."

"I sense that you have a point hidden in there somewhere."

"They aren't scientists and you need scientists. And you happen to have one as a part of the team already."

Sal turned to scowl directly at her. "I won't call Courtney. If she wanted to come to the Zoo, she would have. She has a life and commitments in Philly. I don't want to disrupt all that for her and especially since all we have at this point is pure supposition. It's pointless for her to make a trip halfway across the world until we have something a little more concrete."

He expected Madigan to push a little harder on the matter but she merely tilted her head and smiled.

"Be sure to bring your meds with you," she reminded him and made no further reference to the scientist issue. "Doc says you need them every eight hours and you don't know how long we'll be gone."

With that, the door opened and closed and he was alone in his room.

There had been a time when he liked having his space to himself, but he realized that he missed having her around.

Maybe that was the lesson she wanted him to learn.

CHAPTER ELEVEN

"It's five in the fucking morning."

A low growl of protest rumbled from deep inside Sam's chest at the sound of someone banging on the door. Whoever it was either didn't know or didn't care about what time it was.

Sleep had been at a premium lately with everyone working from sunup to three or four hours after sundown to set the new camp up. This meant that if someone was waking him at this ungodly hour, it was either a matter of life or death or soon would be.

He sighed, pushed off the hard cot he'd called a bed since they'd moved into their little compound, and shuffled to the door. The banging resumed, almost hard enough to break it.

"What?"

His tone was a little more hostile than intended but the merc captain who stood outside didn't appear to even notice. He was speaking on the radio and snapped orders before he turned his attention to the ENSOL engineer.

That already did not bode well for them.

"We have a situation."

Honestly, he was so tired of hearing those four words .

Fix pulled some clothes on and followed the man to where Elke and Chen were already waiting for him. Both looked bleary-eyed and yawned, probably in desperate need of coffee like he was.

"Reports have come in that the primary ENSOL base has been overrun," the captain finally explained once the three were together. "The token workforce we left there to finish packing the last of our equipment made the call."

"Raiders?"

The large man shook his head and played a message that had been sent over the satellite phone.

"Calling...ENSOL base has been...Zoo is...we need more...fuck!"

It was garbled but there was no mistaking the frantic tone of the man who made the call. The interference alone was enough to confirm the presence of the Zoo at this point, and if it had overrun the primary base, they were lucky that a message had gotten out at all.

"The Zoo has overrun the base?" Elke whispered. "How?"

"We're not sure yet. An SOS has gone out to the Algerians, Brits, and Americans, and we've asked them for support. As it stands, we cannot leave this camp unprotected."

It was obvious enough that the captain wanted to go and help the men he'd left as escorts and no one could fault him for that. Unfortunately, he was prevented from doing so by his duty that required him to keep the ENSOL operation up and running as well as he could manage.

Sam felt his pain but his initial instinct to rush back and rescue their people had to be restrained. They had no idea what the situation there was.

"Right." He scratched the stubble on his chin that he hadn't yet attended to. "Here's what we'll do. Get yourself and some of your men in suits and ready to fight. I can leave my lead engineer in charge of the camp with your team members who stay, and we'll be ready to leave immediately. Reinforcements will come to assist here."

"What?" The captain turned to face him and looked confused. "You are civilians. We can't—"

"They are our people," he snapped. "My people. I intend to be there. We'll stay at a safe distance and will leave if it becomes necessary, but we will go with you."

"Agreed," Elke interjected and Sam was surprised that he had her support. "We need to know what the situation is on the first base and it would be better to learn first-hand."

Chen nodded as well. "There's no real point in holding the fort down here if we don't know what caused it. The chances are we will be in as much danger."

The merc looked at the three of them in turn.

It was obvious that he wouldn't convince them otherwise and nothing remained to be said. They would get the work done, no matter what.

"Right then." He shook his head, turned, and hurried away to find his men to prepare them for the change in their plans for the day.

Sam couldn't help feeling a little sick to his stomach,

and from the expressions on the faces of his two colleagues, they felt much the same. None of them wanted to come face to face with the Zoo—even from a so-called safe distance—but they were responsible for those who worked for them. They would go because it was the right thing to do.

"I...I'll get dressed," Chen said finally, looked away from others, and hunched his shoulders as he turned to their accommodation building.

"I should probably see about the logistics," Elke added before she strode in the same direction the captain had taken.

Fix sighed and wondered how they had become so deeply involved. They had signed up to build a goddammed wall, not for the Zoo shit. It had inched around them and gradually pulled them in until they realized they could no longer back away. They needed to help and do their part for the benefit of humanity.

It still fucking sucked, though.

As ironic as it was, this was maybe a situation in which the Brits had been a little too enthusiastic with the plasma throwers.

Sal had assumed it would be the case so was frustrated rather than surprised. The soldiers would have been told to leave nothing to chance, especially this close to home, and they had burned through almost everything. The plasma throwers had done their job well and it was the right thing to do, especially since they'd had a window of opportunity with no animals present. Any incursion beyond the containment of the walls needed to be destroyed with all prejudice and no delay.

While he would be the first to agree that they'd done the right thing, it unfortunately meant there would be little left in the way of evidence for them to work with.

Still, he could only hope there was something for them to study, if not on the ground then at least in the samples and footage they had taken. This was their first job as the official specialists on call for the bases and he wanted to have something to show for their presence.

A small contingent waited to greet them, although it appeared that the man in charge was a sergeant. He looked tired like he'd been up all night. He was probably used to that kind of thing, and while he didn't like it, he would continue to work until the situation was resolved.

"Sergeant Willis, is that correct?" Sal asked as he dismounted from their Hammerhead and approached the group. "You were one of the first to encounter the incursion here on the base."

"That is correct."

It was easy to tell that none of the men present were overly impressed with Dr. Jacobs—a reaction he was used to by now. Even with the knowledge the bases had about Heavy Metal, he knew he did not have the kind of outward presence that fitted the reputation.

He had gained muscle weight since he'd first arrived at the Zoo, but nothing about him suggested the fighting prowess soldiers tended to respect.

"Can you describe what happened?" he asked to move the conversation somewhere productive.

"Trees were growing in the middle of the base. We burned them all the fuck down. Is there anything else you need to know?"

"Do you have a problem with me, Sergeant?"

"I'm not used to being interrogated by a colonial geek, is all." The man's tone seemed almost deliberately disrespectful.

"It's not an interrogation. I'm merely trying to gather information about what happened."

"Well, it sounds like an interrogation to me. Babysitting you all seems like the last thing you need, which begs the question of why you need us."

Sal drew a deep breath. They were all tired and the last thing any of them needed was him to react to a sergeant's rudeness. The man would take it the wrong way, get defensive, and let things escalate into a fight that would create all kinds of ill feelings between bases.

"This is a matter of safety for everyone here," he said and tried to keep his voice low and not sound confrontational. "As I'm sure you know, the beginning to any battle against the Zoo starts with the intel gathered by geeks of all nationalities. I'm not questioning your version of events. Your men did a great job of clearing everything, but it means there's nothing for me to work from aside from video footage and first-hand accounts."

He put no apology in his tone but spoke with forthright honesty. It wasn't quite enough to make them look any more welcoming, but the open hostility softened somewhat.

"Right then," the Brit muttered, straightened, and

schooled his demeanor into politeness. "What do you want to know?"

"The origin point of the incursion. Did you get a good idea of where it all started?"

"From what I was told, there were two points. We noticed it outside the barracks first. The growth was still short at that point but thick—almost like grass but growing like fucking weeds."

Sal nodded. "The Zoo plants get a good start in the dark, but they need sun on them to fully explode. It's a good thing you noticed it before that happened."

"Luck was all it was," the man told him. "I was leading a new patrol with the night crew and we tripped over the growth."

"It came up from under the paving?"

"Like fucking daisies. People are talking about how the Zoo might be burrowing underground to reach us from under the wall, but I call bullshit on it. The mercs who protect our fire teams tracked something in that caused it to grow."

"You have a good mind for this, Sergeant," he commented. "That's what we thought too. A rapid reaction time and thinking like that kept the Brit base from becoming a second act to what happened to the Japanese. Not that they could have stumbled on what happened to them."

The soldiers had a good chuckle at that.

"Our tech people will need to have a look at the footage you have on what happened." It was only one person but there was no need to tell them that. Anja was able to do what others needed a team for. "Could you get that done before we continue?"

The sergeant nodded to one of his men, who jogged off to where he assumed their comms base was located.

"Where was the second area where everything went to shit?"

"The decontamination site near the wall. They took some samples there and said something ate straight through the prefab blocks. I assumed you would have been briefed on the situation there already." There was no challenge in the man's voice, thankfully. He seemed curious more than anything else.

"I'm sure we will be at some point," Sal acknowledged, "but we've been flying by the seats of our pants since we were called in. Wasn't the decontamination supposed to take care of anything that might cause all this?"

"That was what everyone believed. I guess whatever it was got out before it went through the decontamination process."

That didn't sound right, but he chose to not question the man's judgment at this point. It was best to not inspire any doubt in the protocols that were in place.

"We'll have to see what's left of the site near the wall. I assume your men were as thorough clearing it as they were here, so I'm not sure what we can find. Still, we have to do our due diligence."

"Of course."

"Do you want a ride with us?" Sal offered

"Well...we assumed we would have to provide you with transportation so we brought our own."

"It's for the best, I guess. The Hammerheads are meant

to carry ten to fifteen men, depending on how many are suited up. If you put any more than eight in there, you start to feel like sardines or...maybe kippers? Whatever you guys eat that's canned and fish."

"Sardines works. We'll follow you."

He nodded and motioned for the rest of the team to mount up. Anja probably already had access to the files she needed so sending them to her was merely a formality. Given the level of destruction that had been wrought to stop the incursion, it was unlikely that they would find anything. They could as easily walk through the barracks site on their way out.

For the moment, he wanted to make sure there was nothing that required their immediate attention. Once that was confirmed, they could take things a little slower.

It was a short drive, but he could see from how scorched the area was that the teams had been as destructive in the decontamination sector as they had been at the base. In retrospect, it was a pity he hadn't snatched a few hours of sleep before being dragged into this shit.

Still, they were there already and he would make sure people knew Heavy Metal was on the case.

Madigan didn't say much of anything but she glanced sharply at him every time he winced when the Hammerhead's shocks failed to cushion the bumps they went over.

She wouldn't say anything—likely because she knew she wouldn't want to be questioned if she was going through the same thing—but the concern was there. As flattering as it was, he didn't want her to worry about him more than about whatever mission they were on.

Maybe it would be a good idea for her to take lead on

the operations until he was back to one hundred percent again. He pushed the thought aside immediately. She wasn't a scientist, so he had to do what only he could do.

"I'm not sure why you needed us to come," Kay commented as the crew dismounted again. "It's good to see that people are reacting quickly to incursions, but we might as well pick up the cliff notes version, right?"

"True," Sal conceded. "But Heavy Metal has been retained by the commanders of all the bases to lead any investigation efforts. They probably want us to run interference between them and all the corporate labs being moved here."

And if they were paid for it, he didn't want it said that Heavy Metal wasn't willing to do the legwork.

"It looks like they were as enthusiastic here as they were at the barracks." The sergeant stated the obvious. "The footage was on all the time for this, though, so your tech teams will have a full accounting of what happened in electronic form."

"It's not always the best choice but I guess it's better than nothing," Madigan responded and removed her helmet and the others, including the soldiers, followed suit. "Do you see those drains? And the fucking floor over there? It looks like someone sprayed the whole place with acid."

Sal nodded. "It looks like it, yeah. The Zoo seriously wanted to get through the fucking floor."

Something was missing, though. Most other attempts by the jungle to spread quickly included the red-and-blue pita plants. As he turned to the sergeant to ask about them, the man's sat phone buzzed to tell him that communications were incoming.

"I read you," he said into the speaker and his expression changed from bored and tired into something a little more familiar.

It wasn't quite fear but the look a soldier wore when they were told they had to head into the thick of it.

"I imagine you and your team will want to head to the ENSOL camp," he explained once the conversation finished. "Their first base of operations has been overrun, and if you're right and this shit goes ballistic when the sun starts coming up, you might have a great front-row seat to that happening. They're calling for any and all available military assistance."

"Fuck." Sal hissed in frustration. How did these situations happen so quickly? No one had noticed anything that might have warned the bases. He and his team would have to get to the bottom of this or they would spend all their time putting fires out in every sector.

That seemed to be exactly what the Zoo intended, which meant it had something else in mind. His instinct told him it was something way bigger and it wanted their attention to be everywhere but where the real attack would happen.

He made a mental note to look at some maps and determine where the hot spots were so he could isolate which should have been hot but were not.

This was the clearest indicator of where the Zoo did not want them to look. It was like it had turned into a magician of some kind.

"Is that what we've come to?" he whispered and shook

his head as Gregor pressed their Hammerhead's accelerator hard enough that the passengers jerked back in their seats.

"What was that?" Juice asked and leaned forward.

"Sorry, I was talking to myself. I do that from time to time. You'll learn to start tuning me out."

The Colombian leaned back in his seat and checked his assault rifle as they exited the base and increased speed to reach the target location as soon as possible.

CHAPTER TWELVE

It was what they should have expected by this point. Murphy knew the shit would hit the fan eventually and there had been major events that validated this, especially Niger. It had consistently pushed the humans to the limit and when the outbreaks were contained, it had gone quiet again.

But they all knew the uneasy peace wouldn't last. Eventually, the Zoo would stir again and start its *Pinky and the Brain* episode by trying to take over the world. Unlike the two cartoon rats, however, the fucking jungle had the means to do so.

This night was when everything decided to blow the fuck up. There was no real reason why but perhaps it was better than sitting around and waiting for it to happen.

The first call had come in around four in the morning about an outbreak on the British base that was being cleared. This meant that all the bases would be on high alert for any sign of another attack—which wasn't usual but one never knew when the Zoo would break its routine.

An hour later, the jungle had defied the pattern and overrun the ENSOL camp with no warning.

US troops had been the first to respond to the SOS call. Murphy had little information since no further messages had been sent but by now, he had a fair idea what to expect. A thick eruption of vegetation that hadn't been there twenty-four hours earlier and an arm that stretched from there to the main jungle.

His assumptions were partly validated when their group of Hammerheads crested the last dune. The sun had barely begun to beam its searing heat onto the Sahara and the outbreak was exactly where he thought it would be. In the time it had taken him to have a good night's sleep, the trees had already grown to between ten and fifteen feet.

Commenting on how trees shouldn't grow that fast was true but it had been said way too many times at this point. The expanding jungle had already taken over most of the camp. The site was much smaller than the official bases and it had been overrun in the blink of an eye. A few vines had begun to climb sections of the wall, probably to try to crack through it.

None of this was any surprise, however, as he had witnessed the same process in other outbreaks. The problem was that no arm stretched from the main Zoo to where the wall was in plain view and there was no sign of it having breached the wall. It was like the whole fucking jungle had simply thrust from the ground.

"How does it grow that quickly?" one of the soldiers asked as they began to dismount. "I thought it needed biomass to spread like that."

"People were probably in there," another responded.

"My question is how the hell it simply appeared out of the sand like that? Will that shit dig through the ground and appear out of nowhere?"

Murphy shook his head. "Someone tracked something in, most likely. That's what most of the specialists are saying."

"You mean the guys who started the whole fucking Zoo mess?"

"I'm fairly sure everyone who got that shit started are dead or retired already. I guess we'll see if they were right."

Mere soldiers could do nothing except step in to clear the mess and leave the geeks to wrestle with the why and how. He assumed that was why people liked having Jacobs and Kennedy around since they knew more about the science of the Zoo. If the researchers weren't the epitome of why escort missions were such a damn nuisance in video games, they were holed up in the labs.

Not Jacobs, though. He and his team liked to be in the thick of it. The other scientists waited for other people to gather samples but from what he'd heard, when Heavy Metal wanted samples, they went in and found what they needed.

He wasn't sure how it was possible but Murphy knew there were many ways for coincidence to be exactly that and nothing else. Still, he felt like it was divine providence to see that another Hammerhead pulled in behind them. It hadn't even come to a halt before the team dismounted.

They were known for having some of the most unique suits in the Zoo area, which meant it was easy to identify them as they approached. Jacobs' suit was one of the most interesting the captain had seen. It was a hybrid suit from the way that it was designed but with power that could call on magnetic technology. He wasn't sure he would ever understand the workings of it but could appreciate that it enabled the two-ton suit to move like an Olympic gymnast.

What intrigued him most, though, were the extra limbs that emerged from its back when he needed them and the sword he could bring out to slice and dice monsters like he was a chef at Benihana's.

The rest of the team—he noticed there were more of them than before—wore combat suits that looked about as regular as most of the others at the Zoo. Gregor's was a little boxier and evidenced some very Russian traits in the manufacturing, but Madigan's was the real beauty. It was one of the biggest heavy suits ever designed and she walked around like a damn tank on two legs. She could march through almost any Zoo charge and come away mostly untouched.

What worried him was seeing some damage to the chest plate and a few of the peripherals. He'd heard that the Heavy Metal group had been called in a few times lately, but if they had run into something that could do that much damage, it didn't bode well for how the day would go.

"Sal, Madigan, nice to see you guys," Murphy called when they joined the group comms. "I didn't expect to see you up and in business this early. I assumed we'd need to hold the line for at least an hour until the dumbasses who run the bases decided to pay your rates."

"As it turns out, we were already in the area," Sal answered and looked back in the direction they'd come from. "People wanted us to investigate the incident at the Brit base. I'm not sure why because it was already contained and plasma'd. Still, we're now officially the experts so I guess we needed to get in and at least do a site inspection."

"Even though they burned any evidence we might have found," Madigan pointed out.

"You can't honestly blame them." Murphy motioned to the camp that was almost entirely buried by the burgeoning jungle.

Jacobs nodded. "Yeah. They acted fast and it probably saved the base from being completely overrun. And them calling us in early was probably for the best too since it allowed us to get here without delays. We'll need to act quickly to keep this patch of green from connecting to the rest of it."

The captain gestured to the rest of his squad to get into a battle formation, while the Hammerheads gathered behind them as well. They had some firepower fitted and every little advantage would count.

"I didn't know you guys were hiring," he said as the preparations were wrapping up.

Madigan looked up from working on her dented armor. "What?"

"You brought new members in for your team. I didn't know you were hiring."

"Oh. I thought Matt talked to all his contacts about finding reliable people. Didn't he mention it to you?"

"I got his message but I thought he meant you were looking for freelance mercs. Are these guys permanent members of Heavy Metal?" He was curious as to what had prompted the change since they mainly used freelancers when they needed extra gunners.

"As permanent as anything is in the Zoo. Why? Are you interested?"

"I still have a couple of months on my tour, barring any incidents. We'll see if I'm still in any position to take mercenary work afterward. I might end up retiring, though."

"Seriously?" Madigan sounded skeptical.

"Yeah, I have some money back home. My brother's in banking and he handles it for me. I don't have a girl but do have family I might want to visit."

"It's a good plan but I know you, Murph. Some time off will be nice, but you live by Murphy's Law. You'll come back here to make sure the worst doesn't happen without you here to stop it. And when you do, Heavy Metal might be the right place for you. Barring any incidents."

He laughed. "Fuck that. You people will be the last line of defense against the alien monsters and the end of the world. I'm very sure you and Jacobs will lead humanity in rebellion against our new alien overlords when it comes to that."

"Looking that far ahead now, are ya?"

"Murphy's Law," he reminded her. "What can go wrong will go wrong and that means in less than a decade, we'll be ruled by a horde of bug-eyed bastards who like to stick probes up people's asses. They'll probably find willing guinea pigs among the BDSM community, but everyone else will fight—assuming the jungle doesn't devour them first."

It wasn't the most comforting thought, but Murphy had never needed to encourage himself with the best-case scenarios. If they had to enter this battle, he would be honest with himself about how it would go down.

If it meant considering the very real possibility that humanity was in the beginning stages of a guerilla war that would span decades and end with them all dead, so be it. He was willing to accept that as a possibility and fight every inch of the way to make it as difficult for the Zoo to take what it wanted from them.

Maybe Madigan was right and he wasn't the type to retire. Perhaps the best choice was to cash out, head to Vegas, and indulge in every vice he thought was possible and maybe learn a few new ones along the way. After being arrested a couple of times and a few visits to the hospital, he would return and join the fight knowing he'd lived his life to the fullest.

"Do we have any fire teams on the way?" Davis asked as the teams organized. "Our British friends only had the plants to deal with. How many monsters do you think will be waiting for us in there?"

"None or hordes," Sal answered and shook his head. "We won't know until we— oh, fuck me, what is that?"

Murphy couldn't hear anything but he turned and tried to at least see what was happening. They were all used to dealing with almost anything, but there were times when the scientist had some knowledge about what was happening in the Zoo that bordered on the supernatural. The kid was a genius, make no mistake.

The noise wasn't from any sign of the monsters around them but a garbled, static-filled message on the comms. It took a moment to realize that the merc team that was stationed to protect the second ENSOL camp was trying to contact him. Something was going on that made them call for help.

From what he'd been told, they had already moved most of their teams and equipment to a second camp and left only a skeleton crew to finish packing up the first site. ENSOL had played a significant part in getting the wall built this quickly. They all owed them a debt for that, especially since they were civilians who had no real place in the Zoo. Despite all the havoc of recent months, they'd stuck around even though they didn't need to.

"We need help!" a man shouted over the line. "Is anyone there? We're under attack!"

Well, that was never a good sign.

"There are some US teams in the area," the captain responded and noted that Madigan had already brought their team closer. "What's your situation?"

"The fuckers came around the wall through the unbuilt section—locusts, a swarm of them! We have a handful of mercs, some Algerian soldiers, and civilians. We can't hold them back."

"Shit."

"The Zoo...it's growing. The goddammed vegetation is pushing out of the sand. I don't know where it's coming from but it's growing fast!"

Unfortunately, everyone there knew that with two live outbreaks, they now had a critical decision to make. The first site was all but completely overrun, whereas the second had barely begun. Logic said they should throw the full weight of their combined firepower at the second camp before it was too late.

"We need to look for survivors," Sal insisted as if he had

read Murphy's mind. "We can get as many of them out as we can before the whole fucking place is plasma'd."

"Sal…" Kennedy cut him off. "The Zoo is taking over. This isn't a highly-populated area and the Zoo will have hunted anything to add to its biomass. There won't be any survivors."

"We don't know that for certain and can't simply abandon them."

"No, but throwing our people into the middle of it won't save anyone."

He wasn't used to seeing this kind of division between the two Heavy Metal partners, but these were trying times. Murphy had a feeling there was more tension and he merely saw the surface of it like an iceberg. It was their business to resolve that, but Kennedy was right. Heading in without any plan or idea of what they were dealing with would only get more people killed.

"We need to wait for the fire teams to catch up to us," Davis stated calmly and matter of factly. "Our six recruits can enter the first outbreak with two of the plasma throwers and try to reach the buildings as quickly as possible. They'll be able to determine if there are any survivors to save. Is that an acceptable compromise?"

"Hey, who the fuck are you calling a recruit?"

Murphy recognized her voice although if she hadn't been wearing her suit, he would have seen her bright orange hair from a couple of miles away. He wasn't sure what the hell Heavy Metal would want with a known smuggler and small-time criminal, but maybe she'd changed her ways. It seemed to happen fairly often these days.

The fire teams were already starting to arrive, and from the hurry they were in, it looked like they'd been told about what was happening and were acting on it as well.

"What do the rest of us do in the meantime?"

Kennedy studied what was left of the first ENSOL base and turned to the team.

"Sal and I will go in with the new team and two plasma throwers. It's a little smaller, so we should be able to clear it quickly and rescue survivors if there are any. He can collect some samples and maybe discover how this fucking jungle pops out of the ground like goddamn daisies. Gregor, Martin, and Matt can go with the soldiers to the second site and we'll catch up "

"It's a reasonable plan." Murphy motioned for his team to fall in. "Get your asses fucking moving! I want all evidence of the Zoo at the second site cleared before lunchtime."

It was supposed to have stopped by now. The adrenaline was out of his system and the tingling effects it had were gone too.

At first, Sying hadn't wanted to acknowledge that something else was happening. His arm and neck had itched ever since the incident and while he didn't want to cause a fuss, he also wouldn't be able to focus on his fucking work if he felt driven to claw through his protective suit to get at the itch.

Much to his relief, it had ebbed and faded during the day but was now back with a vengeance. He'd noticed a rash too, which meant he had to see a medic. Maybe they would know what he was dealing with.

He could already hear what they would tell him. His aunt was a hypochondriac who could cause symptoms by the stress of worrying about the symptoms she thought she felt.

Maybe that shit was genetic but honestly, he didn't have to worry. The medics didn't know his aunt and he had the visible signs of a genuine problem. All he knew was that he had difficulty focusing on the road when he wanted to get out and scratch his arm on the paving.

It was probably a good thing that he was so meticulous about keeping his nails trimmed or he would have clawed through the skin already.

Thankfully he pulled the vehicle in to park at the medical center only a few moments later. Before he could do anything, he paused and scratched again until the stinging pain overwhelmed the itch. The latter would be back, though, and it was odd how he preferred the pain to it.

Sying looked up and suddenly registered the presence of two people in the parking lot. He recognized both, although he only knew Dr. Han. The other was the soldier who had been injured on the trip into the Zoo.

Both were smoking but they had paused to look at him, likely curious as to why he stopped everything to scratch his arm. He sighed and accepted that an explanation was in order, if only to reassure them that he hadn't lost his mind.

"I know you might have some questions about that," he said and gestured at the vehicle. "But I can explain."

"No questions," the soldier answered. "It's not our business."

Han took a drag of his cigarette before he nodded. "Besides, we know what ails you. It might have happened to the two of us when we were in that containment room, although how the fuck anything got through our suits is a mystery."

Both men extended their arms and Sying was surprised to see that they were dealing with the same thing he was. The soldier's rash appeared to be a little better, pink instead of the outright red that was visible on Han's arms.

"It blisters from time to time," the private muttered. "But sometimes, it goes away like it's dormant or something."

"Are you here to see the doctor about it too?" he asked and shook his head when Han offered him a smoke.

"Well, yeah. Hopefully, he has some kind of ointment for whatever the fuck this is." The young man shook his head. "I wasn't even involved with whatever gave you two this itch."

"We were handling the shit our team collected," Han explained. "It might be that we caught it from something we brought out."

"All I caught was a fucking concussion. The bastard knocked me on my ass with one swipe of its tail."

"You're lucky," Sying told him. "I've seen a Komodo dragon's tail cut men in half or sever heads. I'd say things could have gone much worse for you."

"That's what everyone keeps telling me." He shook his head, dropped the cigarette butt, and crushed it under his heel. "If it had knocked my head off, at least I wouldn't have to deal with this rash."

Neither of the researchers argued the point. Han took a final drag of his smoke, threw the butt amongst others near a trash can, and motioned for Sying to join them as they headed inside.

When the three of them entered the medical bay, a young-looking doctor was already waiting for them.

"Hello, yes…Dr. Han, Private Zhao. And…I'm sorry, I was told that only two patients needed my attention."

"The call was made a few minutes ago," Sying explained. "I didn't know there were others, but if you're tending to the same kind of issue, it would be better that you see all those affected, right?"

The doctor checked his tablet and nodded. The research head assumed that his name had already been added to the patient list as they were all directed to join him in one of the clinic rooms. They sat where indicated and waited while the medic consulted more charts.

"All right," he said briskly and focused his attention on them. "Let me have a look at the affected area."

It almost sounded like he expected this to be some type of STI and was asking them to present their privates for inspection.

He seemed relieved when he saw that it was only their arms and shoulders that needed to be looked at, although the relief was short-lived as he leaned in a little closer and pulled on a pair of gloves.

"How long have you had this?" he asked.

Sying checked his watch. "For Dr. Han and me, twenty-six hours, more or less. The itching started yesterday within minutes after the assumed exposure time."

The soldier leaned back. "It's been a little longer for me. I was in the Zoo when the itching started the day before yesterday."

"That's interesting because it looks like the state of the rash is the same on all three. This means that whatever is causing it is inert in your body or that your body effectively prevents it from spreading. I think we can help with an antibiotic salve that you can apply. It will also stop other infections and bacteria from getting in as well. I'm surprised that something else hasn't appeared already."

He scribbled prescriptions for them to collect from the field office pharmacy, and Sying noted that he marked it as a priority. Without it, they would be left waiting for it for a few days, at the very least.

"Now, we need to look at what might have caused it to begin with. You two were exposed to it in your lab, as I can see, and the private was exposed when the creature attacked him in the Zoo, is that correct?"

All three men nodded.

"It might be that we were all exposed to something on the Komodo dragon," Han commented. "Something abrasive that's irritating our skin."

"Except that I was not ever in contact with the dragon's skin," Sying pointed out. "I didn't even come close to it. Unless it was somehow airborne, I don't see how that could be what caused this."

They all nodded to concede that it was a good point, although no one could think of a decent explanation as to why or how he was affected by it. Maybe it was enough to merely be in the same room, but that would bring up a whole other mixture of issues that would need to be addressed. This would require everyone involved to be quarantined before something major went wrong.

The research head wouldn't make any decisions or offer suggestions on that, though. The medical experts would have to decide the way forward and there was no point in him adding his opinion until they had a better idea of what they were dealing with.

Or until someone asked him for his thoughts on the matter.

"I'll take pictures of the affected areas and share them with my colleagues to get a second opinion. And try not to scratch, as tempting as it might be."

"Have you ever tried to not scratch an itch, doctor?" the private asked, gritted his teeth, and clasped his hands tightly to fight the impulse to scratch.

"Well, the salve should help with that but even so, I would suggest that you make a conscious effort to avoid aggravating the area as much as possible. Again, that could introduce new infections into your bloodstream."

The doctor was right, of course, but so was the private. Trying to not scratch an itch could be as annoying as the itch. Still, they would have to try and hope that the salve helped.

CHAPTER THIRTEEN

The hope that they wouldn't have to deal with any cryptid presence in the first ENSOL camp was soon dashed. Sal knew it was unwise to have such hopes but in the end, if they had to fight any and all kinds of monsters produced by the ever-expanding jungle, he would hope for things to be easier from time to time.

Of course, it meant he would be disappointed fairly often. Maybe if he kept his expectations low he might be pleasantly surprised instead of consistently let down.

But that was how he was. He was a hopeful person by nature and would leave all the debates about how the world would end soon to the other experts. While he firmly believed the Zoo was driven by ulterior motives that did not bode well for humanity, he would continue to hope because the alternative was too depressing.

"We've got incoming!"

The wall was still in place and it was comforting to see how much difficulty the rampant jungle encountered in its attempts to tear it down. Despite this, swarms of locusts flew over the top to join those already there and engage the newcomers with all the enthusiasm the teams had come to expect from the Zoo.

Sal already had his assault rifle out. The humpers weren't a surprise, nor was the presence of the blue-and-red pitas. He had long since accepted that they played a major role in any Zoo expansion effort although he had yet to determine exactly what and how. They were massed in a smallish area close to the damaged gate and confirmed his theory that they grew more densely at the point of origin of the outbreak. From there, the plants pushed into the camp—which explained how the area had grown and expanded so rapidly—although they were spread fairly thinly.

The surprise at seeing so many of the beasts already present faded quickly as the teams took a battle formation and opened fire. Madigan's suit was equipped to handle most of the heavy fire to thin their numbers and Sal conceded reluctantly they were unlikely to find any survivors. By the time the Zoo was this thick, the humpers were already gathering and burying the bodies but still, they had to confirm that no one was trapped.

He moved out in front with one hand ready to draw the sword while he used the other to shoot anything that came too close. It was his job to get as much research done as he could while gunning and running. They didn't need any further samples from the humpers—there was probably a joke in there about DNA samples from the bastards—and it was interesting to see them proactively trying to defend their position. In the past, they tended to be passive and focused on their task until someone intruded on their personal space or attacked them.

Maybe they had marked off the whole area as their own and decided that humans were unwanted. He would have to find out how they did that.

When they weren't throwing themselves into the line of fire, of course.

The two plasma throwers who had joined them worked under his direction to clear a path once he'd checked that no valuable clues would be destroyed. The other teams had already started at the outer edges, which drew some of the mutants' attention from inside. With the Zoo forces divided and the brutal efficiency of the plasma, they were able to proceed at a much faster pace than usual.

It was fascinating how what had once been pure desert sand had begun to transform into dark soil. He still wanted to find out how the goop did that and see if there was a way to replicate it without the side effects, but there wasn't much time for personal projects these days.

Sal knew that Madigan watched him like a hawk but was careful to not react. With a second outbreak to deal with, they had no time to worry about his condition or her anxiety, although he appreciated her concern. Fortunately, the two limbs that protruded from his back moved him out of the way of the attackers and allowed him to react with more dexterity than he would have managed otherwise. New Connie had taken most of the control and her combat suite of programs did the work while they continued to press forward.

He set the pace at the front with Madigan and the rest of the team drove forward behind them. The fire teams would continue their work on the perimeter, but he wanted a closer look before everything was incinerated. They would have to remain alert to avoid the fire when the teams pushed closer to their position, but he was confident that they would be in and out before their comrades had progressed much beyond the perimeter.

An investigation was critical given that there was no indication of how the outbreak had started. The wall was intact and what appeared to be the point of origin suggested that the cause had somehow been introduced.

Hopefully, they would be able to avoid having to use heavy-duty explosives to clear it. Desperate measures like that had been needed when the Japanese base was overrun.

They wouldn't let that happen there, of course. At the same time, they would make sure that the Zoo gained no beachhead beyond the walls so he knew the heavy artillery would always be an option if the conventional approach didn't succeed. The base commanders were under strict orders to hold the Zoo back and if they failed, those in control would inevitably turn their minds to last-resort options. At that point, nuclear solutions would be considered.

People out there already called for them to drop tactical nukes on the Zoo but for the moment, cooler heads still held the launch codes. The reality was that no one knew for sure whether these would have the desired effect or not. Their mission into Chernobyl had provided proof of the goop's ability to overcome the radiation and restore the blighted landscape.

The conservative approach would change, however, if something like Niger happened again.

"We have a whole horde of locusts here," Jim commented as they readied themselves for another onslaught. "Is this maybe time to mention that I have severe entomophobia?"

"Ento-what the fuck now?" Sonja sounded confused.

"Entomophobia is a deathly fear of insects," Sal answered quickly and targeted a few that were perched on the trees that grew over what he assumed was either barracks or storage. "And I think you should have brought that issue up with your superior before being transferred to the Zoo. And maybe every day since. Why haven't you discussed this with the base therapist?"

"I've always been good at controlling my fears and such, which means I use the phobia to drive my need to kill as many of the fuckers as possible. When I was a kid, I was claustrophobic so I locked myself in my closet for a weekend."

"That's...disturbing. I assume your parents took you in to see if you had any of the markers for psychopathy?"

"Oh yeah. The shrinks said the results were inconclusive, which is better than a full-on positive test, I guess. Not as good as a negative test, though."

"Hey, Jim, do us all a favor," Madigan interjected. "Don't ever develop arachnophobia."

"Oh, no, I love spiders."

"Wait." Sal shook his head and settled on his haunches to collect a sample of the soil. "So you have a deathly fear of insects but anything with eight legs or more is a-okay?"

"Darn tootin'. Besides, spiders are the best way to keep

insects away from you so I was always happy to be around a nice little web."

There was no accounting for weaknesses and no reason to dig a little deeper into what made their friend and comrade tick. As long as his issues didn't compromise his ability to do his job, he wasn't a cause for concern. For the moment, they had to focus on what they were there to do and it was better to simply accept how weird their comrade was and leave it at that.

Besides, he was currently nagged by the intriguing possibility that the Zoo was practically daring them to hit it with a nuclear strike. Of course, this implied knowledge of humanity's weapons capabilities and even he wasn't ready to take it that far. He could, however, accept that it was challenging them to throw their worst at it, which in turn implied that it was able to withstand whatever their worst was.

They all needed to take a deep breath at this point and calm down. It was all too easy to slide into pointless specu-lation rather than think of real solutions.

Until they learned more about what the Zoo intended and how it had managed to push beyond the wall, their task was simple. Kill all the fuckers they encountered and obliterate every trace of the jungle. They had accomplished a fair amount of that and the perimeter teams no doubt contributed even more effectively.

The humpers seemed a little less aggressive with the locusts there and they were the easiest kills since their entire focus seemed to be on injecting the goop as quickly as possible. Eliminating them might help to slow any new growth and leave only what was already there to deal with.

A small pack of hyenas rushed into an attack but scattered quickly when two of Madigan's rockets hammered into them. The rest of the team opened fire but it was soon over. A couple of panthers, likely hoping for easy targets when the team was distracted by the hyenas, used the branches above to beat a hasty retreat.

"We should have brought your Christabel plant in here for this," Kolt told Kay, looked around, and nudged one of the vines with his rifle barrel. "You could have released her into her natural habitat and all that shit."

"Fuck you," she snapped and drew a laugh from her teammates as they pushed through the camp.

Random snatches of conversation on the comms suggested that the fire teams were making better progress than Sal had thought they would, but that was probably because the area was small in comparison to other outbreaks and the Zoo hadn't grown to full maturity.

Maybe there was something a little different about incursions that didn't have any direct connection to the original Zoo. That was something else he would have to try to find data on before they were finished there. It also raised the question as to why the jungle had not pushed forward to the wall as it had reputedly done at the second camp. With no wall in place, that was easily accomplished, but this outbreak appeared to be entirely separate. Had it merely been a distraction or was the plan to push out from camp two and assimilate the first outbreak?

Nothing had emerged to provide any kind of insight and he had a constant sense that they were looking for answers in the wrong place—or, rather, looking for obvious answers when the key to it all lay in some obscure direction they might never think of. While he continued to search, he would have to try to think outside the box.

It wasn't long before they found at least some sign of human activity, although given how overgrown the area was, it was easy to tell that it had been a couple of hours since people had been there. A handful of battered and broken weapons lay scattered on the ground and finally confirmed that they would find neither bodies nor survivors.

"Fucking hell," he whispered and drew his sword as a mixed group of locusts and humpers surged toward them. He was done playing nice with them. They would get through the camp and leave the military to annihilate it while they moved on to the next crisis.

Sal lunged and killed two humpers before a third tried to catch him with its stinger. He swung his sword in an upward strike to cut the creature in half at the abdomen before New Connie dragged him back. As a handful of the mutants tumbled over themselves, he rolled away to allow Madigan to finish them off with a grenade before they continued.

A few more of them were gunned down or slashed with his blade before they seemed to decide to focus their attack on the human in the smaller combat suit. They were no match for the combination of his quick reaction time, confidence in what his suit was capable of, and the AI that enhanced his every movement with extra power and speed. He managed to eliminate most of them and distract those that were left.

Finally, he activated the magnetic coils in his boots, which launched him up a solid fifteen feet. A pair of limbs immediately dug into a nearby tree trunk to stop him from falling into the frenzied monsters and he sliced a couple that tried to jump to his position.

Something moved above him and the sound immediately caught his attention. Before he could shoot, the creature launched toward him. Thankfully, it missed its jump due to a burst of rounds from the people on the ground.

It was a decent tactic. His suit let him stay mobile and bound in and out of the fight to draw the attention of the monsters around them. The other team members made most of the kills while he darted around and played like a rodeo clown.

Of course, the downside was that the rodeo clown would eventually be hit by the bull. In the Zoo, it would be an angry, mutated alien bull that probably had fangs, tusks, and a scorpion tail or something.

For the moment, though, it looked like they had pushed the mutants into a retreat. A panther tried to attack him from above but met a concerted volley and landed dead amidst its comrades. This provided even more of a distraction and the firepower from the Heavy Metal team successfully felled all those that had not yet slunk away.

"You're welcome," Juice called as he dropped from his perch in the tree. "That panther had you dead to rights."

"I appreciate it." Sal grinned. "I know I'll be killed by my style of fighting eventually, but it'll be delayed while I have sharp eyes watching my back."

"Yeah, your back," Madigan interjected. "If I said you were a crazy fucking bastard, how many times would that be now?"

"Three hundred and forty-two." The truth was that he'd

lost count, but the random number he pulled out of his head was probably fairly accurate.

"That sounds about right," she agreed. "You might be low-balling it, but I assume it's not counting when I called you only a crazy bastard, nutty dumbass, and numbskull."

"Right. That pushes it into the low thousands."

Juice chuckled. "When you two are done flirting—"

"Never!" Sal declared.

"Fair enough, but maybe you can keep at it while we move forward."

Madigan chuckled and set a brisk pace so that they would maintain a good distance between them and the fire teams. They paused occasionally to eliminate small groups of mutants and for Sal to collect a few more soil samples. He wanted to test them for concentration and activity of the goop and compare them relative to their distance from what he believed was the point of origin.

If he could establish a pattern in the various levels, maybe they would be able to develop a system of early-warning sensors to alert them to possible outbreaks and enable them to stay one step ahead of the Zoo. It was a long shot, but it was his job to find those damn impossible solutions because occasionally, they were the only option.

They needed all the samples they could get.

"The sensors don't pick up any more movement," Madigan said. "We caught this early."

"And the Algerian military has begun the incineration," Sal agreed. "Their reinforcements should have arrived by now so if they continue at this pace, they should clear the area before any other nasty surprises appear."

While some people questioned the Algerians' efficiency

when it came to the Zoo, they had learned the hard way in various outbreaks and had done a good job. They had some experience in the area and had secured and inciner- ated the Sustainagrow project in record time. After Niger, they wouldn't leave even a single leaf or tiny vine tendril to potentially start a second outbreak.

"I've had word from the people upstairs," Murphy advised them over the comms once they had circled the plasma throwers and emerged near their vehicle. "It looks like a sizable force of reinforcements have been dispatched to camp two."

"We're on our way," Sal responded. "But don't wait for us. We can join the rest of our team once we get there. Do we know if there are survivors?"

"Comms are compromised as usual, but the last message indicated that the civilians have taken refuge in one of the buildings and the merc team hired to protect them isn't big enough. It's a matter of time before the Zoo gains the upper hand." The captain sounded frustrated.

"Getting teams to them is the first priority." He sighed and shook his head. "I only hope it's not already too late."

It had been a long-ass flight. She'd forgotten how unsettling the journey was. Even on a private jet, they had to find things to occupy them rather than think about what waited for them at the other end.

Courtney had work to do on the plane and the three freelancers used their awake time to clean and check their numerous toys. It was their first time on a first-class aircraft like this and their tension had remained almost palpable through the long hours. All three were Zoo veterans, but they had left it behind for a reason.

Now, everyone felt like they had to be on the front lines although no one wanted to do it. They knew, however, that a single gunner could turn the tide of a ferocious assault and that when things turned ugly, those stationed at the Zoo needed volunteers to step in and assist them.

It was easy to take things for granted until the Zoo did something to dry the money up and someone had to step in and stop it.

From what she had heard, the corporate interests were kicking and screaming about their forced relocation to the Zoo. The protest was both futile and foolish. If they stepped back and thought about it, they would realize that the move would halve the costs of containment and eliminate transport overheads altogether. It would save them all a fortune in the long run, but the assholes seldom thought long-term.

Chief officers of the companies involved often only wanted to stay with a single company for a few years and then take a pay bump when they moved elsewhere. They would always protest the expenses of relocating to the Zoo. To them, it was like a red blot on their perfect balance sheet. By the time the savings manifested, they would be long gone and someone else would reap the benefits.

She had no patience with their constant bleating about their bottom line. Everyone had issues, some worse than others, and it was high time that they worked on the front line and experienced a little of what their profits demanded from others.

Her unexpected conflict had started shortly before Casablanca. While she had missed her friends in the Heavy Metal team and even the high-risk life at the Zoo, part of her had rebelled. She'd tried to ignore it and the inner push to inform the pilot of a change of plans and instruct him to land in Casablanca. The freelancers could arrange passage to the US base and she could fly home.

With the green smudge now visible in the distance through the windows, she wondered if she hadn't made the biggest mistake of her life. She had come because Sal, Madigan, and the team needed her. Hell, maybe the whole fucking world would need her before the current situation was resolved. So maybe she didn't relish the idea of putting her life on the line but there were benefits as well as risks, and she was a veteran. She was used to living on the edge and would adjust once they landed.

"Is it only me or is the Zoo way bigger than it was before?" Chezza asked.

Courtney looked at the three freelancers, who all stared out the window. They had been instructed to take their seats and fasten their seatbelts.

The woman was right. It grew bigger every day, but it was one thing to read news stories and see footage and another to look down on it. Pilots always gave the whole damn jungle a wide berth because the locusts had a habit of launching from inside to attack them. Even from a distance, however, the thick, green ribbon caught and held the imagination. It sprawled menacingly across the Sahara and conjured fear and fascination in equal measure.

They had arrived and there was no turning back. She hated that she had even thought about it. Sal and Madigan needed her and she would be there for them. They would never have expanded the team unless they had to and it would be impossible for one researcher to keep up with whatever Sal envisaged that required so many recruits.

She could fill a role no one else could and this was where she was meant to be at this point in her life.

The plane touched down at the base and it was immediately apparent that a campaign was in progress. Hammerheads and other vehicles raced to where soldiers and mercs in full armor waited to board. When they were at full capacity, they drove out of the base at a speed that suggested a crisis and she wondered if they had arrived at a crucial moment.

A couple of officers approached as they disembarked and completed the paperwork required on arrival. Courtney approached them immediately.

"What's going on here?" she asked and only vaguely registered that she sounded like someone in charge who expected instant answers.

The two exchanged a look as if unsure whether to provide her with the information or not before the woman with lieutenant's bars shrugged.

"There was an outbreak—no, make that two," she told her. "Every base is scrambling all the troops we can to stop it before it spreads."

"Has the Heavy Metal team been notified?"

"They were one of the first on the scene. The last I heard, they were reclaiming one of the ENSOL camps."

Courtney nodded, turned on her heel, and strode to where the freelancers were overseeing the people unloading the plane. She could understand them being concerned about their suits since they were responsible for maintaining the damn things themselves.

They would work under a different financial arrangement now, though.

"Chezza, Jiro, Trick," she snapped and again sounded like an officer. "We've landed in the middle of an outbreak so will join the effort. I hope you rested on the plane because it'll be a long haul."

"Hell, I love plane rides," Trick answered with a chuckle. "I'm not McFadden."

She realized that it was an insider joke since the other two chuckled but could guess that Taylor McFadden, their previous employer, had a flying phobia.

It was no doubt an ongoing source of amusement between them.

"Well, the Heavy Metal team is already out there, which means you three will go through the trial by fire of a fucking lifetime."

"Do we have transportation?" Jiro asked. Somehow, she knew he was the most pragmatic of the team, although he had an annoying habit of playing with his knives whenever his hands were free.

"We will. Suit up and be ready to move as quickly as possible."

"You got it, boss," Chezza confirmed with a salute that was only half-joking as Courtney turned away and gestured to the driver she'd arranged to meet them when they arrived.

"You picked one hell of a day to touch down," the man said as she climbed in. "Will the others join us?"

"Nope," she answered curtly and put her seatbelt on. "Get me to the commandant's office. And step on it."

There would be no need to talk to Franklin and she had no intention to harass him when he had so many other issues to manage. She needed to talk to the officer who juggled the veritable mountain of paperwork that came with the logistics of moving that many soldiers and mercs into the field of battle.

They would get her and her three freelancers on the next transport to the incursion. It wasn't so much that she felt entitled but rather that she'd had to establish and exercise her authority to overcome significant resistance from her enemies.

Along the way, she'd learned that assertiveness was a necessity in certain situations, and this was undoubtedly one of them.

"Sergeant Greaves," she said as she approached his desk and read his nameplate. The man was all but buried in paperwork, with three phones around him and a squad of soldiers to run errands. Similar scenes could probably be found at all the Zoo bases and she had to respect the men and women who managed the controlled chaos.

"You need to put some people in for the next transport to the front," Courtney told him without preamble. "Myself and three others. Here's the paperwork on them."

"Look, I don't know who—" Greaves paused when his hands automatically flipped the files open and he recognized her name at the top of the list. It was a little gratifying to see that people still remembered her. "Are you still with Heavy Metal?"

"I certainly am. The three freelancers I have with me are

new acquisitions. We intend to join the fight on the front line, and something tells me we can't simply rent a Hammerhead and drive ourselves there."

He shook his head and grimaced at the stack of papers on his desk. "Look, I'll do what I can, but the people moving out now are priorities. It might take a few hours for me—"

She leaned on the desk and made sure her eyes were level with his. "This is a courtesy visit. We will be on the next transport heading to the incursion. I'm merely hoping you can find a way so we don't have to shoot four people and take their places. Do we have an understanding here?"

There was no way she meant that threat but at this point, all he cared about was getting the people from the base out into the field as quickly as possible. There was nothing in his paycheck that justified dealing with someone like her.

And thankfully, her reputation did precede her, which meant she would likely be put on priority if she decided to go over his head.

Courtney could almost see all those thoughts going through his head immediately before he whistled to one of his corporals, who hurried forward and took the four files she had given Greaves.

"Knock four people off the next transport—the lowest priority—and add these four."

The man nodded, no questions asked.

"The next transport is out of here in thirty minutes," the sergeant told her. "If you're not there, that's your goddammed problem. Now get the hell out of my face."

Not many people talked to her like that anymore, but

she wasn't the type to hold a grudge about that kind of thing. Military people would always be high on testosterone and after her challenge, he would find some way to establish his authority again, even if it was only a sharp dismissal.

She had what she wanted and the driver was taking her to where her team waited for her.

They looked up when she climbed out and jogged closer.

"How soon can you get us out?" Chezza asked. "Some people we were talking to have been waiting hours for their helicopter."

"We're on the next one in about twenty minutes," Courtney answered and gestured for the forklift driver bringing her suit to hurry.

"How the hell did you make that happen?" Trick asked.

"You know how Karens are the worst kind of person to have in your face?" She pulled the top of the crate off. "It goes without saying, but a Karen used to yelling through lawyers and sexist corporate assholes is the prime kind of bitch you don't want in your face."

The three freelancers exchanged a look that told her they hadn't expected her to be able to pull that kind of weight at a military institution. It was like they didn't know her at all.

"What do you want us to tell the Heavy Metal team for you?" Chezza asked as they finished with their suits.

"That you couldn't talk me out of coming," Courtney answered and began to pull her armor out and put it on. Gone were the days of heading into the Zoo in a glorified hazmat. She'd picked up a top-of-the-line hybrid that hadn't even hit the market yet, and she'd trained in the sims to keep her mind and trigger finger sharp. It wasn't as good as the real thing but hopefully, it meant she still had the reflexes and skills she needed.

"You're...coming with us?"

"You don't think I flew you out here to work for me while I hole up in an air-conditioned office somewhere, do you?" The gauntlets in particular were one of her favorites, with sensory links that gave her perfect tactile control. "No, you're my posse. We'll head in there together—and out together."

Again, a look of surprise crossed their faces. She had assumed that they merely didn't believe anything they'd heard about her, but maybe they'd not done proper research before boarding the plane. It wasn't the best response from people who were joining the Heavy Metal crew, but time had been short and no one was perfect.

They had no more questions for her as she caught up to them quickly and went through the familiar motions of suiting up and getting ready for battle. Since she had the time, she included the minutiae of running diagnostic checks as she donned the helmet and turned the HUD on.

"Hey, Chezza, Jiro, Trick—it's good to see you guys on the ground with us grunts again. It looks like you're taking the transport with us."

A small troop of soldiers had gathered where a transport helicopter was already coming in. It would be in time to touch down, get refueled, and leave again with another group of reinforcements.

"It looks like we're heading in there," Jiro answered. "We haven't even had time to sleep the jetlag off."

"Well, if it's any consolation, we have been up and at it since three in the fucking morning, so we'll all be dead on our feet. What about your boss? Is the leprechaun joining us there too?"

"Nah, McFadden's taking some time off," Trick replied. "He sent us to pick up his slack and work with the Heavy Metal team."

"But don't you worry, Reyes," Chezza interjected. "He taught us how to kick ass so we don't need some giant redhead here to hold our hand. It looks like you assholes do, though."

"Fuck you."

It was something Courtney had never quite got a hang of. She'd thought she had it a couple of times, but it always felt like a second language. The camaraderie and smooth way they threw insults like banter, always knowing where the line was, remained a skill she had yet to master.

Or maybe it was common respect, a knowledge that nothing said was meant as a deliberate insult. Maybe that was why she was never sure. They didn't see her as one of their own so they never knew if she meant her insults or if it was more playful banter.

"Let's get moving, people!" the lieutenant in charge of the reinforcements roared and his voice carried even over the rotors. "It looks like the front liners are in a bind, which means everyone who can get out there will get out there. If you don't board this chopper, someone else will."

The response was immediate and those waiting scrambled to board. The suit's movements were smooth, almost like it anticipated what Courtney wanted it to do. Maybe she would still need a little getting used to it, but she was one of the first in the helicopter. The moment the refueling hoses were dragged away, they were in the air.

It felt strange to know she would soon be back in the thick of it. A sick, hungry feeling in the pit of her stomach had returned and she took a deep breath while she watched the Zoo getting closer.

She'd missed it.

CHAPTER FOURTEEN

"Do you think they'll ever come up with more combat AIs?" Martin asked conversationally as their Hammerhead approached ENSOL's camp two.

"More of the combat AIs?" Matt turned to face her. "Do you honestly think it's a good idea to send a group of suits out on their own to deal with the Zoo?"

"Yeah, maybe not." She shielded her eyes and squinted to study their destination.

"Damn right, it's not," Gregor declared. "With the way the Zoo can screw with the comms, there's no guarantee that it couldn't simply take control of them and use them against us."

This triggered a half-hearted debate that Matt chose to ignore. He didn't believe that scenario was possible but had long since accepted that the jungle operated by its own set of rules that seemed geared toward surprising the crap out of them at every turn.

While he still wouldn't support the concept of "independent" AI-driven suits, he did wish he had access to a

Hammerhead version of the Connie Sal used in his suit. They could sure as fuck do with the firepower she was able to bring to the party when they'd had to infiltrate the overrun Russian base to rescue Gregor and the other survivors.

He leaned forward and looked out of the window of their Hammerhead as they pulled to a stop. "We can dream about combat AIs all we want but right now, we need to get our asses out there because this clusterfuck won't go away unless we force it to."

They scrambled out of the vehicle and stood for a moment to survey a scene that could only be described as utter chaos. A handful of troops and mercenaries did what they could to hold a swarm back—and did a decent job of it given what they were up against.

It looked very much like how the Zoo reacted to having a pita plant plucked. Murphy was in charge and he had considerable experience dealing with the Zoo, but that only went so far. Eventually, they would be overwhelmed.

"That's weird," Gregor muttered. "That's fucking weird, right?"

Martin nodded. "The Zoo usually sends the vegetation ahead to provide cover for the mutants. I've never seen mutants attacking first."

"Shit," the Russian whispered. "If the goddammed jungle is willing to send them out like this, imagine how many it has in reserve."

It didn't look like any of the creatures cared that they attacked without cover. They rushed forward and into the defenses like they had every intention of soaking up every bullet the humans had to offer.

The Hammerhead immediately turned to position itself so the cannon on top of it could open fire, if only to let the teams know that reinforcements were on the way.

Matt had hoped for more people to be in the action by now, but there was no telling if the other bases were dealing with this kind of attack as well. Either that or they had to be prepared for it, which meant they couldn't commit all their troops to help others without having secured their defenses.

A few of the men had already set themselves up and now took shots from a distance, and picked mutants off to try to draw some attention away from the attack.

"I got word from Franklin," Murphy announced as he strode to meet them. "It's good to see you guys. Reinforcements are on the way in force. The Algerians are sending troops in too but they might take a while to get here."

"US troops will take a while too," Matt responded and shook his head. "It looks like we're the only reinforcements they'll have for now. What's the status?"

The captain shrugged. "Most of the defenders are holed up in the central building that you can see in the distance. They have sharpshooters on the roof and they've established firing lines through the windows."

"But that will only last as long as it takes for the vegetation to grow to full height," Davis pointed out. "At that point, visibility will go to crap and they'll have to fight at close quarters."

Murphy nodded. "If we can divide the mutants and draw some of them off, they'll have a chance, but only if we can get reinforcements in there so they don't have to fight alone. As things stand, it's only a matter of time before they are overwhelmed. Any questions?"

The newcomers had already begun to check their weapons, the only real answer to his question. He slapped Matt on the shoulder and stepped back. "It's up to you now. I'll see you when you get out."

"Yeah. When we get out." It sounded good, but everyone there knew there was no assurance that they would. This battle had already broken numerous accepted "rules" and there was no way to know what the Zoo had planned. It would be much like going in with all their experience and assumptions swept off the board.

The combined teams moved in and immediately fell into battle formation. Matt took the lead alongside the merc leader who had been in charge of the ENSOL security teams. By unspoken agreement, they tightened their ranks, readied their weapons, and pushed directly into the surge of cryptids.

It wasn't quite a Pelennor Fields moment and maybe rushing headfirst into the monsters wasn't the best idea. The truth was, however, that they had to drive through the mutants to reach the defenders and there was no easy way to do that. Given that they were trying to keep as many people inside alive as they could and distract at least some of the horde attacking the building, a direct challenge by a new force might be the best way to achieve that.

If they survived long enough to make a difference, Matt thought grimly.

He loaded a grenade into his assault rifle and launched it directly into where the beasts were thickest. A group of locusts bore the brunt of it but others immediately took their places. It was a mixture of all the usual suspects but with a few of the real dangers hidden in the mass.

None of the dinosaurs, thankfully, but a few Komodo dragons, a handful of the massive sloths that had been seen recently, and even a pack of the mole rats, although they didn't look like they were digging themselves into the ground yet. Maybe they were positioning themselves for when they had the camp fully overrun to make sure that any attempt to retake it by the humans was slowed by having to deal with the fuckers.

"We got us a killerpillar on the left side!"

He wasn't sure who made the announcement. Matt doubted that they were wrong since there wasn't much in the world that looked like those fucking monsters.

Or, at least, not that big. Either way, if it attacked, they would have to deal with it. For the moment, it seemed like the creatures were more focused on taking the camp than dealing with the newcomers, and the teams made a point of making them pay for it.

Another grenade—an ordinary one this time—was lobbed into the shifting, frenzied mass of mutants. A second followed seconds after the first exploded and between them, they gouged a sizable hole in the monster ranks. Others surged in to fill it before the humans could push an advantage and for the first time, the creatures turned to engage the reinforcements.

The first of the panthers was gunned down quickly, and Martin eliminated the other two with a fusillade that was concentrated enough to fell a handful of locusts too. She stepped back when she realized that one of the sloths had seen her and attempted to cut her off from her team.

Gregor noticed it and shifted his weapon to cover her. The creature backed away but a pack of hyenas surged forward to engage them and the larger beast retreated to a safe distance.

One of the mercs watching the flanks was momentarily distracted by a locust swarm that seemed to target him directly. He and the men on either side of him immediately opened fire but it seemed the attack was only a diversion. A massive Komodo dragon lunged from behind the cloud of smaller mutants and before the humans had even registered its presence, it swung its tail in a lethal arc.

The man on the left managed to fling himself prone and the appendage swiped both the center man and the one on the right. One was cleanly decapitated and his head fell on the merc still on the ground, who tried to scramble to his feet while he fired desperately at the beast. The third man backpedaled frantically and caught only a glancing blow, but the power in the swing was still enough to sever his arm above the elbow and gouge a wide patch across his chest plate.

Some of the hyenas bounded forward and dragged him down, but with an artery severed, he'd be dead in minutes. As the mutants tried to haul him away, his teammates unleashed a barrage that scythed through them and battered the Komodo dragon.

Gregor and Martin both fired shots into the giant lizard's acid sacs, although they weren't sure if the old method of killing these creatures was still effective. They had heard that the Chinese had encountered one with acid that had no effect on the beast and there was some concern that the new mutation would replace the old.

Fortunately, this was one of the original kind and it hissed in rage and pain when the sacs ruptured and spewed their contents, which immediately burned through its scales into the vulnerable flesh beneath. It thrashed wildly but another concerted barrage ended its struggles.

A handful of the panthers tried to head Matt off and one of them bounded in from the side and barreled into him with enough force to hurl him off his feet. He landed hard a good few paces away, which left a brief window for the merc captain to open fire on his attacker as it lunged in for the kill.

Shots erupted from the group and the merc grasped his arm and hauled him up. Gregor stepped alongside to steady him and Martin covered them while Davis checked his armor and steadied himself.

"The first round's on me," he told his rescuers and began to move forward again.

The Russian laughed. "And all we have to do is keep you alive long enough to pay for it."

"Although with these odds," Martin quipped, "it might be a very cheap round."

Matt snorted. "If any of you even think about dying on me, I'll haul you back and kick your fucking asses from here to next year. We have people to save and Zoo bastards to kill, so let's get in there Heavy Metal style and get this goddammed clusterfuck cleaned up before the shit completely hits the fan."

The merc captain laughed. "If you're still waiting for that, what the hell do you call this?"

"A warm-up," Gregor replied smartly. "A little flex and stretch before the real business begins."

Being still, even for a second, would mean being swarmed and killed almost immediately, and Matt had no intention of making it easy to kill them. He'd had one brief moment when the panther's hot breath misted his visor and he'd known how close he was to dying. *And today is not a fucking good day to die.*

"We keep moving," he ordered on the group comms. "Even if it's one goddammed inch at a time. Stay in tight formation but work in twos or threes to cover each other, and make every shot count. The Zoo has broken one of its patterns but that works in our favor."

"Oh, yeah?" One of the mercs snorted derisively. "And what would that be?"

He gestured to patches of green growth that had begun to push through the sand. "No full grown trees and vines so no real jungle yet, but that will change." Up ahead, the humpers were already busy injecting the goop to provide the impetus for the Zoo to catch up to itself. "With those little bastards at work, we have a limited window. Before you know it, we'll be waist-deep in green and by the time we reach the defenders, it'll be over our heads. We have a reasonably clear field for now so let's use it."

The mutants continued to pour into the outbreak area from the original Zoo. With this section of the wall still unbuilt, there was nothing to stop or even slow them. The jungle had already thrust a wide spur out that had almost reached the outer edge of the buffer zone.

Another large group of humpers worked feverishly in advance of this growth and their efforts visibly increased the speed of the burgeoning incursion. Within a few hours, the Zoo would meet its new outbreak and all hell would break loose.

Matt increased the pace and the mutants responded with greater aggression. A smattering of gunfire ahead indicated that those creatures that held the defenders under siege were being picked off by the sharpshooters on top of the building, but it wouldn't last.

Two Komodo dragons pushed through the smaller beasts and hissed with rage as they barreled into the combined teams and tried to ram as many as they could off their feet. They were only partially successful, but the three they did manage to knock over weren't able to escape the acid spewed at them before the monsters continued past the humans and wheeled as if to prepare for another attack.

"Shit," Gregor muttered as he set his weapon to auto and joined a few of the mercs to unleash a sustained assault on the lizards. "I've never seen the bastards do that before."

He was right. The creatures usually attacked from the perimeter once the dispensable species had harassed the teams and weakened them. They were fearless but canny and relied on their speed and physical power for lightning strikes that would inflict the most damage as quickly as possible. Usually, these involved the use of the mighty tails, and it was a first to see them attack a tight group and not use their lethal appendages at all.

One of the monsters was almost obliterated by the gunfire but the other hissed a challenge and retreated behind the smaller creatures. Some of the mercs had rushed to the aid of their fallen comrades but only one had survived, and he was badly burned by the acid that had eaten through his armor in mere moments.

The merc captain and two others stood guard while their medic did the best he could, but everyone knew that the victim would likely not last much longer. Two of his teammates stepped alongside him but he retrieved his weapon and shrugged them off.

"Don't worry. I won't slow you," he told them. "I know I won't make it, but I can kill a good few Zoo bastards before they kill me."

Before anyone could protest or argue, another wave of mutants swept forward, led by a large contingent of the scorpion locusts. With their stingers and razor-sharp limbs poised to kill, they pushed forward with the obvious intention to overwhelm the group so the other creatures could finish them.

"Form a circle," Matt yelled, "and stand your ground. Don't let them through." He yanked a grenade from his belt, pulled the pin, and lobbed it into the mass of mutants far enough away from the teams but still close enough to inflict maximum damage to at least some of the front ranks.

Francesca launched two more grenades into the seething horde seconds after his detonated. Two more were thrown by the mercs and the four exploded in sequence to carve a path through the creatures.

The scorpion locusts rallied and three of them lunged at Matt, chittering defiance while their tails swayed ominously, all tipped with a drop of venom. He barely had time to shift his rifle before the first reached him and he fired at point-blank range. The creature hovered for a moment, inches away from his helmet, before it seemed to fall apart in a flurry of limbs and blackish-green blood.

Part of him wondered how the bastards knew he was leading the teams because there seemed to be no other explanation for the way they had singled him out. The other part of him was already focused on the other two and he opened fire instinctively. Martin and the merc captain joined him and the mutants all but disintegrated in the gunfire that also caught some of the mutants that tried to push in to close the gap the grenades had created.

A couple of the mercs lobbed grenades for good measure to clear the path, and the team pushed into the breach with no need for orders or explanation. They knew that in moments, the creatures would push in to close the gap behind them and there would be no going back.

Ahead of them, the mutants fought to block their progress. Matt was about to retrieve another grenade when the wounded merc pushed past him, firing on full auto with one hand while he held a grenade in the other. He'd already pulled the pin and pushed into a jog with a wild bellow before anyone could stop him. A small pack of the hyenas surrounded him and as they dragged him down, he released the grenade.

"Damn fool," the merc captain muttered but led the way into the newly opened breach.

"The pain—" the medic began but cut the comment off. No one had the right to judge a man for choosing how to die.

An urgency seemed to infuse the animals and when distant gunfire could be heard behind the teams, they became even more aggressive. It was as if the entire landscape had been charged with electric tension and the result was immediately visible around them. The trees began to grow at a rate no one had witnessed before, not even from the Zoo.

They thrust from the sand and vines curled up the trunks as the underbrush pushed through between them. It was as if someone had pressed fast-forward and accelerated what would take months or even years in the rest of the world. Even in the Zoo, it usually took the whole jungle at least a few days to grow as much as it had in only a few minutes.

Even when it was taking over the Japanese base, most of the growth needed hours before it was a full jungle. Now, it looked almost like everything had already grown under the sand and simply exploded into existence when it was ready.

It was a horrifying, beautiful sight to see, and Matt knew it did not bode well for them.

"What's your plan?" Martin asked, calm and focused as she reloaded and leveled another volley at one of the mole rats that hadn't yet moved to sandy areas where their traps would work best.

"Nothing's changed," he replied, "except that I think reinforcements have pushed in behind us. We need to move our asses and get to the building before we're completely cut off."

He muttered a curse as a panther made a swipe at him and he fired a short burst through the creature's skull that ended the attack with messy efficiency. At least they were still grounded and couldn't launch their assaults from the trees like they usually did.

The jungle was still pushing, however, and to survive, they needed to reach the defenders before it overwhelmed them. He had a feeling that trees and vines growing that quickly would pose more of a threat to their teams than the swarm was.

Still, they had a job to do, and retreating was not on their list of options. They were already, by his estimation, close to where the camp inhabitants had holed up, although the gunfire from that direction was more sporadic. If the jungle was growing at the same pace there, the sharpshooters had no doubt retreated to safer positions.

"Talk...me, Davis, before...fucking jungle...comms." Murphy sounded irritated and frustrated, which might either be his natural response to the situation or a harbinger of doom.

"We have the fucking jungle going ballistic and growing by the minute," Matt replied amidst the hiss and crackle of static. "I estimate that we're close to the defenders, but the mutants are rabid. We have to fight for every inch of ground and have five fatalities thus far."

"...forcements on...and more... Plasma te...buffer...to push..."

"I hope to God I heard you right, Murphy. Reinforcements on the way and more to follow. Plasma teams dispatched to the buffer zone to push the original Zoo back. The number of cryptids is increasing, but if we can cut this section off we can hopefully slow—fuck." He snorted in disgust. "And that's the end of that. The comms are down and we can only hope like hell that I didn't get the bull by the balls."

The teams, galvanized by the thought that others were on their way, pushed into a slow jog that was the maximum pace the fast-growing jungle would allow. They could no longer see the humpers and Matt wished he'd thought to mention to Murphy that they should try to patrol the perimeter. It seemed logical that they would move on to resume their goop spreading in virgin sand.

He wondered how the other half of their team was doing and how long it would take for them to arrive. They could do with Madigan's tank suit and firepower. Having her there to drive forward would have saved considerable time since the sheer weight she carried could bulldoze through almost anything.

A few members of the merc team hung back a little to act as rearguard and make sure their comrades' backs were covered. Gregor had taken a position on the flank and held the line before his rifle emptied and he paused to reload. He looked away from the Zoo for only a moment but something dark and massive seemed to have waited for his moment of inattention before it rushed forward.

"Goddammit!" Matt yelled, alerted by the odd sensation of the earth shuddering beneath his feet. He looked around to see who was both close enough to help and wasn't dealing with their own issues. "Gregor needs cover!"

Thankfully, the Russian's reflexes were well-honed. His rifle was reloaded and he flung himself out of the way as one of the new hippo mutants made its presence known with a speed and belligerence that would have put its earthly counterpart to shame.

There was no real way to confirm it, but the fucker's

tusks looked even bigger than what Matt remembered from those in the mountains.

"Focus fire!" he shouted, but half the team had already shifted to fix their attention on the hulking beast as it tried to decide which one of them to attack.

All he could be thankful for was that the Heavy Metal team already had some experience in the matter.

Gregor was trying to back away from it and his rounds simply bounced off its hard, armor-like skin. It snapped its head around and barely missed him with its tusks but managed to bowl him over.

As the mouth opened to deliver the finishing bite, Matt stepped in, opened fire, and aimed the bullets into the back of its mouth. Martin did the same, then stepped closer to help her teammate onto his feet when the hippo began to buck and stumble.

The sheer weight of it was a danger. They would have a difficult time dragging Gregor clear if the creature fell on top of him, and they were lucky to scramble away before it fell. The mercs shifted their aim to drive off the smaller creatures that attempted to attack them while they were distracted.

"We made it," the merc captain told them. "The building is directly ahead." He activated the general comms and was able to reach those of his team who had stayed to guard the civilians. It was fortunate that the Zoo interference wasn't a major issue with the teams so close and at least they now didn't have to worry about friendly fire as they made their approach.

As expected, the jungle had encroached to the point where it surrounded the building and effectively trapped the defenders within. Cheers went up as they arrived but they were a little subdued, probably because of their low numbers.

"More are on the way," the captain assured them. "I don't know how long it will take but until they arrive, we'll keep fighting."

"We have to be smart about it," Matt added as he took stock. "Plasma teams have already started work in the buffer zone to push the Zoo back. That should stop mutants from crossing over, and while there is a shit-ton of the bastards, if we can stop the numbers increasing, that's half the battle won."

The wait was harder than the bloody battles they had fought to get there. Matt and the merc captain had discussed their options and both reached the only conclusion—there weren't any.

The main issue was the sheer number of civilians present. Virtually the entire ENSOL workforce was huddled in what was little more than a shed where their equipment was usually stored. They had managed to gather the basics like water and medicines, but there was no food and the toilet facilities were limited.

The first prize would have been to march them all out and push to the perimeter, but none of the civilians had suits, about half had weapons or knew how to use them, and twenty-three mercs plus the Heavy Metal team was simply not enough to protect them against the kind of furious aggression displayed by the mutants.

They had tried raising Murphy although they didn't expect the comms to work. For now, they were a little island of humanity in a rampantly growing jungle and all they could do was sit tight and hope the reinforcements would reach them. There was no guarantee of that given the overwhelming mutant presence, but none of the bases wanted the Zoo beyond the wall so hopefully, all of them would send teams to clear the outbreak before it expanded even more.

For the first hour or two, the mutants appeared to be content to simply surround the shed and keep them trapped—"Like a fucking food warehouse," Gregor commented acidly. He and Martin had organized a few of the mercs to stand ready at the door in case something should gain entry. It wasn't unlikely that a beast like the hippos could batter through what was far from reinforced steel. The remaining mercs and Algerian soldiers had positioned themselves at the few windows.

Tempers were short and a few arguments almost erupted among the civilians, especially when Matt insisted that they start to ration the water. Oddly enough, the sudden bang and thump of what could only be mutant bodies flinging themselves against the structure proved to be the most effective peacekeeper. Perhaps being reminded of their common enemy put personal offenses into perspective.

It was hard to tell what the creatures hoped to achieve. The efforts were random and not concentrated in one place—the door being the most obvious, and Matt had no doubt that they would know where the entrance was. For the moment, it seemed to be the smaller species that were the least likely to be effective.

Matt finally decided that it was an intimidation tactic but he still made sure that their teams were spread throughout the building so no single area was left entirely undefended. They were stretched thin, of course, and God help them all if a concerted attack was launched at multiple points. The structure wouldn't withstand the heavier mutants if they were determined to gain entry.

"ENSOL camp, you have incoming. We heard there was a party happening," a man called over comms in a German accent. "It's a little insulting that we weren't invited."

"The invitation is in the mail," Matt responded. "But come on in. You're the best damn party crashers ever."

"We're about ten minutes out," a Brit told them cheerfully, "so please keep your fireworks for the Zoo bastards."

"We'll stand down," he acknowledged, "and get ready to open the door. I suggest you stay close to one another. We have the mutants battering the building so don't want to let any of them in if we can help it."

"Gotcha," the man responded and a loud barrage in the background drowned his next words.

The approaching gunfire grew louder and the team at the door stood ready, as did the others who fell into a defensive formation to be prepared if those at the front were overwhelmed. A palpable sense of anticipation settled over those gathered, and even the thumps and bangs of the mutants seemed to pause while they waited.

"Knock, knock," the Brit quipped cheerfully. Matt was tempted to respond with the "who's there?" but the door swung open and what must have been a full platoon streamed into the building. Their suits carried all the markers of their Brit and German counterparts and while they looked like they'd been through the mill, they appeared ready to do their part.

"I guess it's not my day to die after all," Matt said and laughed.

"You're fucking right it's not," the German retorted and froze when a loud thud directly behind him made the wall shudder. "What in the hell was that?"

Matt shrugged. "It's the not so welcome gatecrashers. The bastards have been doing that for the last hour although they haven't made any concerted attempt to get in."

"There are a few others on the way," the Brit told them. "The Americans should be first, but the other half of the Heavy Metal team were about half an hour behind us."

"Well, it's damn good to know we're not in this on our own."

"We are very pleased to kick some Zoo ass," one of the German soldiers assured him. "It has been a while for some of us."

"Davis, we're here to save your sorry ass." Madigan sounded surprisingly cheerful for someone who'd been in various versions of the Zoo since the early hours.

"You're early," he responded. "The other team said half an hour."

"Yeah, what can I say? We used their slipstream and snuck through while the Zoo fuckers were distracted by them."

CHAPTER FIFTEEN

The reinforcements were certainly a boon. Without them, they would have been almost immediately overrun when the trees reached maturity. There was no chance of holding it back, not unless some serious firepower joined their ranks.

Still, they had to do what they could and at least now, they had sufficient numbers to take the fight to the jungle.

"We have the surviving defenders manning their stations," Madigan noted as she approached the rest of the group. "They'll be the last line of defense for the civilians inside. I guess we have to say that those civvies held their own well enough, but I want nothing but pros and soldiers on the front line. Plasma throwers, you have to push the plants back from the shed and create a clear killzone. Our defense will be centered around this building."

"Won't that mean we have nowhere to retreat to?" the German leader asked.

She nodded. "There isn't anywhere else that can accommodate the number of civilians so we can't worry about what we can't change. We have to work with what we have. Let's get to it!"

The plasma throwers took turns to attack the encroaching jungle, guarded by the reinforcements who then took positions in the widening killzone. A small team volunteered to set the claymores at strategic points to hopefully thin the mutant ranks if they made a concerted attack.

Some of the ENSOL mercs were stationed inside to guard the windows in case something pushed beyond the other two lines of defense. A few of the best sharpshooters were on the roof, but most of the combined force would be on the ground, fighting directly.

Madigan had tried to get Sal up on the roof, but he saw through that almost immediately. It seemed like the pain meds were wearing off but he wouldn't let that stop him. He would keep going until there was nothing left of him.

"Movement on the way!" a German soldier warned and they readied themselves for the first wave.

The claymores detonated with ruthless efficiency and spewed seven hundred ball bearings each to rip and tear through everything that tried to pass.

They were enough to hold the Zoo advance back a little, but it wouldn't last and once they all exploded, they didn't have more.

Sal was a little surprised that they lasted as long as they did. Sporadic cracks of explosives all around them indicated where the attacks were coming from. Not all sides, thankfully, and it seemed that most came from the side facing the original Zoo.

It wouldn't be long until they were surrounded, though.

The Zoo was growing too fast and it wouldn't stop simply because they resisted. Sooner or later, the plasma throwers would run out and it would continue to push through and around them if it had to until they were all smothered.

He didn't know why he felt that way and tried to ignore the niggling feeling in the back of his head. It was like something was digging into the pit of his stomach and his brain at the same time.

The depth of whatever he'd done to himself had gradually become clearer and ignoring it wouldn't help anyone. It could even end up being a danger. If the Zoo had a connection to him, there was no telling what it would do to and with him.

Gunfire all around him said the men on the rooftop had chosen their targets and made sure that at least some of the mutants were thinned before they came close to the building and challenged the ground teams.

Madigan took a step forward and her rockets flared as the plasma throwers stepped in front of the vines that had begun to spread and attack the buildings that weren't defended. Sal moved forward and his assault rifle kicked against his arm. A sick feeling coursed through him and made it difficult to focus. His shoulder ached and the pain seemed to radiate to wrack his body relentlessly.

From the way things were going, they would need as many guns and bullets at the front as possible. There was a reason why the fire teams were generally pulled back when attacks were initiated by the Zoo. Fire dealt with the plants well enough, but it didn't do anything immediate to the animals.

An awful sense of helplessness washed over him when

the first of the hyenas rushed out and caught fire almost immediately as the plasma throwers were burning at temperatures in excess of anything required to set organic material aflame. The beasts didn't seem to care. They rushed forward while their bodies burned under the flames like they couldn't even feel the pain.

One of the fire team screamed as powerful jaws clamped on him and dragged him into the thick of the flames. His screams fortunately didn't last long. The fire was still lit and the insulation containing the neon that was used to power the throwers was broken.

Sal was a nerd and even he didn't understand how the equipment was built. He'd never liked physics much so maybe that explained it. As the tanks erupted, an electric-blue light flashed brightly enough to make the sun seem dark for only a second. New Connie reacted faster than he could and immediately shielded his eyes through the HUD.

In a single second, not much remained in that area aside from an impressive black scorch mark.

"We might want to start using those damn tanks to fight these assholes!"

The person who shouted that probably wasn't thinking straight. A tank like that could set a burn through the proper channels for days from what he'd heard. What they'd seen was one quick reaction, a very sudden release of gas mostly lost to the atmosphere, although enough of it was caught in the flames to deliver the flashy kind of bang that got people's attention.

It seemed to raise morale despite the fatality, however, and they opened fire again. From the way it was going, they would need more bullets. The monsters surged forward in a wave and explosives detonated at various points. Sal knew this was not the time to push into the battle. If he ended up in the middle of something he couldn't get out of, there was no sword big enough in the world to carve through that kind of a mess.

"We might have to abandon this position and withdraw to the shed perimeter," Madigan shouted as her assault rifle reloaded itself and her mini-gun picked up the slack. "Sal, get the mines turned to cover us if we're forced to make a break for it. "

"Are you on it?" he asked and restricted his voice to New Connie.

"I have already worked the claymores to prevent our people from getting caught in the blast. I'll activate them ring by ring if and when we pass."

"Sure, but keep the outer rings activated in case something starts coming in behind us."

"Respectfully, I think that would be a bad idea."

"Why? We need to be on top of anything trying to flank us." He tried to keep the impatience from his voice but the pain and the queasy sensation made him tense and irascible.

"Our rear is already covered. We have a few members of Heavy Metal approaching with an American contingent."

"What Heavy Metal Members?" He let his assault rifle reload, drew his sword, and stepped into the front as one of the horned gorillas rushed toward him. "We're all here, remember?" he added before he drove his blade through its skull from the side and retreated quickly.

"I still have one Dr. Courtney Monroe listed as a Heavy Metal member, and she is accompanied by the freelancers you hired through Taylor McFadden. They are at the head of the US team that is approaching the base as we speak."

"Oh, shit." Stupidly, he'd accidentally set the commlink to include Madigan.

"Oh, shit?" She sounded like her focus was on almost everything her thoughts could latch onto. It was something she did where her mind went blank and let her body do what it had been trained to do for so long. "Do we have incoming?"

"Yeah."

"The bad kind?"

"Not...really." He almost wished something would attack and distract her.

"So the good kind then."

"I wouldn't call it that either. But we do have the US team headed our way."

The reinforcements arrived almost a full minute later and announced their presence with gunfire and explosions. Three heavy suits pushed in, knocked one of the buildings down, and blocked the main street access to their position as the others began to position themselves to cover the flame and plasma throwers that were burning the Zoo back.

Sal heaved an inward sigh of relief. The numbers they'd had were barely enough to hold their position and keep everything at bay to protect the civilians, but for a limited time only. One by one, they would fall and even if that didn't happen, they would run out of ammunition and the Zoo would win.

The Americans almost doubled their force, which gave

them the extra little push they needed to start driving the Zoo back and reclaiming the lost ground.

"We have more to do. Let's get moving, people!"

He would know that voice anywhere, no matter that he heard it in person for the first time in almost a year. They talked on the phone all the time, but it had a different impact hearing in the flesh, especially when orders were issued with unexpected authority. Courtney had once been a passive person, only interested in the science going on in the Zoo.

Now, she had somehow assumed command of a US military contingent and people were following her orders. It didn't seem real, but he could explore that later.

"Fire teams, push up!" Madigan called and motioned them forward. "Roof team, give us warning if you see surges of either the jungle or animals advancing. We'll revert to the regular scheduled programming here, folks!"

That sounded a little more familiar. He pushed in with them, took a step back, and found a higher position. He had never been much of a crack shot and there was a reason why he liked to do most of his heavy work up close and personal.

New Connie was better at identifying anything Zoo-related and if he could pick off a couple of smaller creatures from a distance, that would work too. The HUD helped with that, and it kept his shooting accurate up to about a hundred and fifty yards. Beyond that required skills and expertise that he simply didn't have.

Either way, it wasn't needed. Courtney had brought enough firepower with her to start pushing the Zoo back, and the fire teams did their jobs quickly and professionally to make it difficult for the jungle to continue its advance.

There was no sign of any red-and-blue pita clusters, though, which he'd expected to be present to power this kind of push. He wondered if something else was driving the expansion. He had already accepted the concept that some kind of cluster density would be determined by the point of origin, but in this case, there was nothing. The wall in the area was still under construction and there had been nothing to stop the creatures or the vegetation from simply spreading into the camp. The fence certainly stood no chance against a concerted Zoo assault.

All they had to be thankful for was the fact that most of the wall construction was automated, or it would have been an even bigger massacre. They had ENSOL to thank for optimizing that, but things could have gone far worse if their workforce was any larger.

In the case of the British base, something was brought in that triggered the outbreak, which explained the tight clusters. That was the only conclusion that made sense but it left him feeling uneasy. How the hell did he identify something that to all intents and purposes was invisible?

The combined forces worked seamlessly to effect a relentless purge and much of the Zoo outbreak was pushed back in less than an hour. Helicopters brought relief teams so those already on the ground could rest while the fresh ones continued the systematic obliteration of the jungle and its denizens.

"Hey!"

That was all the warning Sal had before something crashed into the side of his suit and he almost careened into the sand. Thankfully, New Connie reacted in time, caught him with the extra limbs, and put him smoothly on his feet.

No one could yell quite like Courtney. She was there and he was in trouble.

It was enough to draw a couple of laughs from the onlookers, but it didn't seem like she cared. Then again, neither did he. He wasn't sure what he'd done wrong this time. While he'd done his best every step of the way, there had been mistakes. He merely didn't know what she was currently pissed off about.

"You were going to leave me out of this?" she demanded and took a step forward.

Oh. That.

"You—"

"Don't give me any shit about me being too busy. No one's too busy to come and help with this bullshit. Do you have anything else?"

Sal looked around and tried to ignore the interest they had begun to attract. He knew they needed to figure shit out but no one needed this kind of distraction.

"We can talk through this later," he told her calmly.

"Or we can talk through this now!"

"Or—and hear me out on this one—we can discuss the matters we've been dealing with. Some interesting things have been happening all day and I haven't had the time to think about them."

She knew what he was doing—distract, deflect, and all the familiar classics. But she knew they needed to be on top of the data that was being collected too.

"Fine. What you do have?"

Sal dropped to his haunches, collected a sample of the soil that had been sand not two hours earlier, and stored it with the other samples. "What is invisible, undetectable, and still able to chew through concrete?"

"I assume the answer isn't the most obscure riddle of all time?"

The silence from all around them said that their audience was no longer interested and had wandered off.

"It's something that happened at the Brit base," he told her.

"Then how the fuck should I know? I just got here."

"I guess we have something to work on together. And we can have that talk while we work."

She paused, narrowed her eyes, and tried to decide if he was up to something before she shrugged. Her suit was one of the better ones and she'd trained in it too since the gesture didn't earn her a chaotic reaction from the power functions.

"Fine."

CHAPTER SIXTEEN

Everyone was on alert all fucking day. Eventually, the commanders would realize that no matter what was happening on the other bases, their people needed rest.

Salah had been around the Zoo long enough to know that there would always be something happening—one emergency after another. Maybe that was a tactical decision by the Zoo to tire them out.

Whether it was intentional or not, it was working. Troops were tired, stretched thin, and irritable. It was his job as captain to keep morale up but given that he was as tired and irritable as they were, he couldn't think of any way to correct it for them.

Running into other teams on patrol in the sector was always a good way to enjoy at least some social interaction, which generally helped with morale. He pulled their Hammerhead over and waited for their comrades to stop as well.

They were Yemenis, of course, but it was still a decent chance to give his men a break. It was about time that everyone had a break since they had patrolled nonstop since dawn.

The other Hammerhead pulled alongside and they all climbed out. Standing in the sun while the wind whipped around was better than being hotboxed in a vehicle with a shitty AC any day of the week.

"How long have you been patrolling?" Salah asked and removed his helmet and gauntlet before he retrieved a couple of cigarettes from his pouch and handed one to the other captain. They lit them and took the first drag in silence.

"From the moment the sun came up and people were talking about how the Brits were under attack. Inshallah, if I ever make it home, I will find a desk job, see my wife every day, and make sure my children are being raised properly. Worrying about alien beasts in an alien jungle is making my hair gray early."

Salah tilted his head. A trace of gray had started to appear in the other man's hair and beard, but he had assumed that he was in his late thirties or early forties already. The truth was that he couldn't tell with all the beard and hair mixed in.

He would have to consider shaving, especially in this heat.

"Do you plan to return home?" he asked.

"I have two more months of the mandatory tour," the man replied. "After that, I could stay on for double the pay, but..." He shrugged.

"No money is worth this bullshit."

The other captain nodded and took a long drag from

the cigarette before he dropped it and crushed it under his boot heel.

"Well, you say that. We made some serious cash when that fucking jungle was merely a moneymaker. Most of my money went into building a house for my wife and children. Of course, her father was rich enough for the dowry to be worth it."

That didn't seem like the kind of thing Salah would ever commit to. He had arrived a few months before the lockdown, which meant he hadn't had much time to make any money.

All he wanted to do was go home. His family was waiting for him and all they wanted was to have a son who was in the military. There were political aspirations involved, but he wasn't sure whose they were.

"Good smokes," the Yemeni commented and nodded approvingly. "Did you get them from the French base?"

"A friend of mine has connections there. Depending on how devout you are, he might be able to get you a little booze if you're interested. But don't let your officers see it."

"Are your officers the type who cut hands off of those who bring contraband in?"

"Not so far, but they always confiscate and drink it themselves."

"That would suck."

Salah chuckled. "I've never been caught and I always drink my stash before they can. The hangover is a bitch but still better than letting them have it."

"Sir!" one of the soldiers called.

"I am not quite as religious as some might be, but I am

not one to drink. I do not fault you for your decisions in mood modification, however," the other captain told him.

"That is open-minded of you, I suppose."

The Yemeni tilted his head. "Maybe. Or maybe all the issues I had with it in the past were put aside when I realized what we were dealing with here. Allah would not want his people to suffer in this type of hell without some kind of escape, no matter how forbidden it was."

These were the kinds of allowances that would disappear when they returned to civilized society, but out there, it was the Wild West and anything went.

"Sir!"

Both officers turned to see what the soldier was talking about.

"What's the ma—oh." Salah gaped, lost for words when his attention turned to the wall they were patrolling. What had looked like a cloud rising from behind the wall moved considerably faster than a cloud.

And against the wind, he realized a moment later.

"Weapons! Weapons at the ready!"

He shoved his helmet and his gauntlet on frantically while he tried to make out what the hell the non-cloud was.

It increased speed and began to stream away from the wall toward them. They were locusts, a huge swarm that bore down on them at an incredible speed.

"Open fire! Shoot—somebody, shoot something!"

The soldiers scrambled, opened fire, and attempted to stop the monsters, but Salah knew for a fact that they wouldn't be able to fight the swarm off on their own.

He had no issue with rushing away from the fight. As

the officer, it meant making the tough decisions. In this case, the decision would be to make it to the Hammerhead.

Someone needed to alert the base and he dared not wait any longer. He flung himself in but left the door open in case any of the others decided they wanted to follow. With his weapon ready, he connected his HUD to the comms system in the Hammerhead.

"Can anyone read this?" he shouted and tried to ignore the shooting outside. "We're under attack and outnumbered—need reinforcements! Reinforcements right fucking now!"

The gunfire continued but one by one, the individual shots stopped and the chitters and screeches from the monsters outside overwhelmed them.

Another hard choice presented itself. He drew his sidearm and fired out of the door a couple of times before he yanked it shut.

Any survivors would have to get into the other Hammerhead. He needed to make it and would find a way.

"Please! Someone pick up!"

He already knew that none of them would listen. No one would answer. He climbed into the driver's seat and reached for the ignition.

Salah stopped himself in time. He realized that he couldn't stop his hands from shaking and it made his suit take that and turn it into him having a seizure somehow.

There was no way he could drive out. He couldn't even start the damn vehicle, but it would be all right. He knew a way out. There would be nothing heroic about it, but he would survive.

Huddled in the Hammerhead, he could hear the beasts

chittering and yammering outside as they tried to find a way in. They didn't try too hard, though, and he wondered if they were satisfied with the lives they'd already claimed.

He turned and aimed his weapon at the door, waiting for them to come through, but the swarm seemed to lose interest.

The chittering from outside was replaced by the drone of wings and soon, even those faded. They were gone. He had no idea where they went but they would be back. Salah knew that, although he had no idea how he knew it.

They would be back. Hopefully, he would have recovered the use of his hands by then. But he wouldn't leave the Hammerhead. The bastards would be back and he was alone.

Another attack redirected the team from their homeward journey before they had even reached the US sector. Sal had a feeling the incidents would continue and perhaps even escalate. The Zoo was determined to catch their attention and hold it, perhaps to make sure that everyone was too tired and engaged to think of the places where it wasn't attacking from.

That was his current theory. Something wanted them running around like chickens with their heads cut off until the real endgame was revealed.

For the moment, though, until they gained more insight, headless chickens was the only option.

"Do you think we're going to find out what the Zoo has planned?" Courtney

Sal looked at her. It was weird to hear his thoughts echoed like that and way too rare.

"We're fighting the Zoo," Madigan answered. "That's the mission for now. Saving lives and doing what we can to find out what the fuck is happening is all we can hope for at this point."

"The attack on the Middle Eastern Sector is weird, though," Sal interjected before Courtney could answer with something cutting that would start a fight. "No trees or other vegetation, and no sign of any effort by the Zoo to push across the buffer zone. Reports are that locusts came over the walls and attacked a patrol—well, two patrols. They managed to overwhelm them all before they could put up a decent defense. Someone got word out, which is why we're heading out to deal with them."

Silence settled over the team for a long moment while everyone tried to consider what was happening and what the endgame might be.

Or maybe they were all too tired. Sal scratched his jaw and drew a deep breath. It had been a long day and all he wanted to do was take a quick nap.

"I'd say our reactions and response times are being tested," OJ commented. "They're trying to find out where to attack us with full force."

"Nope." Matt shook his head. "We're being distracted. We need to find out where nothing is happening on the map because that's where the Zoo doesn't want us to look."

"You're both right," Madigan interjected before an argument could ensue. "They aren't mutually exclusive. Think about it. A tunnel with escaped hippos that don't attack the locals. Strange gunk spat at British soldiers and then the base is compromised. Solodkov reports that a weird spur pushes to the wall but does nothing. This random attack and the attacks on ENSOL."

"Wait, what's happening at the Russian base?" Courtney looked around. "Sorry, I've been a little out of the loop these days."

"Only a...like a Zoo arm that grew up the wall and stopped," Madigan explained. "It had the Russians on high alert but nothing happened."

"Oh. Well, the ENSOL outbreaks are at least explainable. To some degree, anyway. If there's anything the Zoo does want, it's to stop the construction of the wall. I remember when it tried to manipulate the landscape to destroy the wall that way, but I guess it decided that killing the humans involved was the way to go instead."

Sal remembered that too, oddly enough. It had been there in the beginning and then simply stopped.

"True." He leaned forward. "But that doesn't explain the randomness of what we're looking at. The only thing that connects them all is the Zoo."

"What are you saying?" Courtney asked.

His mind turned furiously as a new option occurred to him.

"With the Japanese base, it was a single massive attack and it drew an equally massive, concerted response, right? But what if it attacked in different places and committed to different strike points simultaneously?"

He didn't like where his mind was going, but it made more sense the more he thought about it.

"So it is testing our response times." Madigan shrugged. "We've already mentioned this. But if it's trying to see where we're the most effective, the question is why? What is it looking for?"

That was something Sal had no idea how to answer. All he could do was close his eyes and try to think, which became increasingly difficult. His whole shoulder felt like it was on fire at this point.

"Divide and conquer," Jiro said softly, flicked his knife up, and caught it deftly. "It's classic warfare and has always been the most successful means of attack. It knows that we will unite against a common foe. But if the common foe is everywhere and attacks from all sides, we will always prioritize our own safety and leave the weaker points to fend for themselves."

The silence this time was heavy as the team considered what he'd said. No one wanted to face the possibility, but it did make sense. And God help the world if they were right.

"We need to finish this site visit as quickly as possible and get back to the compound," Sal decided immediately. "All we can do now is sift through the footage and the reports to see if we can find anything that might provide more insight. I don't want to have to raise an alarm over something that might not exist but there's a clock now and we're working against it."

"That and you need to take your pain meds," Madigan reminded him. "Don't think I haven't noticed how you wince and brace yourself every time we hit a fucking bump."

"Pain meds?" Courtney looked sharply at him. "And you let me punch you?"

"I…had a choice?"

"Well, no." She sounded a little smug beneath her concern. "But still, what happened?"

"He got himself trampled by one of those hippo mutants," Madigan told her bluntly.

"Jesus fucking Christ, and you let him go out into battle?"

"I tried to stop him, but Sal has something of a Messiah complex if you haven't noticed."

"Right. He does, doesn't he?"

It was good that they were getting along, but Sal couldn't stop his mind sliding back to the ticking of the clock. Every second now was another step in the long, arduous countdown to the end of the world.

CHAPTER SEVENTEEN

This was the third day in a row and Bolin was not impressed. Big things were happening all over the Zoo, and he was stuck on the night shift again. Maybe it was because his scores in the damn sims were some of the lowest on the base. He reminded himself that they were in the top eighty percent, but they were still shit compared to others.

He was almost sure it was because of his shit sim scores, but maybe that was a good thing. From what he heard, people were dying during these attacks. While he could appreciate the safety advantages of his current duties, he wished they would put him in the kitchens instead. He had always loved to cook.

"Shit, I shouldn't have thought of that," he muttered and peered over the edge of the wall. It was dark below, faintly illuminated by the stars but with no moon out, and at two am, it was difficult to tell what was Zoo and what was sand.

And now, of course, he was hungry. That was what he got for thinking about being in the kitchens. It was all political. The dumbasses in the mess were a group of idiots who had all the right connections.

Meanwhile, he was left on the top of the wall at two in the morning, freezing his nuts off while he tried to see anything in the pure blackness. The only comfort was the tiny reinforced guard office where he could sit for a moment each time he entered his hourly patrol report on the computer.

The least they could have done was put him in with a partner or something but these days, everyone was spread so thinly that he was lucky to have pulled a guard shift on the wall at all.

They were already talking about ending those and leaving all the work to drones. Honestly, it was a good idea and besides, drones could see in the dark. The only downside he could see was that they would be very tempting to the locusts.

"It'll be another boring night." He was starting to develop a bad habit of talking to himself. At least this time, he wasn't fantasizing about being in pro baseball with a massive contract playing for the Yankees.

Even with all the excitement in every sector, he was sure nothing would happen and he would be left wondering if joining the army and coming to the goddammed Zoo had been the right decision to make for his life after all.

"Still, it could be worse. I could be in the middle of all that mess and be killed by one of the monsters the Zoo keeps churning out. That's not the choice I'd be interested in—right, Mei?"

The video game bobblehead on his desk nodded after a

light tap. He'd even gone so far as to buy her ice gun, although there was no way he could pass for her in cosplay at the conventions.

Holy shit, he missed going to conventions. Assuming people still held them. Was there any kind of normal in the world?

"Fuck." He swatted at something that brushed against his left leg. It felt imaginary at first—like his brain had conjured something out of boredom—but the next touch was far less feathery.

It felt more like a poke.

"Damn it, Delun. If you're screwing with me again, I'll report you and have you sent straight back to China, you little shit!"

His voice fell on deaf ears—or no ears at all—and another hard nudge at his leg made him jump up from his desk. He turned the light to investigate.

Something cold, painful, and unsettling spasmed down his throat when he realized there was no trick and no joke from the shit sergeant who was located at the opposite side of the base. He was no doubt patrolling the top of the wall since they alternated times to ensure two patrols every hour.

Instead of the expected—and hoped for—practical joke, something green, long, and covered in real leaves had slithered into his office. He gaped as it poked him in the leg again.

"What the fuck?"

The words failed to cover the sheer horror of what he was looking at, although there was no sign that it intended to attack. From the way it moved, the vine appeared to be exploring and now tried to decide what in the hell he was.

It couldn't be real. Shit like this wasn't supposed to happen. The walls were safe and he wouldn't believe that one of the goddammed vines had crept into his office. His one little sanctuary away from the mess the whole fucking base had turned into could not be invaded right now.

He'd fallen asleep, his mind reasoned desperately. That was what had happened. This was all a very bad dream. There was no need to worry about it and certainly no need to panic.

Right?

Bolin blinked and rubbed his hands over his eyes to get them to focus again. He felt a sharp pain in the back of his eyeballs and he saw weird shapes that came from rubbing them a little too aggressively. That shit should be enough to wake him.

He opened his eyes and his mouth dried when he realized the damn vine hadn't disappeared as he had hoped it would. It was still in the office and its tip waved gently from right to left much like a snake would. There were no eyes on it, but he couldn't help the feeling that it watched him anyway and waited for him to do something.

And he had to do something. He was stuck in his office with a goddammed Zoo slithery so what fucking choice did he have?

A second of thought was all he could spare before he dragged in a deep breath and fixed his gaze on the intruder that seemed to follow his movements to the desk.

No, his brain was playing tricks on him. It was a vine. It had no eyes or ears to tell it where he was going.

After another look to establish that as a fact, Bolin turned to the desk, scrambled for the alarm radio, and clicked it on.

"Delun...Delun, are you there?"

"I hear you. Do you need me to read you a bedtime story?"

This was no time to feel annoyed at his shift sergeant's commentary. "There...there's something here in the office with me. I don't know how but a vine got in."

"What?"

"A fucking vine!" He drew a sharp breath when he heard the hint of panic in his voice.

"Bullshit. I know you're short of friendship these days, but this is some pathetic shit."

The line cut off and there was nothing else to it. The shift sergeant was probably taking a quick break to piss over the wall—he liked to brag about that to the other soldiers—and didn't want to interrupt it by coming to check on what he was sure was a hoax.

In fairness, Bolin wasn't quite sure he believed it either, but he wouldn't tolerate the damn slithery's presence any longer. He scrambled to reach the alarm button on his desk and pressed it down with all the force he could manage.

His moment of gratification at the ear-splitting wail of the alarms as all the outdoor lights turned on was short-lived. Something flickered in the corner of his eye and before he could register the change, the vine moved again, this time toward him.

He tried to step back but the tight confines left him with nowhere to go. The intruder was suddenly very aggressive as if it understood that it had been discovered and would not take any chances or prisoners.

"Shit!"

It wrapped around his ankle and it was all he could do to avoid falling and hitting his head on the desk when he was yanked toward the door.

Nothing could have prepared him for this kind of attack. That was what the damn suits were there for, but as its hold on him tightened, he reacted out of instinct. It wasn't the first time he'd faced anything, however, and he yanked out the pocketknife he carried everywhere. There was no chance he could get to the box with weapons in the corner of the office.

The damn lockup needed a key anyway. Bolin wasn't sure when he started screaming, but it was something wild, primal, and unplanned as he flicked the pocketknife open and tried to find something to hack at.

His first fear of accidentally cutting his leg was assuaged when he missed entirely. Thankfully, the blade wasn't damaged when it struck the floor instead, but his second stroke was more successful. He'd missed his leg and dug the knife into the vine as deep as it would go.

There was no reason why a vine would utter a cry of pain when it was stabbed. He wasn't sure why he expected something like that, but now was not the time for him to dig into possible problems in his subconscious mind. He hacked at it repeatedly until the pressure on his leg released.

Bolin scrambled to his feet, still screaming as the vine began to retreat without most of the tip that had been wound around his leg.

The section that had been severed showed no signs of life, but he had a feeling that would change the moment he put it in water or soil. That was how the Zoo worked and they would have to burn it.

He straightened and tried to understand what had happened and decide what he would do next. It wasn't wise to sit around and wait for the next damn vine to show up— or worse, his superiors, who would ask him why he had triggered the alarms. Instead, he hurried out of his office, still carrying the pocketknife.

Unfortunately, he still didn't have the time to break out the firearms that were under lock and key for the moment.

After a moment's thought, he rushed to the gun place- ments. The damn things were big enough to rival anything installed at the other sectors. Their superiors wanted a message sent that the Chinese were not in the Zoo area to fuck around.

Bolin rushed up the steps and tried to access the manual controls. They had been given instructions on how to use the gun placements without having to rely on what- ever wonky-assed software had been brought over.

A proper HUD was set up there as well, which meant he would be able to determine where the attack came from. The whole damn base was galvanized by the alarms by now, but he would make sure they knew where the threat originated.

He shifted the turret to face inside the base instead of out and scanned the open area to try to see where the vine had come from. A patch of green just shy of the wall and close to the base hospital caught his attention and he paused to study it.

It wasn't a fully grown Zoo yet, but a small semi-circular patch directly below where he stood was considerably more advanced than the rest. That was likely where the vine had come from.

This little core area struck him as odd. It looked like everything had started in a rough semi-circle, almost like three people had stood perhaps in conversation, and it radiated from there.

Troops rolled out of the barracks and raced into the open, and their presence made Bolin feel a little braver. He moved to the box on the gun placement, unlocked it quickly, and retrieved the assault rifle stored there. Out of habit instilled during his training, he checked it quickly to make sure the bullets were loaded and nothing was out of place.

He peered into the open area again and immediately noticed something start to climb the wall again.

"Motherfuckers!" he shouted and leaned over the railing. Just because he'd crapped the bed when it came to the sims didn't mean he wasn't a good shot with regular rifles. He'd been out hunting for his dinner with his dad from the moment he could walk, and he decided he would be dead before he took an attack like this lying down.

The assault rifle punched into his shoulder when he pulled the trigger and fired a three-round burst. The shot was good, caught one of the vines, and sent it slinking back to where it came from.

One down, only another million or so to go. It wasn't that boring an evening after all.

Sal yawned and leaned back in his chair. His body screamed for more rest but his brain still refused to cooperate. It had dragged him from the sleep of the dead around midnight and almost three hours later, continued to churn relentlessly through endless questions he couldn't find answers for.

He had woken to the conviction that they had missed something vital and the intensity of it was such that he had crept downstairs, made coffee, and loaded the first of the footage they had been sent. It was tedious and time-consuming but far better than tossing and turning helplessly with no hope of falling asleep again.

"Fuck this." He stretched and tried to shift into a different position to ease the stiffness. "There has to be something here we can use as a starting point." He recalled his challenge to Courtney the day before, issued partly as a joke to divert her from the vent she'd had primed and ready. It had worked but it also left him with the growing fear that what they were up against was indeed invisible.

Another stretch reminded him that he hadn't taken another painkiller and he realized that he didn't need to. The pain hadn't gone completely but it was significantly less than it had been the day before—courtesy, no doubt, of the goop he'd so foolishly ingested.

That had probably been the single most stupid decision he'd ever taken, but he'd soothed his recriminations with the certainty that he could use the Zoo within him to thwart the Zoo without. Now, however, it felt like all it was good for was to trigger the weird primal instincts that unsettled him and left him feeling vulnerable along with an inner knowing that things were poised on the edge of disaster.

"Okay, ten minutes and I'll make more coffee." The team would have to use their downtime to work through the footage as well. Perhaps he simply couldn't see the jungle for the leaves.

He pressed play but paused it a second later when his phone rang. The tired half of him groaned because he knew it was yet another exercise in futility. At the same time, relief swept over him—he could stop his fruitless searching and maybe this time, the incident would provide some clue to break the stalemate.

"Let me guess," Franklin said when Sal answered a moment later. "You couldn't sleep either."

"Yeah. I've been looking through everything we have hoping to find what we've missed."

"Well, I can add a new one to your list—the Chinese this time. One of the night patrollers alerted the base to the fact that a new Zoo had appeared out of nowhere."

"In the base itself?" Sal frowned as his mind flipped through what he knew to find similarities.

"Yes, and with no activity from the real Zoo—no spur, no sudden growth, and no mutants as yet. They caught it early."

"Like the Brits." His mind cataloged the similarities and the commander grunted assent. "Did anyone there have a run-in with one of those spitting vines?"

"That was my first question too," Franklin told him, "but it's still unclear. They are doing a little digging while they wait for you to see if anything unusual happened that wasn't reported."

"Wait—they're waiting for me?"

"Not happily but they agree that it makes sense for you to find any evidence before it's incinerated. I didn't specifically mention the Brits but they made the comparison anyway."

Sal pushed to his feet. "I'll get the team up and ready. Will you send choppers?"

"They are scrambling as we speak. ETA twenty minutes."

The commander cut the call.

"Connie, wake—"

"Already done," she said briskly. "You might want to make yourself useful and put the coffee on before you get dressed."

"Dammit, Connie. Do you listen to every call?"

"Of course. How else would I know everyone's business?"

CHAPTER EIGHTEEN

No one would get much sleep tonight. It didn't matter if they had the time for it. The people running logistics all around the Zoo had put in the work to make sure the teams worked in shifts. They organized it as quickly as possible so they would get the best out of everyone while still making sure no one was at the front line too long.

The idea was to make sure no one was burned out by the end of this. He wasn't sure if it would work, but that wasn't a failure on the part of the people in charge. The Zoo seemed determined that they would all be burned out with these constant attacks coming from all sides.

Sam had been one of the skeptics before he'd arrived at the Zoo. He'd never believed all the talk about the jungle somehow being sentient and able to plot and plan its attacks on the humans who tried to fight and contain it. While numerous witness statements and specialists all mentioned it, they'd talked about aliens too and he wasn't buying into that either.

He couldn't state outright that there was no such thing

as aliens, of course. That was illogical, but all the talk of probing and visitation and shit had never made an impression on him. He was very much on Occam's Razor when it came to that kind of thing. It was a possibility but far from the most likely possibility. More probable, in his mind, was that the witnesses were lying or maybe had misremembered. Or they were high. Any of the above had merit.

From his perspective, probability had always factored in and the probability of an entire fucking jungle being a sentient hivemind was fairly low. That was until he saw it up close and personal. He'd seen hundreds and thousands of animals throwing themselves mindlessly into the line of fire, working together, and making tactical decisions. The probability was rising and even worse, he couldn't think of a damn thing that would explain what he was looking at other than aliens.

Now, even the experts seemed to concur and not only said that the jungle was sentient but that it was being powered by aliens of some kind who were using it as a means to terraform their planet. Many seemed to think this meant getting rid of all the annoying, pointless humans who were ruining things for everyone.

Sam turned on his cot and tried to put it from his mind. His white noise machine had been lost in the attack, which meant he was stuck listening to nothing but the ringing in his ears and the painful memories of what they'd all seen in the past couple of days. He liked to think he'd done rather well in the circumstances. As a civilian thrust into a military scenario, no one had singled him out as a problem that got other people killed. That was a win in his book, even though he secretly carried the guilt for the deaths of his people.

None of that made it any easier to sleep, and since the lights of Chen's phone and Elke's tablet were still on, it looked like no one on the ENSOL team had managed to get much sleep.

He wished he could say that it was only nerves from being thrust into a combat zone, but this was different and he could see the impact it had on all the people who had to deal with the situation. They were as much victims of their evolutionary response as they were of the battles. Their bodies constantly produced large amounts of adrenaline because they perceived themselves as under attack. While it was a natural survival mechanism, it would make things difficult until they managed to adapt themselves to it.

Either that or things would simply get worse until they were all dead.

He turned in his bed again, drew a deep breath, and tried to calm himself. Part of the problem was the constant activity of the large contingent of soldiers and mercenaries assigned to the camp now that it had been retaken.

"You can't sleep either, huh?"

He turned to see that Elke had pushed to a seated position in the bed.

"I don't think anyone would be able to sleep, which is weird. I'm about as tired as I've ever been, but it's not coming."

"White noise machine?"

He grimaced. "The jungle destroyed it. I lost all my shit so it might have been personal."

"Your clothes too?"

"Yep. And my laptop. I'll have to order another one to be delivered out here. They said they could get my personal effects transported from home in a couple of days but until then, I'm screwed."

She nodded. "Well…yeah. Do you have any clothes?"

"Only what I was wearing. I managed to get some from the requisitions office, but I only had access to what isn't restricted to the military people. You know, with logos and names and shit. People in the US can walk around with clothes marked with the Marine Corps and Navy and whatever, but it's a little different when you're on a proper military base. So I'm stuck with tank tops and shorts. In this case, they might suit me, but I've never been a tank and shorts kind of guy."

Elke shrugged. "People change, especially in the circumstances we're in."

It was a valid point. They would have to find ways to survive their situation, and they would have to dig deep to find resources they never knew were there to get out of this.

"What have you been up to?" Sam asked and sat in his bed as well to try to peek at her tablet.

"The insurance company is giving us the runaround. It feels stupid that they're trying to play with us like this given the lives that were lost. We might have to call in some help to pressure those assholes." Her sigh was one of frustration.

"Do you think we can hire a handful of mercs to show up at the insurance office and intimidate people?" He found the idea extremely tempting.

"Eventually. You know, if they don't cooperate. But

since we're doing work for governments all around the world, you would think some of them would be able to intercede on our behalf."

"They should. It doesn't mean they will, though." He'd long since learned that lesson. "If I know anything about how governments work, they tend to avoid getting involved in helping anyone with anything related to efficiency."

"They'll have to make an exception for us, though. This isn't the time to start pinching their pennies now, as you Americans say."

Sam shrugged and shook his head as he rubbed his eyes. "I'm learning not to put any faith in human beings knowing what is best for them and what is in the interest of their survival. But still, we can hope. Why the hell are they making things difficult?"

"It seems they're not sure if their policy covers the damage done by alien jungles and monsters. Then again, there were no issues raised when we informed them of the work we would be doing. Everyone knows that ambiguity in the policy favors us in that case, but they're still making things difficult. They'll probably fold the moment we bring litigation, but they might be counting on the fact that we're out of the country and hope that means we won't litigate."

"Sure, why not gamble with people's lives simply to save your company a few extra bucks?" Sam shook his head. "It's people like them who give the insurance business a bad name."

"Yeah, people like them," she agreed. "Not all the people in the insurance business."

"I have friends in the industry and they aren't assholes.

It's the numbers people, the pencil pushers who end up making the decisions based on what will give them the bigger bonuses. Straight-up psychopaths, the lot of them." He snorted in disgust.

She laughed and leaned back against her pillow. "Well, I have the plans for replacements all ready to go once someone signs the checks. I don't care who."

"So that's all you've done? I've been trying to sleep for hours now."

"Not at all. That took me about five minutes. What I started on next was something I know we have the funding for. We're still getting a steady stream from the different bases to hire the mercenaries who help to keep our work going once the Zoo is cleaned out. I've looked at resumes—mercenaries and workers. You'd think there would be a limited number of people who are willing to work here, but nope. Many people with recommendations too."

"I would assume there's something wrong with them if they actively want to work here," he remarked dubiously.

"Sure, that's something I've had to consider. It's hard to work a psych profile out of a resume." She sighed. "But we need to replace the people we lost. I compiled a list of what we needed while getting the names of the people we lost to Franklin so he could notify the next of kin. Or find somebody to notify the next of kin. That's mostly what I've done to pass the time."

"What about Chen?" Their younger partner had been almost withdrawn since they'd been allowed to return to the camp.

"I thought he was putting more videos up about what happened, but when I had a peek at what he was up to, I saw he was reviewing and taking the videos that he put up down. I think he's reconsidering the message that he's putting out there."

Both of them jumped at a loud crack from outside their building and grasped the weapons they had placed next to their beds. Everyone was armed at this point. No one wanted to be left with nothing to defend themselves against the monsters out there.

He wouldn't get to sleep tonight. Although he was exhausted, sleep wouldn't come. He knew himself well enough to recognize that much, at least. There weren't many things in the world that terrified him, and the Fixer was rather proud of himself that he was able to survive the horror. He'd tuned out to some degree and merely went through the motions while he was in the middle of it all, but now that he had time to think about what had happened, he was still amazed that he'd not shat his pants in absolute terror.

That was what he was afraid of, as it turned out.

"I expected sleep to be difficult for people right about now," Elke muttered and patted her pillow before she lay down again.

"And why is that?"

"Well, people are generally afraid of nightmares. But when nightmares wander the world in the flesh, it infects dreams too. It makes people think about everything that could come for them when they fall asleep."

She turned to look at Sam, who had an eyebrow raised.

"I had a few psych classes in university and even participated in a sleep study. It was an excuse to sleep a little more and they offered money and extra credit."

"Universities in Germany certainly know how to treat their students." He chuckled for the first time in what felt like days.

"No system is perfect, but I did like my time in Hamburg, yes."

Tension defined every person who had logged into the video meeting. Peter Tellisman had expected that given the news that began to spread across the world at the speed of light. His Zoo Overwatch group had come together fairly often recently. It had been founded to monitor the situation in the Zoo and gather data they could use to compile a report to generate awareness of what the jungle represented. All of them believed the purpose of the goop was to terraform the planet and that the aliens would return to finish what the Zoo had started.

Their ultimate purpose was to convince governments and power players the world over of the need to begin developing space defenses in preparation.

"The Zoo is attacking," Lidgton commented, her platinum hair held up in a bun. "We received regular reports from Anja. She isn't the kind of person I expected to work with, but I suppose there is a first time for everything. The reports have military and biological backgrounds, which tells me that Jacobs and Kennedy are writing them. Our Russian hacker merely compiles them and adds her commentary here and there."

"I always appreciate having first-hand views of the situation," Peter answered thoughtfully. "But we don't know what's happening. Well, no, that's not quite right. We know what's happening—on a surface level at least—but we don't know why. What the purpose behind it is."

"I thought we had a theory," Katz stated and leaned forward.

"As theories go, it is barebones at best." Kondo shook his head. "Aliens attacking us with a jungle does have a few spaces between that need to be filled."

"The missile that was sent to earth didn't quite do its part." Schafer rested his chin on his hand and stared into his camera. "If I attacked this planet with something like the goop, I would have it disperse in the atmosphere. Having said that, if it had landed, say, in the Amazon Rainforest or the oceans, it would have exploded and decimated humanity in days. Instead, we brought it down and it spread into the most deserted part of the world not covered in ice."

"It's a good thing we didn't send it to Antarctica as originally planned. Fighting it there would have been a nightmare." Lidgton sounded a little defensive. This was a thorny issue since not everyone agreed with her sentiment.

"There would have been fewer chances for it to find biological material to work with," Schafer retorted.

"As far as we know. It could have found something under the ice that would have resulted in the same thing or worse."

"Enough." Peter drew a deep breath. He hadn't even followed the discussion. It was in their blood to debate these kinds of things, but the time for debate was over. They needed action. "The situation with Gregory Hall and his clandestine lab has advanced as foreseen, and it should be aired soon on all major newscasts. It's encouraging but it's been a little overshadowed by the escalation in Zoo activity."

"Do we think it's a reaction to the events in Niger?" Lidgton asked. "It is the closest the Zoo's ever come to a major outbreak that could have entrenched it as a secondary alien jungle location beyond the wall. Of course, how the Zoo would know that is unanswerable, but it's a possibility."

"Or Niger was merely one of its more successful attempts to extend beyond the wall," Kondo surmised. "It knows what the most viable means of transmission is and is using it. While there is much we do not know, I think we can all agree that this series of attacks has all the hallmarks of a calculated and concerted sequence of events. There is nothing random about it, yes?"

No disagreement followed, only an uncomfortable silence among those gathered in the online meeting.

Peter cleared his throat. "The Zoo is trying to fulfill its prime directive. We know this is a preparation for the return of whatever sent it, even though we're far away from proving it in a manner that would stand up to peer review. All we can hope for is that Salinger Jacobs finds some answers. Until then, we can continue to sift through the reports sent in case someone sees something that might have been overlooked."

The collective sigh from the group expressed a feeling that he experienced as well—frustration. They were used to having the answers but instead, they had to wait for word from others and hope against hope that someone would tell them what they could do to help stop it.

CHAPTER NINETEEN

The workload appeared to be expanding since nothing had truly been closed and could be set aside. If he'd been a cop, he'd probably have talked about open cases. All that came to mind, however, was unresolved clusterfucks. It seemed appropriate.

Sifting through all the details of the missions and trying to find anything they'd missed through the magic of recording HUDs was the type of work he'd never enjoyed. It felt like reviewing his own work, and he'd never been much good at that.

They wouldn't review any of this for a while yet, though. Sal knew what was happening at the Chinese base was a disruption, a distraction by the Zoo to keep them focused everywhere but where they needed to look.

And he wanted to know why.

"What's the situation in there, Colonel?"

Madigan had already made contact with the superior officer in charge of the Chinese response to the attack.

They'd managed to get a full-bird colonel to deal with the situation or at least oversee it.

"Most of the mutants have been eliminated," Hou Tengfei answered. "Fortunately, they have only recently appeared so there were not as many as there could have been. The teams are standing by to begin incineration."

"We appreciate you holding off until we can collect evidence. I'm sure your troops are anxious to start."

"They've been convinced that it's necessary."

Sal ignored the soldiers who stood somewhat sullenly near the gate. They might have been convinced but they certainly weren't happy about it.

"Commander Franklin from your base suggested that we wait before we incinerate everything until our resident experts had a chance to take a look. We've burned any attempts it makes to grow beyond its current area and killed any mutants we've seen. Mostly the humpers and locusts, but a handful of the larger creatures too. A young killerpillar was killed not that long ago. It was rather cute, if you ask me."

"You're the kind of person who has bugs pinned to a notebook at home, aren't you?" Sal raised an eyebrow, surprised by the statement.

"How barbaric." The colonel sounded slightly offended. "Of course not. I keep them all in the terrarium."

"Right. How foolish of me."

"From what we've seen," Hou Tengfei continued, "it takes time for the mutants to be generated, and word is that our experts are curious as to how that is accomplished."

He nodded. "I always assumed it was the result of the

goop which is possibly bioprogrammed with the DNA of the required species, but that doesn't explain where the goop came from in the first place. Do your people have a timeline, Colonel?" he asked. Madigan had already begun to ready their team to move in. "How long until your orders are to burn the whole damn thing to ashes?"

"We have no specific timeline, but I don't need to tell either of you that this situation is tense. My men have orders to hold off on burning through the vegetation for as long as they can and I trust their judgment."

It was the best call. The decision had to be made by the people on the ground since they had to fight anything the vegetation produced. It was annoying that his need to study everything coincided with their need to destroy everything.

"We'll be as fast and efficient as we can," Madigan assured him. "I guess there's nothing else to tell your people. We don't want you to put the base at risk in any way, not even for us."

"That is appreciated." Hou Tengfei nodded formally. "I shall see you when your investigation is complete."

It seemed his fantasy of sleeping for a week would have to wait for now. Sal felt like they had been working nonstop although the numerous cups of early-morning coffee had certainly helped.

He was still tired, though, and it was likely to get worse.

"All right, team," he said and connected to the group commlink. They all turned to face him. "Record everything, I don't care how small. Leave your HUDs recording and all the sensors on to pick up on everything. Anja's managed to program the operating systems to filter what you need to your visuals while keeping all the data stored. It should only record for a couple of hours since the hard drives on these are fucking pitiful, but we do our best with what we have. Any questions?"

There were none, but he wouldn't answer any even if there were unless they would affect a successful outcome. They were there on a fact-finding mission and he wouldn't have them put that aside unless their priorities shifted again.

A young lieutenant strode toward them and looked like he would have much preferred to be on the front lines with the other soldiers. That was an assumption, of course, but a fair one.

"You...are following me!" the young man said and motioned for them to join him.

Maybe he hadn't been impatient and merely tried to memorize his lines. It was well-known that while most bases made a point of sending troops who had some knowledge of the English language for easy communication, the Chinese were interestingly reluctant on the matter. Perhaps they had no interest in collaborating with everyone else.

The Heavy Metal team followed their guide across the grounds to where they could hear the sound of gunfire ahead of them. They were being escorted to whatever was happening.

The reports said it had simply thrust out of the ground and Sal had a feeling they would find something very similar to what had happened at the British base. Something had broken through the road and the prefab to enable everything to grow from the soil that was once sand beneath.

The Zoo was predictable in all the worst ways, and top of the list was its unpredictability. He couldn't help wondering why it would repeat one attack when all the others appeared to be frustratingly different.

"Lieutenant, why are we going to the top of the wall around your base?" Madigan asked.

Sal startled and frowned when he realized they were doing exactly that. "That is a good point. Why are we doing that?"

The young man said something quickly, and he realized that his English wasn't merely bad. It was non-existent. Thankfully, most of the HUD OSes were fitted with translators that helped with the communication kerfuffles. It wasn't quite a seamless solution but was better than hand signals, he supposed.

His words were quickly translated for them, like subtitles running across the HUDs.

The view is denser from the wall.

"That...doesn't explain anything," Francesca Martin pointed out.

The lieutenant repeated what he said and again a third time when it was clear that they hadn't understood.

Finally, Sal grasped what he'd meant. From a distance, it looked like it was simply a thicket starting to grow, but as they got higher, the vegetation somehow looked thicker and denser. He wasn't sure which was the illusion and which was reality.

Something was different than what he'd seen recently.

That was immediately apparent when they were guided into a position that provided a view directly over the burgeoning jungle. A clump of red-and-blue pita flowers grew almost in the center. They were concentrated in the area, which suggested that this was the origin of the incursion.

"I'm going down there," he announced. "Try to keep people from shooting at me. I don't want anyone to think I'm one of the fucking monsters."

"I'd suggest not using your extra limbs down there, then," Madigan cautioned.

He nodded. It was still dark enough that if someone saw him and counted six limbs, they would assume he was one of the monsters.

After a deep breath, stepped over the edge of the wall, and let New Connie assist him to land directly beside the pita flowers.

It was still a hard landing and he absorbed the impact by dropping to a knee, extending his other leg out to help, and supported himself with a fist on the ground as the other hand drew his assault rifle.

"It's been a while since I've done one of those, eh?" he called as he straightened slowly.

"You're a fucking dumbass." Madigan growled her annoyance.

"I'm fucking cool and you know it. Otherwise, you wouldn't be staring at my ass."

"The ass covered in half a ton of armor?" She snorted.

"And you're still staring at it."

"Could you guys not do the flirting while we're on a mission?" Matt asked.

"When else would we do it?" Sal asked.

"When we're not on a mission?"

"Do you have any idea when that will happen?"

Davis had no answer to that. There was no telling when they would have time off or even if there would be any time off from this point forward.

Sal approached the cluster of pita flowers and tried to decide on the best way to approach them. After a moment's thought, he drew a portable seismic sensor from his pouch and planted it carefully in the transformed soil. On its own, it was able to detect anything that made the ground shake and little more than that, but he had discovered that with three of them and a little movement he created, they were able to map anything that was underground. It was useful for making sure nothing could tunnel into the compound.

After what happened to the Japanese, they had all decided it was a good idea to plan ahead for that kind of thing.

He could hear the people on the top of the wall wondering what he was doing, especially when he jumped in place a little to generate some seismic activity for the sensors to start mapping.

"That's funny," he muttered as he studied the readings. "The plants are all connected by a network of roots, which is kind of what the Zoo does. It's how they consolidate the goop. Go farther out, though, and the plants stop but the roots continue. Even in the places where they've been burned by the Chinese military."

Sal had defaulted to his old habit of thinking aloud. He'd realized early in life that if he did that, people would tell him when he stopped making sense. Even more importantly, hearing his ideas out loud was a great way to decide if he didn't think they made sense. His brain was a weird place to be when it was quiet.

"The roots extend beyond the growth." He retrieved another sensor and established a square instead of a triangle, which would hopefully help him to get clearer details of what he was looking at. "It's not that important, though. That's how plants grow, and if they were growing before but were stopped, the tops of the trees would be gone but the roots would remain unless they were dug out."

"What are you muttering about?" Gregor shouted at him.

"Shut up, I'm thinking."

"You're talking."

"I'm thinking aloud."

There was still no evidence of how it had all started. With nothing else to work with, he still wouldn't risk taking a sample of any of the plants. There was no telling if the active organic material would die or start a whole new outbreak. A few samples of the soil, though, might contain clues. It was easy to keep soil contained.

Once he and Courtney had gathered samples and secured them, he moved to the wall, activated the coils in his boots, and jolted as they launched him to the top. The jerk was unfortunately enough to make his shoulder ache slightly again.

"We don't need to go through it after all. There's nothing more to discover here," Sal said softly and turned to the young lieutenant. "Contact your commander. You can go ahead and send your fire teams in."

"Son of a fucking whore."

Anja was happy sometimes that she turned her microphones off when she took one of her power naps. It had been a great idea to move a couch into her little den slash server room and the power naps were a real booster, especially now. With so much happening, she had begun to rely on them more and more. A quick, powerful coffee and a fifteen-minute nap worked wonders.

Someone had woken her early, though, hence the cursing. She pushed off the couch and grimaced when she noticed she'd drooled on it. It wasn't the first time so she ignored it, returned to the computer, and dropped into her chair. The familiar creak brought a smile despite her irritation.

"This had better be something important, Connie," she muttered and rocked in her chair a couple of times simply to hear the comforting sound.

"Ah, yes. I forgot you were only up and about for the important stuff. Remind me—how important was it for you to make all the current political leaders of the G9 to lip-sync to 'What is Love?'"

"Incredibly important. It allowed me to pass the time while I waited for the results from what Sal collected to come back, for the system to connect to those assholes on the Overwatch group, and filter out the bullshit from the Chinese feeds. The computer does much of that on its own so I kept myself busy and entertained. Do you have a problem with that?"

"Generally, no," the AI replied, "but in this case, you might want to have a look at what woke you."

Anja looked at the computer screen, where red lights flashed. "Oh. The compound alarm. What's going on?"

"Assuming you don't want to be consumed by the Zoo with your fucking eyes closed, maybe stop with the power naps, open them wide, and look at the exterior feeds from the wall."

She didn't like Connie telling her what to do, but the fact that she hadn't thrown a dirty limerick or two in with her berating meant there was probably something serious for her to take note of.

"Oh...fuck me."

"That's what I thought," Connie agreed.

The Russian drew a deep breath, rolled her neck until she felt something crack comfortably, and pulled up the other camera feeds. She hoped this was all some kind of trick—Connie wasn't above altering the feeds to mess with her—but each of the feeds began to tell the same story.

A jungle had appeared barely a few yards away from the compound.

She gritted her teeth as her heart beat faster and thudded against her ribcage. Her mouth was dry and she didn't even have any cold coffee to ease it with. Panicking wouldn't gain her anything, which meant that as much as she wanted to lose her shit, she had to remain calm.

"This is exactly what I stay in the goddammed server room to avoid," she whispered and kept her hands away from the keyboard, which also meant avoiding doing anything stupid. "If Sal and his merry band insist on gallivanting all over the place, the least they could do is build me a safe room or something."

"If you're done throwing a fit, you might want to take a second to inhale. It will bring oxygen to your brain and help you think."

"Thanks, Jill Nye. *Cyka blyat.*" She paused, shook her head, and dragged in a deep breath. Before she even attempted to do anything, she had to calm herself and try to get the oxygen to accommodate her rapidly rising heart rate.

"So you feel better now?"

"Sure. I only...had the weirdest sense of deja-vu, is all." She put out an alert quickly and sent the feeds directly to Franklin at the US base. There was no telling if or when the Zoo's famous ability to block communications would kick in, so she set the man's computer to record just in case.

Besides, she didn't want to talk. She wouldn't turn the lights on and even moving would be kept to an absolute minimum.

"Anja, I'm picking the feed up." Franklin responded almost immediately. "Is this live at the Heavy Metal compound?"

She leaned a little closer to her mic and spoke in a hushed tone. "Yes. Please send help."

"Help is on the way. Hang in there."

He said that like she had a choice in the matter. While her first experience with the Zoo had been nothing like this, she couldn't help but make the comparison—alone in the dark, knowing something was out there, and waiting for them to come in to get her.

"I need to get something to eat," she mumbled.

"What?" Connie sounded almost outraged.

"My blood sugar is already tanking. If it goes any lower, it won't matter how much oxygen I have pumping through my blood."

It was better to not sit around waiting for something to happen too. While she couldn't do anything to help herself at this point, the people who could help her had been alerted.

"Oh, fuck."

"What's the matter?" The AI had somehow found what might be genuine concern, although maybe that was what she wanted to hear.

"I forgot to tell the rest of the team."

CHAPTER TWENTY

Zhao knew what was coming. The base was still in an uproar and confusion abounded but eventually, someone in a suit who had never experienced military service would decide that he was responsible for what had happened.

Still, something niggled at the back of his head and made it impossible to relax as they set up in the mess hall. He had never been the kind of person to care what other people thought of him or even why they thought those things in the first place. Guilt had always been a foreign concept to him.

He felt it now, though, or maybe something similar. Like many in the Chinese military, he had joined to see the world and to make some money. He'd never even imagined that he might be the reason why people would die. In the past, he'd done some bad shit—robbed graves, stolen, killed the odd person, and parked in front of a fire hydrant once.

But this was something new. He had never felt it before and he didn't like it. The worst part was that there was no real way to make it stop.

The only explanation for what had happened was that he had brought something back from the Zoo trip. He wandered to one of the exits, stepped out, and stared at the area in front of the medical bay where he had stood with the two researchers. Something had happened. His arm no longer itched and the Zoo had appeared out of nowhere.

Zhao pulled his sleeve up and ran his fingers over the smooth skin that had once been red and blistered with what had appeared to be an infected rash.

All the symptoms had gone now. Either the balm he'd been prescribed was incredibly effective, or the rash and the itch were something far more sinister.

"Are you all right?"

The young private snapped around at the sound of someone's voice and his eyes widened when he realized he was standing in front of the commander of the base.

"I'm sorry. I didn't see you there, sir!"

The man stared at him for a few long seconds before he raised an eyebrow. "Well then, are you going to answer my question?"

"Question, sir?"

"I asked if you were all right."

"Oh. Right. Quite all right, sir."

"You might want to tell that to the rest of your face. You look like you're about to throw up. That and the fact that you failed to salute me when I approached you."

Zhao winced and raised his hand to his forehead so fast that he couldn't stop it in time, which made both the hand and forehead ache.

At least that drew a laugh out of the commander.

"Don't worry. Usually, there would be consequences,

but today has been an odd day for everyone. It's hard to be a stickler for routine when you're staring in the face of worldwide destruction."

"I appreciate that."

"And so I ask again. Is everything all right?"

He looked around and tried to think of something he could use as the reason why his mind wouldn't work the way it was expected to when he was at the front line. No good lies came to mind and he lowered his head, closed his eyes, and drew a deep breath as he came to terms with the fact that he had to tell the truth, no matter what kind of trouble it landed him in.

"What happened here..." He gestured at the confusion happening all around them. "It might have been my fault. Not only my fault, but I am to blame as well."

The commander's eyes narrowed as he took a step closer. "What do you mean?"

"When I was struck on the head by the Komodo dragon, I didn't think much of the rash that appeared on my arm and neck afterward. As it turned out, a couple of researchers had the same rash. We talked to a medical officer about it but none of us considered the possibility that there might be some other kind of danger. Well, we considered it but not too seriously."

The man's eyes darkened. Not in a threatening way, but Zhao wondered if it was because they were still trying to determine how the Zoo had spread to them. He couldn't tell if the commander's promise to not inflict punishment for not saluting would extend to this. Maybe people needed to be punished given the lives lost while containing the jungle that had gained a foothold because of them.

"Right. What are the names of the researchers you mentioned?"

"Oh...I..."

"Never mind. I have their names."

That didn't sound good. The commander motioned for a few soldiers to approach him, shouted orders for them to find the two researchers, and even called them by name. It seemed there was more to this than he realized and he was escorted to the temporary medical center that had been set up while something a little more permanent was being established. He was put into quarantine and it wasn't long before the two researchers joined him inside.

They didn't look like they had been woken from their sleep, but who would realistically be asleep at this point? It was all hands on deck, and that included the scientists.

"What's happening?" Dr. Han asked and looked around the quarantine area like he had no idea why they had been dragged there.

"It would appear that we might be responsible for what happened." Dr. Zhi Sying pointed out the obvious and shook his head before he looked at Zhao. "I suppose you might have had something to do with that?"

The private shrugged. "I assumed it was obvious enough. We had the rashes caused by the Zoo, and now they're gone. I thought everyone knew it and it was only a matter of time before they isolated us. It's better that it got done as soon as possible. Who knows what else we might be spreading?"

He could tell that neither man liked the idea but they also knew that he made a good point. Instead of questioning him, both pulled their sleeves up and immediately checked their arms. Like him, it had taken them this long to realize that they no longer itched.

And like him, when they revealed their arms, the skin was as smooth as it had been before like nothing happened.

"That salve the doctor prescribed to us was effective, huh?" Zhao asked and raised an eyebrow.

The sarcasm dripped from his voice but they refused to believe it until they inspected their arms closely to make sure it was all gone with not even a hint of redness.

"Shit," Han whispered and looked at his companions. "How did we not notice that?"

"Many reasons," Zhi answered, his frown thoughtful. "The rash came and went, so it wasn't there all the time. We went to bed and while we were asleep, all hell broke loose. Some things are bound to fall through the cracks."

Their conversation was interrupted when the doctor was brought to the quarantine area. The escort was a little larger than the one used for the private or the researchers.

More importantly, it looked like they were being joined by the commander. Zhao had no idea how the officer knew that this particular doctor had treated them. No, that wasn't right. Almost everything was monitored and inspected on the base. The question was how he had managed to get that information so quickly.

Usually, anything they asked for took three or four days and paperwork about a kilometer long. There was no other way around it. The bureaucracy was the kind of thing that applied to some but not all. Political connections had a way of slicing through any red tape.

"You can see these men now," the commander stated bluntly, clearly continuing a conversation that had started before they entered. "Does it look like their rashes aren't something to be worried about?"

The doctor pulled his glasses on and inspected their arms, which were exposed for his scrutiny.

"They weren't supposed to heal that quickly," he commented once he had inspected all three. "But the salve did do its job. I don't know why I was summoned here in such a hurry."

"Because the rash disappeared in time for our base to be attacked. If you think we believe that to be a coincidence, I can assure you it is not the case."

Zhao looked at the two scientists. Their eyebrows were pulled in a frown and they had begun to show some concern. He took that to mean that while there was no real confirmation, they were worried about how plausible the idea was.

It appeared as though the commander came to the same conclusion. He sighed and shook his head. Most of the military officers would have erupted in a litany of curses at this point, but he showed a great deal of restraint. Maybe he had something against foul language?

"The Heavy Metal team is waiting for me in my office. I don't know what they might do with this information, but I suppose anything is better than nothing at this point."

Sal generally didn't like to immediately associate his doctorate with his name unless he was in a situation where there were peers to whom the qualification was significant.

This was a circumstance in which he hoped no one

would think he was a proper doctor—a physician—since he was looking at pictures that pertained to medical information. He wasn't sure if he was somehow expected to know what in the hell he was looking at.

Which made the next question easy to ask. "What in the living fuck am I looking at?"

"The after picture," the commander said. "The before picture is here."

"Oh...fuck me," Madigan muttered. "Ouch. Okay, yes. I guess you might want to keep something like that from spreading, but I'd say you would need to put them in quarantine and issue a shitload of penicillin. I don't know why you would need us to look at that."

"It isn't an STI," Courtney interjected. "What kind of infection are we looking at here?"

One of the Chinese researchers took a step forward. "According to those who were infected, it started when they came into contact with Zoo material and disappeared prior to the incursion, although they cannot be certain of the timeframe. The assumption is that something from the Zoo inserted itself between the skin layers, and what you're looking at here is a response from the immune system trying to drive it out."

It was an interesting concept, although Sal wasn't sure how it was possible. Maybe it was some kind of mite. He wasn't sure why they hadn't seen something like that before.

But if the creatures did manage to attach themselves to humans, something must have prompted them to lie dormant between the dermis and epidermis and remain viable despite heavy attacks from the body's attempts to drive it out.

"You think that whatever infected your men caused the incursion," he whispered.

"Precisely," the commander confirmed. "Well, that is our current hypothesis, at least. We would have needed some samples from the tissue while it was still infected to try to confirm this. As it is, all we have are pictures."

"It's a good hypothesis," Courtney told him. "And something for us to work off. The Zoo will adapt to the people it infects, though. If you can run periodic tests on anyone exposed to anything from the jungle and check for any rashes and infections, you might be able to catch something like this early and nip it in the bud. It might be beneficial to run tests on your people even if they don't have any symptoms."

Sal nodded. "It might already be adapting its system to find a way that allows it to settle into the carriers without showing any symptoms. Do you think we should send word to the bases to make sure that all soldiers, fire teams, and researchers who have any contact with the Zoo are tested?"

"Tested for what?" Matt asked. "It's not like we even know if anything will show on any tests that we might run."

"It can't hurt, though." He approached one of the pictures and narrowed his eyes. "There is no indication of what was transferred once the incursion started or how it was transferred. Or where for that matter. For all we know, it might be invisible and undetectable."

"Yeah."

He appreciated the support, but when he glanced at Courtney, she looked concerned. He recognized the expression as her trying to dig deep for some kind of helpful insight but was coming up blank for the moment.

Before anything could be tapped for inspiration, though, something buzzed inside his suit.

"Your phone is ringing," Madigan pointed out.

He nodded and pulled the device out from where it was stored. The screen told him it was Anja and he handed it to her.

"Can you find out what's going on?"

She nodded, took it from his hand, and moved outside. At least this time, she didn't make a snide remark about being his secretary. They needed to continue with the discussion and he didn't want any conversations to be held where intelligence and spies would be able to take anything away.

"So, what are you thinking?" Courtney asked, still focused on the pictures.

"Me?"

"No, the other world-class biologist in the room."

"I did win the Max Delbruck Prize three years ago," one of the Chinese researchers mentioned but paused when both Courtney and Sal turned their gazes on him. "I...do believe she was speaking to you, Dr. Jacobs."

"Damn, they don't hand that prize out to simply anyone," she whispered.

"Hey," he chided. "Be nice."

"I am. I paid him a compliment."

"It's not a compliment if it drips with sarcasm."

"Whatever." She sounded impatient. "What do you think?"

"I think we're looking at the very real possibility that the Zoo might have already adapted to circumvent issues with human immune responses and could be spreading itself in asymptomatic carriers."

"Funny, I thought the same thing—"

They were interrupted when Madigan rushed in. She hadn't been able to get the heavy suit into the building, which had forced her to climb out of it and do most of her work in her regular sweats.

"It's Anja!" she told them bluntly.

Sal resisted the urge to roll his eyes. "Well, yeah—"

"Shut it! She's in trouble. The Zoo pushed to the wall of the compound. US troops are on the way and she's alive, but she's about to lose it."

"She has good reason to," he snapped. "We need to go! Commander, we'll have to cut this visit short."

"Of course, your home needs you more than we do. I will be in touch."

He stood as they hurried from the room. The rest of the team who had waited with the helicopter were ready to go and the pilot had begun his warm-up.

Anja's experience in the Zoo would come back to her now. She didn't like to talk about it, but Sal was very aware of how much being alone in the dark in the middle of the Zoo while the monsters prowled had affected her.

Hopefully, this wouldn't add to the trauma.

CHAPTER TWENTY-ONE

They hadn't been kidding or exaggerating. Sal had hoped for one or the other, although something deep within him knew it would be all too accurate. He wasn't sure how in the hell the Zoo had reached their compound so quickly, but there was no need to make any assumptions.

The US troops were in the area, still busy driving the Zoo spur back from the wall. There was something to be said about how effective the military had become in this day and age. Franklin and Murphy put the work in to ensure that they were about as ready as they possibly could be.

He had no doubts that if the Chinese talked about what was happening, they would make sure that any and all personnel who came in contact with the Zoo were tested for any trace amounts of Zoo material, especially if any rashes manifested. A host of STDs and STIs would be made public knowledge by it, which was a win all its own.

Unfortunately, they didn't know what they were looking for or where to look. What was to stop the Zoo from hiding deeper, entering the bloodstream, and becoming even more impossible to detect?

He shook his head firmly. There would be time for all that later. At this moment, their focus had to be on Anja. It looked like she was safe but he knew the physical attack was far from the only damage that the Zoo could do.

"Get the team working, coordinate with whoever's running the operation, and see if they need any support," Madigan snapped. "Sal, go inside and see if Anja needs help with anything. Gregor, you go too."

She had a good instinct for how to deal with people and was far better at it than he was. He would have gone in to see how she was doing anyway but hadn't thought about the benefits of bringing Gregor. A familiar face would always be a welcome sight in this kind of situation.

Sal knew he would have liked to have a familiar face to turn to after his first time in the Zoo, but none had presented themselves since he'd been sent across the world at a moment's notice. He'd adjusted eventually, but the nightmares hadn't gone for a while.

Anja looked a little hyper, despite the bags under her eyes. She clasped her hands tightly like she was trying to stop them from shaking when they entered. Her eyes widened and a smile appeared on her face when she saw them.

"Baby Jesus fucking H Christ, it's good to see you guys." She rushed forward to wrap Gregor in a warm hug.

He muttered a few words in Russian and patted her shoulder gently. Although he seemed uncomfortable with the hug, he tolerated it for her benefit.

Sal moved closer to squeeze her shoulder and she turned and grasped his hand as a show of appreciation.

"I...I was taking a nap," she said and pulled out of the hug. "Only a cat nap, not like I was sleeping on the job or anything. I need some fucking rest from time to time, you know? Anyway, Connie wakes me and doesn't do it with some perverted joke or another, so I get to the screen and it's....it's fucking there. I don't...it was there, and I started to call people and then I needed to get something to eat. I needed to chill out, and the Zoo was outside, and I forgot to call you guys, and there was...there... Oh, fuck...and it was like it was looking for you guys—like it knew you were here, and I freaked the hell out, but I'm okay now."

She brushed her hands quickly over her eyes, which suddenly brimmed with tears, and rushed to the kitchen to yank a few paper towels from the rolls. Her efforts to push the tears away were almost aggressive.

"Hey, hey, hey." Madigan stepped inside, out of her suit again, and pulled Anja's hands away from her face, which Sal could now see was reddened from her overly rough wiping. "It's all okay now. You need to get some rest. I'm serious."

"I...I need to get back to work. I can't see anything when I'm like this—I need to be...I need to get—"

"Come on." Madigan's voice was soft and even a little calming as she pulled one of the paper towels from Anja's hand. "Everything's all right now. You don't need to sleep but you shouldn't work anymore tonight, do you understand me?"

The hacker looked into the woman's eyes in confusion and tried to understand what she was doing. Sal could understand her current state of mind. All kinds of survival responses kicked around in her head at the moment, and he knew that if she kept trying to push, she would burn herself out.

He nodded. "The situation is under control. Your quick response made sure the reaction team was here in time. You saved the compound."

"I know, but—"

"But nothing. If I have to institute a 'save the compound from being taken over by the Zoo, get some time off' policy, I fucking will and you know it. We all need rest, and if I know what your sleep schedule looks like, you probably need it more than most of us."

She still looked confused but the panic attack had passed and she had collected herself a little.

"Okay...I need something to eat. Some chocolate, I think."

Madigan nodded and let her go to the kitchen before she turned to Sal. "Save the compound from being taken over by the Zoo, get some time off?"

"Too much?" He smirked

"No, I thought it was good. Did that just come to you or have you waited to use it for a special occasion?"

"I thought about pulling it on the Brits when they came asking for recommendations. You know, give the people who saw the incursion early a reward. I'm glad I got to use it, though."

"Do you think she'll get any sleep?" She darted the hacker a concerned look.

"I hope so. She needs it and after a day like today, I think we all need it. Most of the attacks are being handled at this point, but there's no telling when something bright, new, and scary will show its face. I want the Heavy Metal team rested and ready for when that day comes."

She nodded. "Right. I'll check and see what's happening. If the response force is making good headway, I'll tell the team to take eight hours."

"Thanks. And...thanks. I'm not that great at...you know..."

"We're partners, Sal. You're good with the science. I'm good with the—well, better with the people. Now, you should take some of your advice."

Sal nodded as she pulled away and headed out the door. There was no need to burden her with the issues that plagued him. Anja had said that the Zoo was there looking for them. It could have torn through without pause but it had stopped and let the American team reach them.

It wasn't impossible, but he didn't want to think that the jungle might want him specifically or worse, why it wanted him.

And if he said anything about it to Madigan or Courtney, he would end up on the bench again, which meant he couldn't tell them. Not that he had any real proof to back it up but they would trust his gut instinct and tell him it was time to stay as far away from the Zoo as possible.

Fucking hell, they would probably be right to do it too. Of course, it was equally possible that this was merely a big fucking coincidence.

Exactly like the Russians also had a spur develop in their sector not twenty-four hours earlier—all simply a coincidence.

This wasn't quite rest but oddly enough, she found it restful. She was working on something familiar again and back on the front lines. While all they did was study soil samples, something about working with Sal again was relaxing.

It was far more challenging than heading Pegasus up, but this was something she was trained to do. All her time spent in the States was plagued by one hell of an imposter syndrome. She always felt like she was out of her depth and pretending to be something she was not.

The feelings were accurate, though. She was a biologist and this was where she was supposed to be.

The only downside was that the soil samples she studied revealed nothing to her. Maybe she'd been away from it all too long, but Sal looked equally as frustrated and he leaned back in his seat.

"There is nothing microscopic that I can pick up," he whispered and rubbed his temples. "Nothing that could cause what we were looking at. Only some...supercharged soil. Honestly, we have thousands of people out there who would pay millions to get a sample of this. You'd be able to grow...three, four crops a year if you could replicate it without the inherent issues."

"The issues that would come from every cornfield in Iowa turning into the Zoo two-point-oh. Honestly, there would be far more people who would pay millions to sit on this information, even if it was safe."

"What do you mean?" He frowned at her.

"If too much corn hits the market, prices go down and

too many people lose their annual bonuses. Believe me, they would be far more invested in making sure nothing like this hits the market."

"It could solve world hunger," he pointed out reasonably.

"If excess corn could solve world hunger, it would have already. Huge quantities are dumped because no one buys it or because they can't transport it before it starts rotting. No, the way to use this would be to make it available to areas where people can't grow shit. But again, too many people who would want to stand in the way of that."

Sal sighed softly and rocked slightly in his chair. "Well, I guess you'd know better."

"Damn right."

"Do you have anything over there?" He sounded hopeful and she hated having to disappoint him.

"Nothing visible. We might have to do some chemical tests but whatever these things are, they would have to be...submicroscopic. I don't suppose you know any specialists in the area?"

He sighed. "A couple. It was never my interest. I liked macrobiology and avoided sticking my eye to a microscope. I paid my dues, of course, but I never liked it."

"It seems we need to get going on those chemical samples. We have so much to learn about what might have secreted itself in people's skin. Hell, it could be the cause of what happened in the Czech Republic, Niger, and fuck knows where else. This opens a whole new world of contact tracing that I know people will love."

There was a knock on the door and Courtney looked

up to where Madigan peeked through the tiny porthole. Sal waved her in, and she closed the door behind her.

"Did you find anything?" she asked and approached the samples.

Courtney shook her head. "I hoped we would be able to see something like mites crawling in these samples but no such luck. We might need to look into some chemical tests —the kind that change color if they come into contact with biological material out of the Zoo. I'm merely not sure which would be appropriate for something this small."

"Dr. Yuri Masuka works in the US base. He's an expert on microbiology and we'll make contact with him in the morning," Sal continued. "In the meantime, I'll try something a little more brute force. Failing that, we could probably approach the Pegasus lab. They probably have better equipment for this kind of thing."

Madigan nodded. "I'll take your word on it. I've talked to Matt, Anja, and Connie, and we all agree that it's time to invest in better long-range sensors to stop something like this from happening again. I thought we should find seismic sensors to pick up anything coming underground. Connie says she thinks she can run the detection without it getting tripped every time someone drives along the road."

"Our defenses are primarily focused on human invaders too, not the jungle," Sal pointed out. "All things considered, I'm very sure Connie would be more than happy to see her defenses set up with plasma throwers."

"We might need a centralized missile launch system too," Madigan suggested. "Something like what they have set up on the walls. That kind of firepower would be more than enough to drive any Zoo attacks back."

She wouldn't have suggested it in the past. At any other time, she would have said they had enough to defend the compound against a Zoo attack, but something had her on edge. Sal looked it too. They were generally the most relaxed when it came to the Zoo, but something was different about them now.

The cause was obvious too, but it felt like there was more.

"I guess we've had things easy up to this point," Sal commented and stared distractedly at the samples he had studied. "The Zoo never came knocking at our doorstep before."

"It was only a matter of time," Madigan agreed and she studied him closely.

Maybe she thought he was hiding something from her, but Madigan was a keen student of the human condition and wasn't that good at hiding shit.

He scratched his arm, almost like he felt the same itch they'd been told came with the rashes, and leaned closer to the microscope.

"Are you okay?" Courtney inched her chair closer to his.

"I'm fine," he snapped and immediately regretted it. He looked around to make sure he hadn't angered her or Madigan. "I...feel a little on edge, is all. I think we all do."

She was right, she knew it. Sal was simply the worst at hiding shit and Madigan could tell it too, but there would be no point in pushing him further on the matter. He had told her there was a reason why Madigan had tried to bench him before.

And he'd said that he still remembered what it felt like when they'd encountered that tentacle monster in Chernobyl and while retaking the Russian base—the loss of control and peering into the mind of a powerful being like that.

He would never admit it but it had almost broken him. If they didn't need every hand on deck at this point, she would talk to Madigan about making sure he no longer went anywhere near the jungle.

Unfortunately, they couldn't afford that.

"I'm fine," Sal insisted, almost like he was trying to convince himself.

"Right." Madigan cleared her throat. "I'll head to the rest of the team and see how they're doing. You guys need to get some sleep before too long, you hear?"

CHAPTER TWENTY-TWO

It had been a long night for everyone. Franklin knew that better than most. The Zoo was the most active it had been since the beginning of its growth, and no one was sure what to do with that knowledge.

He had more reason to be cantankerous than most, though. The US had the largest military presence in the area, which meant they were expected to help whenever something went wrong.

"I'm still in touch with Kimura on what we see from the Zoo," Solodkov muttered.

"How's he doing?"

"Recovering much better than he should be. I guess it's all the clean living he engages in. Either way, we've been in touch since it appears that the Zoo pushed out another odd spur toward the wall. This time, it was closer to their side, which I guess explains how they saw it first."

"That's more your schtick, isn't it?"

"I hope you don't think I'll comment on that. Of course,

I've heard that your neck of the woods has developed similar spurs. Two of them over the course of the night."

"Well, yes." Franklin adjusted his glasses and inspected the reports in front of him. "One on either side of the base, but too far away for it to have been directed at us and missed. One of them was mere yards away from the Heavy Metal compound, though. There are also reports from the Brits and the French about one each for them as well, but I haven't been able to confirm those."

Oddly enough, the Russian hadn't been able to either. He didn't like being on equal grounds with someone on anything, especially when it came to intelligence.

"The Zoo is up to something, there's no doubt about that," he muttered and studied the satellite images that had been pulled up from all sides of the Zoo. "But there is no real rhyme or reason behind any of these incidents. It might be that it's simply trying to tire us, torment us, and make sure we're spent and exhausted for when the real attack comes."

"Or it might be harassing us to prevent us from seeing what it's doing—the worst game of three-card monte ever." Franklin smothered a yawn and wished that for once, he could enjoy a good night's rest

"Three-card...what?"

"Three-card monte? You know, the game with the cards where you have two jacks and a queen, and you move them around and the other person has to guess which card is the queen."

"In that case," Solodkov asked in confusion, "is the queen not usually among the three that the...mark has to choose from?"

"Exactly. Meaning that while our attention is on all these fucking attacks in every sector, something is slipping through our intelligence network."

Neither man liked that idea much.

"The scenario is always the same." The Russian commander growled in irritation and rasped his fingers over the stubble that he had yet to deal with. "The spur grows overnight and reaches the wall, but it's pushed back by the flame and plasma throwers and puts up little to no resistance with mutants or...anything. Everything simply goes back to the way it was and it repeats the process. All the while, we're waiting for the other penny to drop. Is that the term?"

"I think you say waiting for the penny to drop, meaning someone finally understands something. You would be waiting for the other shoe to drop." At least that was one question Franklin could answer.

"Right, right, the other shoe to drop. I keep mixing the two up for some reason."

"I would assume it would have been part of your training to learn all about English idioms and how to use them properly in context."

"Well, yes." For once, Solodkov made no attempt to evade mention, however vague, of his previous career. "But that one always did confuse me. I understand the penny dropping since that is what you wait for when you do a coin flip, but why the shoe?"

Franklin narrowed his eyes. "I'm...not sure. But I do know that the penny dropping idiom comes from the penny-in-the-slot mechanisms they used to have in British public bathrooms. They would get jammed so you would have to…you know, wait for the penny to drop."

"Interesting." The Russian laughed

"Yeah. Besides, you do the coin flip with quarters, so if it were an idiom, it would be about the quarter dropping."

Solodkov looked like he was genuinely thinking about that for a moment before he shrugged and pushed past the point in their conversation. It was not the most important part of what they had to discuss but it was a little relaxing to see that he was not quite the master of disguise Franklin had begun to fear he might be.

"Is something on your mind?"

The US commander realized that his gaze had drifted to the reports coming from all around the Zoo.

"It all seems pointless, you know? Like it's wasting its resources on throwing itself at us. But the problem is that we can't assume it's pointless because we know better."

"If we're lucky, all it's doing is testing our defenses, trying to judge our response times and our readiness. That comes with the hopefully good news that the only reason it's still running those tests is because it hasn't found a location that is sufficiently weak or vulnerable. Of course, wishful thinking like that will only get people killed."

"Except that it is the most logical answer." Franklin sighed. "Still, we can't simply accept it as such."

"Agreed."

Sal could see skepticism in the commander's eyes as he studied the reports they had put in front of him. Stacks of them were gathered on every available surface in his office and made it look smaller. Anja would lose her shit if she saw it and complain to Franklin over their inability to digitize their system.

When all this was over, he wondered if she would be willing to work for the US base for a few months to get their servers up to snuff in terms of security and efficiency. All this paperwork was a goddammed fire hazard.

"Let me see if I have this straight," Franklin said and looked like he was still struggling with some of the language in the report. "Something...what? Burrowed under the skin, caused the rash, and burrowed out again to start a new Zoo when the time was right?"

"Burrow is a good word for it," Courtney agreed. "The current assumption is that whatever it is burrowed between the dermis and epidermis, which is what caused the rash when the body's immune system fought back. We assumed it was some kind of dust mite, but closer inspection of soil samples showed no microscopic creatures. I sent a few samples to my labs and we're running a few more."

"But it is the present hypothesis," Sal interjected when he saw that Franklin's eyebrows still bunched low over his eyes. "Whatever it is, they burrow into the carrier until they're ready and then drop out. We assume they carry goop as well, which makes them the primary vectors to bring about these...surprise incursions."

"Assume." The commander's scowl remained and he looked like he hadn't had any sleep since first word of the attacks had come thirty-six hours before. It wasn't quite fighting at the front lines but his was still draining work.

He thought the soldier in Franklin might have preferred to put a suit on and head out to fight monsters instead of reading reports and working through red tape to keep other soldiers alive.

"Doubts are good," Courtney pointed out. "At this point, it's merely what they think is the most viable way for it to have moved beyond our defenses without being noticed. That and the sudden appearance of these soldiers with rashes is certainly something to keep an eye on."

Franklin shook his head. "This is all…way too science fiction for me. I don't even know where to start. Besides, no one on the British base had any rashes."

"True." Sal nodded. "But they also reported having something spit gunk at them like there was with the Chinese researcher. In those cases, the gunk was the carrier. It was brushed off outside the British barracks and the armor was taken to the contamination unit."

"Which brings up another issue," Madigan stated.

"Yeah," the commander muttered. "If you're right, it means our current decontamination protocols are ineffective against whatever it is."

"Right." Sal cleared his throat. "We talked with Sam Jackson at ENSOL, and he said the Algerians brought two mercenaries with them when they called at the camp. Both showed similar symptoms and scratched their arms, but since they were in custody and were moved to confinement, no one knows what happened to them."

"We can assume they are currently strumming harps, sitting in clouds in whatever particular afterlife they happened to believe in," Madigan added snidely. She looked around and tilted her head when her comment failed to get a laugh. "Tough room."

"Are we honestly considering the possibility that the Zoo was tracked to the ENSOL base as something that burrowed into the skin of these mercs?" Franklin shook his head as if unable to grasp the logic or the implications.

"There's what happened in the Czech Republic too," Sal pointed out

"No rashes were reported," the commander stated hastily.

"That we know of. But it was confirmed that the outbreak was blamed on illegal pelts transported to a tanning facility there. And there was the situation in Niger too. If some of the mercs decided to go home while they had that kind of a rash, the burrowers could easily have transferred in the first villages where the outbreak triggered."

"Do you have any better ideas?" Courtney asked and sounded exasperated. "Because we're open to hearing anything."

"I'm not the one who's supposed to come up with ideas. That's what you're here for."

"Well, yeah." Sal cleared his throat. "This…this is one of those ideas."

"Right." Franklin shook his head. "Well, I'll look into it. And we'll look for money in the budget to get that testing you're recommending here. I'm not sure I'll be able to sell it to the people upstairs, but maybe we can get the corporate people to foot the bill on that. It would be an even tougher sell, but maybe Ms. Monroe here might be able to convince the right people."

"Dr. Monroe," Courtney corrected him. "But yeah, I'll see what I can do."

"Of course. And...sorry."

"No problem. Most people assume I'm another corporate suit these days."

Madigan tilted her head. "Well..."

"Yeah, sure. The other woman rolled her eyes. "That's what I've done for a while now, but it's not like it erases the years of study, research, and time in the Zoo on top of that."

"Right."

Sal narrowed his eyes. It was an interesting interaction —like the two women tiptoed around each other as if unsure of how to act.

"You should get some rest too," Sal noted and patted the commander on the shoulder. "No offense, but you look like a man who's been up and working for the past two days."

"That sounds about right. It feels like it's been a fucking week, though. How in the hell do we deal with something we can't see?"

The Heavy Metal team exchanged a look at the question but none of them had an answer for it.

"We'll find a way," Sal answered and cleared his throat. "And if we don't, we'll probably be dead inside a month and it'll be someone else's problem."

"Is it a bad thing that it would be a relief at this point?" Franklin smiled but it didn't last.

"Probably. Which is why we generally don't say that part out loud."

CHAPTER TWENTY-THREE

"I'm very sure that no one cares if we take a little of our time on duty for ourselves."

"Is that the same very sure that allowed you to commit to trying to smuggle weed and set up a dealership on the base?"

Aaron glowered at his comrade. "That was...a legitimate misunderstanding that was cleared up quickly."

"It's interesting that it was cleared up when the army needed as many bodies in the Zoo area as they could get. And that it resulted in a demotion too. Nah, man, we know you got caught red-handed trying to sell weed to an MP you had a crush on. The only reason you weren't shipped back home, court-martialed, and sent packing without honors was because the higher-ups decided keeping you here as buck-assed private was a better punishment than anything they could have come up with."

It was true. He liked to think of himself as a creative entrepreneur and when the money coming out of the Zoo dried up suddenly, he found another revenue stream rather quickly. That, however, was where the story deviated from reality. He'd dated the MP chick a few times and even slept with her before he decided they weren't compatible.

She disagreed and decided to rat him out when she couldn't change his mind. Or maybe that one last time was her trying to find evidence in his private residence, although he liked to think she had tried to win him back and turned him in when her ploys didn't work.

He preferred to think it was the romantic in him.

The lenient sentencing had been something of a disappointment. They were never able to prove intent to sell, which meant that possession was all they could get him on. Under any other circumstances, they would have shipped him home and kicked him out of the military, and he would have spent a couple of months in prison for it before moving on.

Honestly, at this point, it was preferable to what they faced in the Zoo, but he had accepted whatever decision they made.

The sergeant sighed and walked where they stood. "What are you guys working on?"

"A little poker," Aaron answered.

"You don't have any cards," the man pointed out.

"Au contraire, mon capitaine."

"Sergeant."

"Well…yeah." He resisted the urge to roll his eyes. "We had an app downloaded to the suits before we left the base. It lets our suits connect and we can play some good ol' Texas Hold'em. It's merely a little something to pass the time. We can hold off on playing if there's a need to head out and pick the game back up when things calm. No problems there, right?"

"Officially? Any number of issues. Unofficially?" The sergeant shrugged. It was well-known that the soldiers in and around the Zoo generally got away with all kinds of shit, and that included playing poker when they were supposed to be on the job.

"It's not like we're doing anything here anyway," Aaron continued, folded his current hand, and turned his attention away from the rest of the hand. "I still don't understand why they don't sweep this area with planes or helicopters and call people in when there's something to kill or burn."

"They have sweeping planes collecting pictures five or six miles up in the air. Our job here is to be on call and quick to jump into action when anything does present itself. They've set teams up along these dunes every three or four miles to make sure there's support available. Since we're here, we might as well watch the Zoo."

"It's not like we can even see much out there," Aaron pointed out. "They've talked about constructing observation posts since forever, but someone somewhere didn't approve the funding or something. Now that we need to see the Zoo clearly, there's a fucking wall in the way. We can see the jungle and a portion of the buffer zone from this dune, but the rest is blocked. We might as well play cards until someone with a better view catches sight of something they need us to look into."

"Fine, whatever. How do I get in on it?"

"Connect to the Bluetooth on our suits and it'll give you the option to join the game."

The sergeant nodded and moved to where the rest of the men were gathered. They were a little surprised that their CO now joined the gambling, but once it was established that he had put some of his paycheck into it, there was no problem.

Aaron smiled. The creative entrepreneur had struck again. He needed extra cash after the pay cut—not that a sergeant's pay was much more than what he made as a private. Cleaning his fellow soldiers out when he could was a nice way to get a little more spending money, and he also made half the ad revenue from the app, splitting it with his friend who'd developed it.

It was a decent way to make extra money. He was well on the way to a respectable bank account back home, which would make it easy to retire and live off the proceeds.

The simple truth was that he was lazy to his core, which was why he needed to be creative to make up for it. He was a firm believer in the theory that all the great thinkers and inventors in the world shared this particular trait. It took considerable dedication to laziness to fight that hard to make the world more efficient.

But even he needed to be occupied by something. Watching the Zoo do nothing for hours on end was not his idea of a good time.

Something shifted over the wall, and Aaron took a step forward, narrowed his eyes, and made his HUD zoom in on what he was looking at. The small wisp of movement might have been a cloud except he could see it moving over the top of the wall. Oddly, though, it didn't appear to move closer.

"Sarge, you need to see this."

The sergeant turned to see what he was talking about and he immediately highlighted the area he was looking at.

"Shit. Locusts. Hundreds of the bastards."

Sure enough, with every second that ticked by, more of the shadows appeared on the wall. The wisp had become a cloud now and the winged mass rose from the jungle canopy and hovered over it.

"They're just...there," one of the other soldiers pointed out, and the rest looked like they had something to focus on aside from the poker game. The pot was looking rich too and Aaron began to regret ducking out early. It wasn't like he had a good hand but there was always money to be made when people threw it around.

"And they're only hovering," the sergeant agreed. "That's weird, right? Shouldn't they be attacking something by this point?"

"Maybe they saw one of the spy planes and thought that they could fly up and catch it?" Even as Aaron said it, he knew that it was bullshit. If they couldn't see the planes or even hear them, nothing in the Zoo would be able to detect them. Probably.

"I'd better call it in," Sarge mumbled and keyed his suit's microphone. "Just in case. Base command, do you read me? This is perimeter team seventeen."

A few seconds of silence over the link seemed to stretch uncomfortably before someone finally keyed in on the channel.

"This is base command. We read you, PT-Seventeen."

"We're seeing some...interesting activity from the Zoo, base command."

"Define interesting activity, perimeter team."

"Well, we're looking at a shit-ton of locusts hovering over the canopy. They aren't doing anything but are out in clear view."

"I didn't even know they could hover for that long," Aaron muttered.

"Roger that. We'll send another team to rendezvous with you in case you need some support. Hold on out there."

"Will do."

The connection was killed, which left them with nothing else to do but watch the creatures that made no effort to do anything. There was no interest in continuing the poker game. Everyone sensed that the unusual behavior heralded something ominous and waited for whatever it was to happen. None of them were sure what it would be, but they were damn sure it wasn't something good.

It wasn't long before two Hammerheads rumbled to the crest of the dune beside them. The moment they stopped, soldiers poured out, their weapons at the ready and aimed toward the wall.

"Aren't you all ready for a fight?" Aaron snarked.

"Why aren't you?" the new CO retorted. "We're looking at a horde of Zoo bastards maybe seconds away from launching an attack."

The comm links came to life and the whole team jumped and grasped their weapons like they expected the Zoo to come out after them. It was unsettling, but Sarge keyed in calmly.

"We have more reinforcements coming in, perimeter

teams," base command called out. "We're picking up a lot of movement in your area, so stay sharp."

"Yeah…you don't say…"

Sarge's voice trailed off and the teams stared fixedly at the scene ahead. What little of the buffer zone they could see was suddenly engulfed. Even at the distance they were at, something that large was hard to miss and especially so many things that large. The hippos were hard to mistake for anything else.

They immediately disappeared, but no one was stupid enough to think they were gone. Soon after, the horrible sound of tusks on prefab shattered the almost silence of the area.

"Hey, base command?" Sarge sounded disbelieving.

"We read you, PT."

"You might want to tell those reinforcements to grow wings. We have a fuck-ton of hippos and it sounds like they are charging headfirst into the wall."

"On top of the shit-ton of locusts?"

"Yeah!"

"And? That whole buffer zone is slag. Even if they did do some damage, there's no way the Zoo can move close to the wall."

"I don't think so, base. We have about fifty of the fuckers that each weigh about eight tons apiece. With them cavorting around on that slag…well, I wouldn't put money on it lasting much longer."

Anja was better off at the base. While she'd put up the same kind of protest she had before, there was less of a fight this time than there had been the other times. She knew she would be safer and get more work done, and there was help readily available if they were attacked.

And if something attacked the base, they were all fucked anyway.

"Thanks," Sal whispered as Madigan took her seat across from him in the Hammerhead.

"What for?"

"You know, helping Anja."

"Sure. She knew this was best for her but doesn't like the idea of leaving the compound."

He frowned. "Should we have left someone there to keep an eye on it?"

"Connie's there to keep an eye on everything." She smirked. "Between you and me, Connie might be the best solution. She has full control of the defenses. If anyone got out of the compound alive, they would know to never come back." The AI was likely to leave them with some very vivid nightmares about the Heavy Metal compound.

They traveled in silence for a while and as they approached the target location, the unmistakable sound of the cannons on top of the wall confirmed that an attack was in progress. The weapons would need to be reloaded before too long, but most of the systems were automated. Sal wasn't sure about the VI they had running the whole operation, but there was much about the defense systems he didn't approve of.

Gregor ground the Hammerhead to a halt, and Madigan pushed out and moved the tank of a suit that she wore like it was her own skin and bones. The rest of the team scrambled out behind her. Sal brought up the rear.

He noticed immediately that something was wrong with the wall. Prefab tended to hold its shape no matter what, which meant the material wouldn't lean, but a bulge had formed around the base. In the temporary lull while the weapons were reloading, he heard the mutants bulldozing into the other side and the grind of tusks in prefab was almost like nails on a chalkboard.

Murphy's Hammerheads pulled up beside them and formed a line so the heavy artillery had a clear line of sight on the wall. The soldiers hurried to position themselves to make sure that if anything got past the heavy artillery, they were there to stop it at the wall and prevent a full breakout.

He glanced at the Heavy Metal team that Madigan had already organized into a defensive formation at the center of the line. His gaze settled on Trick who clambered onto the roof of their Hammerhead and settled himself comfortably. The freelancer had earned his name through the insane shots he could take with his rifle. It would be good to see some evidence of that.

"If the wall comes down, that's your signal to start shooting at the goddammed hole until I tell you to stop," Murphy roared and made sure people could hear him whether they were on comms or not. "If you run out of rounds and didn't have the presence of mind to have a reload ready and waiting, I will gun you down where you stand! That's right. You will have wasted my bullets too by riddling your useless fucking corpses with them. Let's move, people!"

Sal was only seventy-five percent sure that Murphy was

joking by that point but although the rant drew a few laughs from his men, there was every indication that they responded to the intention behind it. If anything got through, they would be ready to open fire immediately.

It was debatable whether they would be able to get through the damn wall but at this point, he had to concede that their violent efforts had compromised the massive structure enough to raise concern.

"We have teams from the Brit and French bases rolling in," Madigan pointed out and immediately highlighted where they could see clouds of dust kicked up by those approaching. "We should be able to make it a damn good fight if nothing else."

"It's always nice to hear your vote of confidence, Madigan." Courtney laughed.

"That was my vote of confidence."

The other woman sighed and stepped forward. "Do you guys see that? On the sand over there?"

It took Sal a second to see what she was talking about. It was almost like she had deliberately looked for it because the odd motion was almost undetectable unless one focused hard.

"Ripples in the sand," Madigan whispered. "We all know what that is."

"The fucking mole rats." He frowned as he tried to determine how many there might be. "They burrowed underneath the wall somehow."

"That's not possible," one of the soldiers said and gestured to the wall. "The damn thing is...it's supposed to be reinforced to some ridiculous depth."

"It's also not possible to knock the goddammed thing

over," Sal snapped in response and aimed his rifle at the section that had begun to bulge outward even more. "I don't know how they did it, but the burrowing bastards are probably the reason why it's about to come down."

Jiro shook his head. "There is a strategic benefit to what they're doing. They have air support from the locusts, the hippos are the heavy cavalry—the shock troops—while the mole rats do the grunt work and act as guards on this side. It's a process of slow infiltration until the whole thing collapses and the main force pushes through."

"Has anyone ever told you that you're an unsettling kind of man, Jiro?" Courtney asked.

"They never stop."

"Oh. Okay."

"Air support." Murphy approached them. "Fucking air support. I wish we had thought about bringing some AA guns."

"Do you think some of your heavies might be able to pick up that slack?" Sal asked.

"They will have to. You heard the man! I need four heavies ready to deal with anything that shows up in the sky."

Four men called that they would take the work on and their targeting assignments changed on everyone's HUDs.

Murphy still didn't seem happy with the situation. "We'll have to see how effective they are—"

His voice cut off when something else filled the air. It sounded like it came from all sides at first but they could soon distinguish between the echoes and their source directly in front of them. Cracks appeared in the wall and they spread in jagged arteries toward the top. The sound was almost like that of something being sucked down a noisy drain.

As the defenders stared in silent disbelief, the weak points widened and a sinkhole appeared at the base of the wall. In seconds, a whole portion fell into the chasm. The prefab rubble filled it to create a rough but effective bridge in their brand new gateway to hell.

CHAPTER TWENTY-FOUR

There was only one way to describe what they were looking at. It was an army, organized and ready to attack the moment the wall came down. The hippos had battered the wall with their tusks but if anyone expected it to slow the fuckers down, they were in for a rough surprise.

A green shield was all they could see at first, covered by the shadow of the wall. An arch was still in place where the prefab held shakily together, but there was more than enough space for everything to move through the hole.

All the familiar species rushed forward. The humpers led the exodus along with the hyenas. A few panthers used the ragged edges of the gap to scale the wall, where they looked down like they expected something or someone to attack from close quarters.

Above them, the locusts began to swarm and the low drone grew louder as they gathered and pushed forward, ready to attack.

Larger figures loomed and prowled in the background, waiting for their moment to push forward.

The artillery opened fire and rounds battered the locusts, although their numbers seemed to increase at this point. Some of the barrage continued into the wall and enormous chunks of prefab were gouged loose to crush any mutants caught beneath them. The fatalities were merely drops of water lost in the ocean that surged toward them.

They were doing damage but far from enough. The shelling impacted the cannon fodder for the most part, and while large numbers of the locusts were dying, enough were getting through to replace them.

"Madigan!" Sal shouted.

"I got it!"

The mini-guns on her shoulders wound up and in seconds, the air was hot with rounds that ripped through the creatures as they tried to reach the artillery. The other heavy suits began to do the same. Trick was already selecting his targets. He fired on semi-auto, but the rounds came out fast enough that it might as well have been on automatic.

Each shot felled its target, drilled through, and struck three or four that came in behind. The precision was uncanny like he was shooting three or four times instead of only once.

"You should be in a fucking circus," Sal muttered.

"I'll take that as a compliment."

"I'm surprised I hadn't heard of you sooner."

"That's on you, brother."

The adrenaline filled Sal and drove him to be in the middle of the action. Maybe whatever was in the Zoo wanted him in a heightened state of aggression but its control wasn't quite enough. It wanted him to be in a fighting mood and it got him in a fighting mood but was unable to use that to its advantage.

Other troops began to move forward, opened fire, and positioned mines to slow the creatures. He joined them at the front lines, his sword already in hand. Jiro stepped beside him, also holding a sword. He seemed like the kind of guy he should have heard of before too.

Maybe they had been among the smaller merc groups and never quite able to make a decent name for themselves.

They were making it now. Chezza was with him too, as were the six newcomers. Madigan had outfitted Leo and Jim with heavy suits, although not quite as heavy as hers. All the rest were in regular combat suits except for Kay who wore a hybrid similar to his. Running and gunning was their business now.

There had never been an attack like this. Vines thrust from the sand without warning and those at the front wound around the ankles of the men closest to them. Screams and shouts were heard as they were dragged away, but most of them were already dead by the time Sal reached the forward positions. His blade cut through the vines and pushed them back like they were tentacles. It even looked like they could feel pain.

Thankfully, the line was still holding.

Grenades were lobbed as the first wave of monsters swept in. It might as well have been an all-out war with the Germans, Brits, and French ranged beside the Americans. With all the other bases covering their asses, it was likely that this was as much as they would see in immediate reinforcements.

"Murphy!" Sal called over comms and ducked when one of the horned gorillas rushed at him. "You have better already have Solodkov on the line!"

"I've got everyone on the goddammed line and told them to send helicopters, bombers, and fucking everything! This is it! This is the attack."

They were chilling words to hear and the kind Sal had hoped he never would. This was the attack and they would be swamped by the monsters that poured endlessly through the breach if they couldn't plug it soon.

He rolled under the gorilla's sweeping horn and New Connie moved him out of the way of the creature's grasping hands before he thrust his blade forward and through it. The rest of the Heavy Metal team now joined him and he had had a feeling Madigan had told them to keep him alive. at all costs.

Courtney surprised him with the fact that she had lost none of her previous Zoo skills. She must have practiced in sims or something to keep her reflexes and abilities sharp while she was in Philly.

More of the vines snaked forward and behind these, the first wash of green from the burgeoning new jungle began to spread and grow before their eyes. The defenders were pushed back since none of them wanted to be caught in the tree line and cut off from the main force. A few fell here and there to the tentacles but that number would spike when the attacks came from all sides.

The claymores began to detonate when the trees pushed through in front of them and a few decimated some of the tentacles. The hyenas turned, abandoned their attack, and threw themselves at the mines instead to clear them so the vines didn't take any more damage. Sal would have assumed it would be the other way around and the tentacles would clear the way for the monsters, but maybe the Zoo knew its vines were doing more damage than the monsters were.

They were used to dealing with mutants and cryptids. There wasn't much training to deal with the fucking tentacles but the line was still holding.

His body chilled when the hippos rushed forward. The ground shuddered and shifted under the troops, and Sal realized they were being funneled into the path of the hippos by the suddenly treacherous sand disturbed by more of the damn mole rats.

A few of the men didn't move fast enough and almost a dozen were ensnared by mole rats the size of grizzlies. Their fangs and claws ripped the men and armor apart. Some had the presence of mind to pull the pins on their grenades before they were killed and in the seconds that followed, pops came from all around them as the soldiers who knew they were as good as dead chose to take the mutants with them.

It wasn't all of them but it was still a reflection of the kind of mindset their people were in. They were willing to die but it would be on their terms.

The artillery continued to fire but the locusts were getting through. The soldiers who were assigned to protect them put up a good fight, but too many of the monsters had learned how to streak in under the fire. Two of the guns were already being swarmed. Sal resisted the impulse to rush back and help them. It wouldn't be worth it, not with the hippos making their rush.

"Madigan, we need some of your firepower over here!" he yelled.

A bright green checkmark appeared over her head on the HUD and the rocket launchers engaged. White plumes of exhaust trailed behind as the projectiles streaked into the line of charging hippos.

It wasn't exactly where he wanted them. He'd hoped to have the ground cleared around them and for the rockets to eliminate the mole rats so the humans could evade and flank the charge, but maybe this was for the better.

If they could slow the charge, the hippos couldn't rush through the sinkholes either. This would give the defenders the opportunity for a countercharge, and Sal wouldn't waste it. The blasts shook him to his bones but he pushed forward, moved as fast as his suit could go, and watched for any sign of the mole rats rising from the sand to attack him.

Against all odds, the line was holding.

Jiro joined him with the rest of the Heavy Metal team on his heels. The jungle had surged in behind the hippos that were still recovering from the rockets. Five of them were dead and a few more wounded.

A handful had been blinded by the blast and blundered into the sinkholes where the mole rats attacked and killed them almost immediately. That was something to keep in mind, at least.

Trick had abandoned his position on the Hammerhead at some point and fought alongside his teammates. He now fell back, dropped to one knee, and raised his rifle.

Instinctively, Sal knew what he was looking for and that he was crazy enough to help the sharpshooter. He continued to sprint directly into the path of one of the larger creatures that was half as large as the one that had trampled him in Niger. While he still wasn't sure if the males or females were bigger, this one clearly led the charge. He highlighted it on his HUD and got a checkmark from Trick, who watched and waited as the creature opened its mouth and exposed its tusks to attack him.

In that moment, the round struck home, punched through the back of the mouth, and severed the spine. It continued through to punch into the eye of the one behind. The second strike wasn't a killing shot since the round lost too much velocity penetrating the other one's skin, but the mutant was blinded and it turned and accidentally gored one of the others.

Trick was one hell of a good name for the freelancer.

Before the largest creature could fall, the coils in Sal's boots kicked in to launch him onto it. He opened fire on the next group with one hand while the other swept to his right with the sword to catch a hippo that tried to rush past. The blade opened it from neck to ribs and then the belly to spill its guts in a rush while the other monsters barreled forward.

He bounded up from the beast he still balanced on. The flesh gave slightly beneath him but he still traveled high enough that he was out of the path of the tusks of the next one to attack. The blind one had already been killed by the tusks of the others and he wanted to capitalize on that.

Their charge had slowed but the locusts, mole rats, and vines still gained ground.

With fresh waves of mutants ready to reinforce those already in position, the line wouldn't hold for long.

Sal landed, rolled smoothly, and let the AI get him on his feet. He drove into the center of the charge and continued to fire and swing his blade to good effect. His aggressive tactic forced the beasts to veer away and many fell victim to the mole rats' traps. He couldn't keep track of how many had died already, but if the hippos got beyond this point, it would be a massacre. And it would be the end for all the bases around the Zoo besides.

He shifted to the side and sliced his blade halfway through the neck of one of the monsters before something hammered into his hand and he sprawled awkwardly, flung back by the force of the blow.

It wasn't a hippo this time. The trees had multiplied enough to reach this point and while they weren't tall enough for the sloth to drop from a high branch, they did provide cover for the beast to launch a surprise attack. The claws had barely missed him and he assumed that New Connie had saved him from being slashed down the middle. Unfortunately, his whole arm was numb from the impact and his sword was still buried where he'd left it, and more of the monsters surged toward him.

The sloth moved in to finish him when Kay stepped in, covered by Courtney. The former pumped two rounds into the sloth's chest before she hammered her fist into the creature's head with enough power that it was knocked completely off. He realized that her suit's left hand had been modified with the same coils he had in his boots, which was where the power came from.

"KO." He grunted as Courtney helped him up. "I get it now."

"We need to get back," she warned. "Solodkov has already scrambled the bombers. We have to get clear."

"Too bad we don't have any helicopters to give us cover, eh?"

"What?" Kay looked around in confusion as she yanked his sword out of the dead hippo and handed it to him before the three of them hurried to where most of the soldiers were gathering.

"Nothing…never mind."

The line tightened and held.

They were buoyed by the news of the incoming Russians. Gunships were already helping to clear the locusts from the artillery guns and more soldiers streamed in before they heard the scream of bombers overhead.

Two white-hot blasts almost blinded Sal when they struck close to the breach in the wall and spread. The shockwave traveled far to hurl the locusts from the sky and stun the monsters—even those underground—which made them easy targets for the fresh troops who bolstered the ranks of the first responders and gave them a brief respite.

He was flung back by the force and landed heavily, although his suit cushioned it somewhat.

"Maybe this is why I avoided football," he muttered and winced when his whole body ached as he moved it.

"If you don't have the good sense to avoid trying to tackle a creature ten times your size, maybe that's a good thing."

Madigan's heavy suit lumbered closer and he wondered

how long he'd have to tolerate her hippo-focused disapproval. "It looks like we did it."

"This part," Courtney corrected her. "But we still have a look at that goddamned so-called invincible wall."

"Yeah," Sal agreed. "What the fuck would have happened if the Zoo had done this to all the sections where it had pushed to the wall in the last few days?"

"The end of the world as we know it," Murphy suggested as he strode toward them, his suit splattered with locust and panther blood. "Of course, there's nothing to stop the bitch from making another attempt."

"I hope she gives us at least a couple of days to recover from this one first," Madigan retorted.

"She?" Sal raised an eyebrow.

"Fuck yeah. She."

CHAPTER TWENTY-FIVE

What have they done to this place?

The whole area looked like it had been carpet-bombed. Black scorch marks streaked the sand and it had turned to glass in some places.

Still, Sam hadn't expected so much damage to the wall. It had been necessary, he knew that. Something had tunneled under, broke through the foundations, and damaged it for about three kilometers, maybe more. They would have to dig it all up and start from the beginning. It would start with assessing the damage, and a massive troop presence still in the area at least reassured him that their inspection would be relatively safe.

He would have preferred completely safe but there were fears that the fucking mole rats might still be lurking, which meant they had to be alert and cautious to move around without stepping on something that could rip them apart.

While everyone wanted the wall repaired, more of them had begun to doubt that it could keep the Zoo in check.

The equipment was en route to make the repairs, but it was on him to see what had happened to damage it in the first place.

He wasn't surprised to see Franklin, Jacobs, and Monroe already present with Chen and Elke. The group worked under a small tent even though the sun hid behind a light cloud cover.

Who would have thought that light cloud cover and in the Sahara would ever be used in the same sentence? It was the first time he'd seen it since he'd arrived at the Zoo and it told him a massive environmental shift was underway in the region.

"The Fixer is among us," Franklin announced as he approached. "I hope to God you have it in you to fix this shit."

"I do what I can," Sam answered. "Chen, you had something you wanted to show us?"

The younger man nodded and pulled his tablet out. "We managed to get some pictures in from the area. This is where your problem started. Something corroded the prefab and straight through the reinforcement. You can see it around where the diggers found a way through. Do you see that?"

Jacobs nodded and took the tablet Chen offered him. He leaned a little closer and his eyes narrowed as he zoomed in on the picture. "What the hell is that?"

"What?" Monroe asked and stepped closer to him.

"That…film around the corroded pieces. It looks like it's almost glowing in the shadows. I thought it was maybe a little overexposure from the camera."

Chen approached and studied the image. "The picture's

fine. But yeah, there's a glow there. What do you think it is?"

"Some kind of residue," the scientist responded. "It looks almost like the substance on the Komodo dragon's scales in the images the Chinese sent us. They believed it prevented the acid from eating through it, remember?"

Monroe nodded. "Do you think that might be what weakened the structure?"

"It might be."

Before she could respond, her phone pinged and she raised a finger to excuse herself before she backed out of the tent.

Elke approached the picture and inspected it closely. "I know of no corrosive agent strong enough to do this kind of damage in such a short time."

"Nothing man-made, anyway." Sam gestured around to the Zoo. "But out there?"

She shook her head. "It still doesn't make sense that something could achieve that."

"I can think of something," Monroe interjected when she returned to the tent and handed the phone to Jacobs. "The goop could pull that shit off."

He studied her phone screen carefully and handed the tablet to Chen.

"Goop?" Franklin asked, his heavy eyebrows hanging low over his eyes. "We've never known it to have any corrosive properties before."

"Not now," Sal agreed. "But the original payload was extremely corrosive to anything man-made that it came in contact with. Classified reports from when it was brought down talk about how it dissolved the suits of three of the first people to handle it. Their deaths were covered up as industrial accidents."

"So how would that get here after all this time?" the commander insisted and his frown deepened into a scowl.

"The burrowers," Sal told him "We finally know what they are."

"Well, don't keep us in suspense." Franklin sounded terse but it could have been from misgivings as well as impatience.

"Technically? A programmed cross-species virus intended to manipulate cellular and molecular DNA for pre-programmed purposes."

Jacobs looked around the tent and was met with a series of blank faces. The young man sighed and shook his head as he tried to think of a simpler way to put it.

"They're...alien nanotech."

"Oh," the commander muttered. "Why didn't you say so?"

"The point is," Monroe interrupted, stepped forward, and let her annoyed expression say more about what they faced than words could, "that these little bastards produce what we could call pure original goop. That explains the wall and it explains the painful rash."

Franklin sighed heavily. "So how do we deal with them? If nothing can cure the rash and the contaminants don't work, what the fuck else do we have left?"

A long silence settled over those in the tent. No one met each other's eyes as they considered the implications of what was being discussed.

Finally, Sam felt like it was his turn to say something.

"It's a long shot, but I have a friend in Interpol. They've

been keeping an eye on a man named Badawi, who basically confessed to capturing and shipping the horned gorilla to the Saudi Prince that caused that little incident. It stands to reason that he might have been involved with the pelts that were smuggled into the Czech Republic—those everyone believes triggered the outbreak there."

He shrugged. "Either way, if he's in the Zoo regularly, he or his men might have picked up this rash...the burrowers or whatever you want to call them. Given that there is no indication of an outbreak wherever he is, it might be possible that he's found some way to deal with them. He might not even know it, honestly, and could have assumed that it was merely a rash."

Jacobs tilted his head, a sour expression on his face. "It's worth a try if nothing else. Franklin, do you think you can put us in contact with this bastard?"

"I'll see what I can do. It looks like we'll owe favors to a long list of people around here."

"*Lieber Gott,*" Elke whispered. "To think we have to rely on a smuggler to save the human race."

It was refreshing to not face any real pushback for once. The Protocol Committee was surprisingly cooperative and made no attempt to protest or argue.

Sal hadn't thought they would see it in his lifetime.

"The idea that there's something out there now that can break through the wall puts a damper on our plans," Courtney explained via the video conference call. "The fact that it's something we've suspected since the beginning is even more unsettling. I won't lie. Things are looking bleak at the front lines."

A moment of silence followed as the committee considered the reality. He recognized it for what it was, having felt the same thing when he'd been presented with the news. A very real moment was needed to confront their mortality before an enemy that could not be bargained with, reasoned with, or escaped. Not unless the billionaires of the world delivered on their promise to start colonizing Mars. Hell, Sal was a little curious to see how the goop would do at terraforming the Red Planet.

"I'll say it since I know it is on everyone's minds," Solodkov stated finally and leaned forward. "What happens when—not if, when—the Zoo tries again."

Sal rubbed his eyes to get a little more feeling into them. "We're adapting to better handle the slew of incidents and attacks from all around the Zoo, and we shouldn't expect that they will slow. If anything, we will see them escalate in the coming weeks and months. We have to start work on a plan with a worst-case scenario in mind—mitigation and damage control."

"The worst-case scenario is that the Zoo attacks us at all the points where it's pushed the spurs to the wall," the British commander stated bluntly and her voice carried easily over the feeds.

A flurry of horrified exclamations and curses followed and Sal was happy to let them get it all out of their systems.

Franklin wasn't. "If that's what the worst-case scenario is, we need to work on ways to prepare for it. To stop it or at least contain the damage."

His voice was calm—perhaps a little too calm.

"Well," Sal answered almost without thinking, "the best plan at this point would be to stop playing defense and get on the offensive. We should retaliate and do something to force the Zoo to turn aside from its current campaign to protect itself."

He expected the suggestion to be met with mockery and was surprised when there were nods all around along with murmurs of approval.

Finally, the German commander leaned forward. "What do you have in mind, Dr. Jacobs?"

That was probably the most surprising point of their little meeting. He always felt he was pulling teeth to get these people to listen to what he had to say, and he knew Courtney and the other researchers had similar challenges.

The silence all around the room was coupled with expectant, hopeful, and almost desperate looks on the faces of all those in attendance. He realized that they all hoped he would come up with some kind of answer for what they faced.

He'd walked right into this one. There was no one to blame but himself but who would have thought that people would listen to the experts on the matter?

"Well," he started, not entirely sure what insane thought process was at work," it would have to be something so bold and fucking crazy that it'll catch even the Zoo by surprise."

AUTHOR NOTES - MICHAEL ANDERLE

NOVEMBER 2, 2021

Thank you for not only reading this story but these author notes as well.

Coming back to *Heavy Metal* is like coming back to old friends. For those who have recently picked up the series, you will have NO idea what I'm talking about.

Presently, I'm writing these author notes from Sharjah, UAE (I'm here for the 2021 Sharjah Book Fair as a guest speaker). The *last* book in the *Heavy Metal* series was released on Sept 26, 2019, which was just over two years ago.

That seems like *forever* to me. We rarely go three months between book releases, much less two years.

Part of the reason is I took a little side story (and character) by the name of Taylor McFadden for a spin (and sixteen books) before reintroducing him to the Zoo and the group Heavy Metal in the stories.

Well, when McFadden (affectionately referred to as Tay-Tay, to his major annoyance) and Banks ended up back in the Zoo, it seemed like we needed a couple of additional stories with Heavy Metal to seamlessly introduce the ZOO timeline once more.

So now I'm heading back out into the deep dark to introduce some additional stories in the ZOO Universe a few hundred...or thousand...years in humanity's future before possibly returning to explain a bit more.

The aliens who sent that lone missile toward the blue planet have *no* idea what they wrought.

If you have not read the *Cryptid Assassin* series, you might want to check out Taylor and the gang. If this is later than first quarter of 2022, you might want to investigate the *Dead Evil* gang ;-)

(Hopefully, Zen-Master-Steve™ can drop in the cover here to whet your appetite!)

Have a great week or weekend, and talk to you in the next book!

Ad Aeternitatem,

Michael

CONNECT WITH MICHAEL

Connect with Michael Anderle

Website: http://lmbpn.com

Email List: http://lmbpn.com/email/

https://www.facebook.com/LMBPNPublishing

https://twitter.com/MichaelAnderle

https://www.instagram.com/lmbpn_publishing/

https://www.bookbub.com/authors/michael-anderle

OTHER MICHAEL TODD BOOKS

PROTECTED BY THE DAMNED UNIVERSE

PROTECTED BY THE DAMNED*

8 Book series

WAR OF THE DAMNED*

8 Book series

DAMIAN'S CHRONICLES*

4 Book series

WAR OF THE ANGELS*

8 Book series

ZOO UNIVERSE

BIRTH OF HEAVY METAL*

10 Book series

APOCALYPSE PAUSED*

12 Book series

SOLDIER OF FAME AND FORTUNE*

12 Book series

TEAM SAVAGE *

3 Book series

Dungeon Core TV*

6 Book series

Dungeon Rails*

3 Book series

Hellspawned Chronicles*

3 Book series

The Sheva Chronicles*

6 Book series

Unlikely Bountyhunters*

6 Book series

House Drakonnen

The Accord

The Anchor's Inheritance Saga

*DENOTES COMPLETED SERIES